Dedication

For children everywhere who love and are loved by lots of parents, grandparents, and siblings. You are blessed and just as perfect as can be...

And for Ted, always.

Loving Logan

Return to Welcome, Volume 2

Bonnie Edwards

Published by Bonnie Edwards, 2023.

This is a work of fiction. Similarities to real people, places, or events are entirely coincidental.

LOVING LOGAN

First edition. January 20, 2023.

ISBN: 978-1989226179

Written by Bonnie Edwards.

Table of Contents

For children everywhere who love and are loved by lots of parents, grandparents, and siblings. You are blessed and just as perfect as can be...

And for Ted, always.

Chapter One

Elle Foster's beater crept to a halt, crunching gravel and sighing with the added exertion of pulling her rented moving trailer. When the engine stopped knocking, she slammed the shifter into park because she needed to slam something. She pasted on a smile, turned to her eldest son, Daniel, and said, "We're here. My family's property." Half of this acreage was hers.

The back half, apparently. Her brother, Clay, had built his new house on the front half.

"Finally," Jorja said from the back seat.

"I'm hungry," said Liam. But he always said that, hungry or not. But he probably was. Lunch was a long time ago.

The baby, Clarissa, slumped in her car seat drooling adorably in her sleep.

"Everyone climb out quietly and don't slam the doors. We don't want to wake her."

Once outside in the rain-threatening air, they stood shoulder to shoulder at the front of the car, staring at the sweeping lawn and back deck of her brother's house. Elle was struck dumb at how different the property looked. No brambles to catch at her skin and clothes. No dark, gloomy trees blocking the sun and the very air. No trash barrels or rusted-out hulks of cars. No pile of beer cans tossed off the deck.

No single-wide rotting from the inside out.

"What'll we do if Clay's not here?" Daniel asked.

"We wait." She could hardly believe the place he'd built for himself and his little girl. First off, she'd almost missed the turn into

8

the driveway because all the overgrown brambles were gone. The front of the lot had been cleared and the house sat in full view of the road, as if the Fosters, finally, had nothing to hide.

A trickle of unease started as she looked around. With the drapes drawn in every window, the house looked closed down. Daniel jumped the two steps up to the deck and peered into a window, cupping his hand around his eyes to see better. "No one here."

Her resistance to this move had made her balk at calling Clay about their arrival. Also, she needed to keep her phone minutes for emergencies. She'd long ago given up her data plan and had had to switch to pay-as-you-go minutes.

Being out of work with four children had forced her return to Welcome, but being stupid about calling ahead was all on her. Weary, she turned her attention to the backyard. A cedar hedge stretched across the property and delineated the lawn. She could only assume the double-wide Clay had installed for her was on the far side of the hedge. The gravel drive continued and swung to the left just past the six-foot cedars. She thought of climbing into the car and driving to the back lot, but Clarissa woke up, screamed her indignation at finding herself alone in the car, and Jorja opened the back door.

They all needed to stretch their legs and Elle wanted to delay the inevitable until the last possible moment. Once she set foot inside that double-wide, Elle Foster would truly be back in Welcome, a place she'd hoped to never see again.

She squeezed her eyes shut and blew out a breath. Giving her head a brisk shake, she collected the baby from Jorja, swung the diaper bag to her other shoulder, and headed across the lawn toward the back of the lot.

GENERALLY SPEAKING, burglars didn't bring children to work. Logan Hughes sent a text to his buddy to confirm his suspicions. He'd parked, seen a vehicle and a do-it-yourself moving trailer and then opened his window only to hear high-pitched, childish voices and happy squeals.

Logan: "I'm at your place to check things out."

Clay: "Security cam only picks up the front of a car in the driveway. I don't recognize it. And a guy just stuck his face up to the kitchen window. Don't recognize him either."

Logan: "Are your sister and her kids due today?"

Clay: "Can't reach her. Maybe."

Logan: "I hear kids."

Clay: "If it's her, the keys are on a hook by the kitchen door. Make sure she has everything she needs."

Logan: "Will do."

Clay: "If it's Elle, good luck. You'll need it."

"That was cryptic," he said aloud as he shoved his phone into his pocket. Elle Foster had a rep as a badass, but surely she'd outgrown her feistiness. Logan climbed out of his SUV and listened again to high, thin voices drift from the backyard. The screeches sounded happy and inviting and reminded him of his own childhood. The Hughes family had sounded like this once. He tried to make out the words. No luck.

In Washington State, June could bring the last of the cold Arctic air and some days the wind held a nasty bite. Today was one of those days. He zipped up his windbreaker and walked by the trailer and ancient sedan that squatted in Clay's driveway. At the far end of the yard, near a cedar hedge that bisected the lot, Clay's sister, Elle Foster, or whatever her married name was, shepherded three children toward the trees. A cute, smiling baby dressed in pink clung to one hip. On the other hip bounced a diaper bag that slid around with each sway of her hips.

He jogged to catch up to them.

Excited screeches came from a boy and girl who were hopping around like live wires while a taller boy walked sedately beside Elle. With his hoodie up, it was no wonder Clay hadn't recognized his nephew as the kid had peered into the window. A camera could only see so much.

The baby on Elle's hip was the first to see Logan as he approached. She smiled wide and he could just make out some teeth. Dark-brown eyes glued to him, she bounced and wriggled on Elle's hip, as if she couldn't wait to meet him.

He smiled back at the pretty curly-haired baby with the Cupid's bow lips and gave her a wiggly-fingered wave. She giggled—a high, pure, sound that lit the air around the happy group. He covered his eyes with his hands and suddenly popped them wide open. She screeched with laughter.

Peek-a-boo. He was reduced to peek-a-boo to impress a little lady. He chuckled and lost a slice of his heart to the cherub.

He didn't remember Elle Foster as a beauty back in high school. She'd been hard-looking as a girl. Her natural black hair had been bleached to white, her makeup harsh. Tough and gruff and bold and older than him by three years, Elle had not been a girl for a guy like him. He'd been intrigued and had wondered what secrets she could reveal because she'd obviously learned a few things he hadn't yet.

The picture she offered today was completely different. She was softer, rounder, and her voice had gentled over time. Her hair had returned to black and with the bright-blue eyes he remembered, Elle was a female version of her brother Clay.

Maybe it was motherhood that had smoothed her edges. Maybe it was time. Maybe she'd grown up and come to terms with who she was.

Whatever had happened in the years between then and now had changed everything about her. She was gorgeous and looked as if she could mother a brood without turning a hair. Easy, graceful, her gait was smooth, even with the baby on her hip. Her head tilted to hear what the younger auburn-haired boy was saying. She patted him on the shoulder and returned his comment in a warm voice. An older girl, with her mother's coloring, bounced up and down in excitement. Her ponytail swung as she screeched so loudly her words were indecipherable.

As he strode closer, he picked up bits of their conversation. "We have more bedrooms?"

"Yes. How many times do you need to hear it?" This from the oldest boy, but the tone was affectionate.

"This house looks new!" It was the girl this time. Logan supposed she could see more of the double-wide through the trees. From where he was, he couldn't see much, but Clay had switched out the old single-wide he and Elle had been raised in and replaced it with an almost-new double.

He heard no shushing or sharp-voiced comments aimed at the children. Elle carried the bouncing baby was if the weight on her hip was nothing. She turned to see what the baby giggled at and her cobalt-blue eyes widened at the sight of him. Toned and fit, Elle possessed a body that couldn't possibly have delivered all these children.

"Can I help you?" he asked as she drew to a halt. He stopped, too. At his words, the eldest boy, who'd been talking with his younger brother, whirled to face Logan. The boy stilled and then hunched his shoulders, narrowing his gaze.

Unfazed, Elle scowled. "Do I look like I need help?" she asked coolly and raised an eyebrow. "Who are you and what are you doing here?"

Elle Foster still had a smart mouth and a fierce protective streak. Had the Earth Mother image been phony?

He put on his most reasonable smile, which usually smoothed his way, but Elle only looked more suspicious. "Okay, I guess you are Elle Foster." At the mention of her name, she raised an eyebrow. "The neighbor noticed your arrival and called Clay, who asked me to swing by to see who was poking around his house."

"Oh." Her gaze slid to the fence that separated Clay's land from the neighbors. "Was it Karen Bowler who called?"

"Yes," Logan replied. "If you're trying to move four children into the double-wide, from that rattle-trap moving trailer" —he hooked his thumb over his shoulder— "then yes, I'd say you could use a hand. And Clay asked me to see that you have everything you need."

"My brother's all the help I need." She faced him squarely and the second oldest boy narrowed his eyes exactly like his brother had. This family was a team. Elle snapped her fingers and the three children ringed her without argument. Each child watched him suspiciously. But the middle girl jutted her chin as if she'd rather punch him in the face as look at him. He held tight to a grin.

He ignored the wolverines ready to pounce and focused on Elle. "Clay's still out of town. They won't be back for at least a week, maybe longer." At this information, she bit her lip and her shoulders sagged infinitesimally. "Clay didn't tell you?" Then Logan remembered Clay's text that he hadn't been able to contact her.

"My phone died and I haven't had a chance to charge it." The shift of her eyes said she wasn't giving him the whole truth. He shrugged. Some families didn't share day-to-day plans. She jabbed her chin in the direction of Clay's house. "You have a key?" She passed the baby off to the eldest boy, who looked too young to shave, but old enough for hair gel. He caught a whiff of some too-strong cheap cologne. Yes, early teens. He suppressed another grin.

"I have a key," he replied, keeping his gaze on Elle's. "I'm Logan Hughes, by the way. I remember you from Welcome High, but we're three years apart. I doubt you'd remember me."

She ran her gaze up and down his body. "You're right. Forgettable," she said, and he felt the dismissal like a slap in the face. He cocked his head and said nothing.

When she didn't speak either, he rocked back on his heels. Ten seconds and counting. Even the children went solemnly quiet. Someone had to break the standoff. "My offer still stands. If you need a hand, I'll lend it." He raised his face to the sky. "More rain coming."

"It's Welcome, Washington, there's always more rain coming," she snapped and walked past him toward Clay's house. "Let us in," she demanded. "We all need the bathroom and the little ones can stay out of our way while we unload the trailer in the rain." As she strode past, she gave him a sidelong glance that looked a bit like guilt.

Maybe apologies came hard to Elle Foster. Logan dealt with people all the time, he was good at reading them and she knew she'd been rude. He could choose to react to her rudeness in kind or put it down to a tiring drive with four kids and a crappy trailer full of everything they owned. Elle Foster had returned to Welcome and, clearly, it hadn't been by choice.

ELLE GRITTED HER TEETH as she passed Logan on the way to Clay's house. She'd been surlier than usual and regret for her tone bubbled under her fear. Snapping at people had become second nature in the last year. Some days it was all she could do not to lose her shit all over store clerks and gas jockeys. "Look," she said, half under her breath, "I'm not used to people offering help unless they want something. And I'm prickly as hell these days, so that doesn't help." Not exactly an apology, but she was too tired to find pretty words.

Logan nodded but didn't say anything. At least he didn't veer off to head for his car. The sky threatened and the wind picked up. She still had a lot to do to get her children settled. Maybe he really would stay and lend a hand.

"Thanks for the help," she said in a mollifying tone.

"You're welcome."

Her churlishness had become her first line of defense when she'd realized she had nowhere to go but back here. All she wanted was to be anywhere but in Welcome, but she had no choice. The children needed to have a proper home and a stable life.

Giving them those things meant she had to accept this return to Welcome.

But she didn't have to like it.

As she walked, Elle recalled that Logan had been gorgeous in high school and he'd actually improved with age. *Men catch all the breaks.* He had sandy-colored hair and gold-brown eyes that danced when he smiled. Yes, she remembered a lot about Logan Hughes. His being younger had made him off-limits, but she'd noticed him in a very female way. She recalled a lunch period when she learned about his reputation as a nice boy; a good kid who respected the rules. Boring, she'd thought at the time; boring and of no value, because nice boys were no fun. *No fun at all.*

And then Tad the bad boy had come along and there'd been no one else for her, until Ben, another bad boy. She shook off the mistakes and reminded herself she'd never make the same ones again. She was immune to bad boys in all their forms. She mentally dusted her hands of all the messes she'd gotten into.

Being attracted to a younger man seemed exactly like another mess to avoid. She was thirty-three, a mother to four children, and broke. What the hell would a younger man want with her? Besides, Logan looked successful. He wore expensive clothes she'd call business casual, and topped off his slacks with a high-end windbreaker. She glanced past him to the driveway and saw the top of an expensive-looking SUV parked behind her car and the wobbly trailer she'd rented.

Men like him weren't for women like her.

All of which only strengthened her resolve to steer clear of men, period. Good guys as well as bad boys.

She followed Logan through the French doors into her brother's house and slammed to a halt in the dining area next to the kitchen. The place was like something out of a magazine. There was a gallery hall upstairs and a huge rock fireplace at the front of the house.

There was a play kitchen, a box of toys, and a stack of books in a corner of the living room. Clarissa was already eyeing the bright primary colors of the play area. She'd be safely entertained here.

"Wow, I guess vet school paid off." Stupid thing to say. Clay had brought in a double-wide just for her. That should have been her first clue that Clay was rolling in cash. And that had happened before he married the movie star, Mercy Talbot.

Still, it was a shock that her little brother was this well off. Times had changed, she thought with a touch of envy. If she'd made different choices, stayed in school, hadn't got knocked up, her life would have been different. The baby squealed and she took her from Daniel with a coo to distract her.

But then she wouldn't have her children and there was no one she loved more. She ruffled Daniel's hair. "Find the bathroom, change her diaper, and then come back outside to help." To her middle children, Jorja and Liam, she said, "Make sure Clarissa is safe and let her crawl around. I doubt she'll wander far from that corner full of toys, but don't take your eyes off her. I'll be right outside if you need me." She could look into the house on her trips back to the moving trailer from the double-wide. They'd be fine.

She looked at Logan, who watched her closely. "What?" While she waited for his answer, she went to the key rack by the door and grabbed the set Clay had left for the double-wide.

"Nothing. It's just—"

She spun back to face him. "What?"

"You're like a general with the troops." He cocked his head in surprise and then stepped out the door. Again, she followed him. "Why not pull the trailer up the drive?"

"Can't be that far from the kids, and I need to peek in to see how they're doing."

"Right." He frowned. "I didn't think of that."

Once outside, they opened up the trailer and unloaded boxes. The ones marked with the children's names she set aside for Daniel to take. "Put these in the largest bedroom for you and Liam, and take the girls' boxes to the second largest."

After that, she and Logan wrestled with mattresses, box springs, and bunk beds. She probably should have her disposed of her old sofa, but it was all she had to sit on in a living room. Whenever she walked back to the trailer she looked inside the house and saw Clarissa trying to pull herself up on the furniture. "She'll be walking soon," she said to Daniel.

He nodded and spoke low. "Who is this guy?"

"Nobody to worry about. He's a friend of Clay and Mercy. She worked for him for a while." Mercy had quit her job when her career had taken off. Maybe Logan still had an opening. When she turned back to face Logan she gave him her very best smile. He caught it and looked curiously back at her, eyebrows knitted.

She felt a raindrop hit her cheek. "Time to hustle," she said and set aside her thoughts to work faster.

Logan lifted her boxy, heavy television. The strain of the weight in his arms made his muscles bulge and she enjoyed a long look before she glanced away.

THE RAIN LASTED TEN minutes, but when the shower was over, the lawn was wet and slippery. Half an hour after the rain stopped, Logan closed the back of the trailer and wiped his hands on his jeans. That was the most pitiful move he'd ever seen, and in the real estate business, he'd seen a lot of household goods and furniture get carried into homes. Elle's children had one small box of clothing each, very few toys and only one old bike to ride between them. The bulk of the furniture consisted of a sofa for the living room, a collapsible soft mesh play yard for the baby and an old boxy television that weighed a ton. He couldn't recall seeing a crib.

Elle Foster was dead broke. Her children looked well fed and healthy and he figured that her cash was more about feeding them than having things. People shouldn't have to struggle this hard.

The older boy named Daniel had been a steady worker and had the flat determination needed to get the job done. Logan hoped the kid was too tired to give him any more flak, but teenagers had an amazing recovery time. He expected more verbal shots the longer he hung around. Daniel set the old bike by the door under the awning as Logan watched.

As careful as Daniel was, the chain still fell off the rickety bike. Logan moved across the lawn to help.

Daniel glared at him. "I'll do it." He gave Logan his shoulder and squatted beside the bike.

"Okay, I'll head into the big house. I'll get you a drink box or something. Your uncle must have juice for his little girl."

Daniel shrugged in apparent disinterest.

On the stroll back to the house, Logan texted Clay.

Logan: "They're in."

Clay: "Good. TY. How is she?"

Logan: "Crabby, tired."

Clay: "LOL her usual—the kids?"

Logan: "Great."

He was glad they weren't face-to-face during this exchange. Logan wasn't sure he could hide his true thoughts; one, that Elle was beautiful and appealing, two that the older kids were hard nuts, and three, the baby made him want one of his own. Truth in texting was best avoided. By the time Clay and Mercy returned home, Logan would be over his mild awareness of Elle Foster.

As Logan entered the house through the French doors, he saw Elle answering the landline. "Hi, Clay," she said. "He texted you? Yes, we're in. All's well. Yes, Logan was a big help." She smiled at him like she had before; high wattage. He wondered what that meant.

Can't be good. Or she wanted something. That was it, he realized, as she jutted a hip and flashed him a grin. "I'll ask him. I'm sure he won't mind." With that, she smiled her mega-watt again. Something wary woke up in his chest.

She said goodbye and slipped the receiver back into the cradle. "Can you give me another hour or so?"

He checked his phone. "I have a meeting in two hours. Better be quick."

"I need to turn in the trailer and get groceries. Would you mind staying with the children? I'd take them, but they're sick of being in the car."

Daniel walked in just as she asked. "I'll stay. He can go."

She faced her son. "You don't know anyone around here to call for help."

Logan raised his hands. "I'll be back up. Daniel's got more experience with kids, but I've got my car in case of emergency."

"A diplomat," she muttered. "I'll go right now."

He accompanied her to her car. "Want me to back the trailer out for you?"

"No."

He reached for his wallet. "Need a few bucks? I noticed you didn't bring much food to put in the kitchen." He'd carried a box containing flour, sugar, other dry stuff, spices, and some cereal, but her fridge was empty.

Elle straightened and glared at him. So the wide, beautiful smile wasn't about needing money.

"I provide for my children," she snapped. Then she blinked and her shoulders moved in an awkward shrug. "And I got my child support this month, so I'm good." She climbed into her car and opened the window. "Thanks for the offer anyway."

He ran to his car and moved it out of the way so she could back out. He flagged her to a stop as her car came abreast of his. "Do you remember where the grocery store is?" he called.

She frowned darkly at his question. "I remember every damn detail of this town."

Chapter Two

ELLE RETURNED FROM the grocery store to find her brother's house empty. She went back to the car, climbed in and drove farther along the driveway to her new place. She'd been shocked to her fingertips to see the almost-new mobile home Clay had installed for her. Relief had immediately chased the shock. She didn't have to bring her children to the same trailer she'd been raised in. She didn't have to see the ghosts of her childhood lurking in every closet and cupboard. All those hiding places were gone.

In the living room where they'd make happy memories to override the hard ones, she found Clarissa asleep in the play yard, her thumb in her mouth with her index finger snugged over her nose. A clattering noise from the bedrooms called her to the back of the house. Daniel and Logan worked together to build the second bed in the master bedroom. The room was so large that the beds didn't even have to be stacked. Her boys had beds on opposite walls, giving them both more space. Elle drew in a breath at the sight. She silently watched them work for a moment.

Seeing Daniel next to Logan made her realize how grown up her son looked. Like a man, he worked quickly and efficiently, following Logan's lead.

Next, she checked the second bedroom.

"Hi, Mom. We've been busy," Jorja said. Her bed had been put together and she was busy trying to put on the fitted sheet. Elle bent to help by lifting the corner of the mattress for her. Jorja's tongue stuck out of the corner of her mouth as she focused on the task. "Done," Jorja said with a gusty sigh.

"She's making me help *her* instead of Daniel," Liam said with a frown. "I wanted to do the bunk beds."

"Daniel has Logan to help him, so *I* need you," Jorja interjected in a haughty tone. She unfolded the top sheet on her mattress. They'd done so much in the short time Elle had been gone.

Her mismatched twins were often mistaken for singles. Jorja had hit a growth spurt and was taller than Liam by a couple of inches and had Elle's black hair while Liam had burnished-gold hair like their father.

Odd that it was also the color of Logan's hair.

Jorja jabbed her brother again. "We been real busy," Liam confirmed. "And hungry. Clarissa's the only one who ate."

"Yeah, *he* said he'd order pizza, but it's still not here. He musta *forgot*," Jorja added with a seven year old's disdain.

"I fed the baby the food in the diaper bag," Liam said. The emergency packs of fruit and vegetable goo. Elle supposed this was an emergency. She couldn't fault Liam's logic.

"Thanks. So she's had the oat cereal? And the rest of the jar of meat?"

At her son's nod, Elle relaxed. "Good job. I'll feed you as soon as I can," she said, holding up the two bags she'd brought in. She emptied her frozen food into the freezer and gawked at the size. Clay had spared no expense. All the appliances seemed new and too fancy to use. *Really?* She was supposed to know what all the buttons were for on the microwave.

As she inspected the oven a throat cleared behind her. She looked over her shoulder to see Logan trying not to check out her butt. His gaze flew to the ceiling when she tilted her head at him.

"Hi," he said. "I've got my meeting soon so I wanted to get your beds put together before I left. Can't have you all sleeping on the floor your first night here."

She straightened. "My bed's done too?" She'd put her bed in the third bedroom. Since she slept alone she didn't need a large room and the kids needed the roominess of the larger bedrooms.

"It's jammed into the corner. The chest of drawers is in the other corner." He set a toolbox on the floor. "I'll leave this here. I showed Daniel how to use the tools."

That brought her up short. Since Ben left, she'd been the one to screw things in or use a hammer. She'd never taught Daniel how to avoid stripping a screw or how to line up a nail before tapping it. She lifted the toolbox to the kitchen counter. "Safer here. Clarissa gets into anything she can reach."

He looked chagrined. "I didn't think of that."

"You don't have kids?" If he'd had children he'd be more apt to think twice about leaving a toolbox on the floor. Any number of things in there could hurt a curious, eat-anything baby. And he hadn't seen the need for her to check the big house while they moved her goods across the lawn.

"Someday I'll have a family," he said. "I like kids."

She'd noticed his immediate bond with the baby. In her experience, men waited until a pregnancy before thinking about kids. Logan could be the exception, though. She'd heard a rumor that men like him existed, but she'd never believed it.

The doorbell rang. She had a doorbell? Logan got to the door before she did, whipped his wallet out, and, before she knew it, had paid for a pizza delivery. When he turned back to her, he had a sheepish grin on his face. "They were hungry and I wasn't sure how long you'd be out."

She reached for her purse as he slid the delicious-smelling boxes onto the counter beside her grocery bags. "What do I owe you?" Two large pizzas would cost a pretty penny. Maybe more than she had available.

"Don't worry, I'll eat my fill." Just as he said that, the kitchen filled with hungry children. He flipped the lids on the two boxes and amid the excited chatter, she found she didn't have the heart to start an argument about paying for the food. This had been his choice, after all.

Instead of protesting, she pulled milk and juice out of the grocery bags. "I need to find the cups."

"There's a box of dishes here, Mom." Daniel opened it and dug out a couple of plastic cups.

Logan checked his phone for the time. "How'd the food run go?" he asked right before he tore the tip off a slice of pizza. He chewed with determination.

She leaned against the counter and pretended she wasn't agog at the gorgeous open plan of the kitchen and living area. Her stained sofa, the thrift-store television and the play yard were all she had to put in the space. After bedtime, with the play yard in the girls' room, this area would be even emptier. No matter. Possessions weren't as important as food on the table and her fridge and cupboards were stocked for now. "The grocery store was a treat."

"I bet it was." Logan chuckled at her sarcasm and offered her a slice.

Elle took it. "Thanks for the help and this. It was good of you." Nice guy, Logan Hughes. She guessed some things never changed; the good and the bad. "I saw people from high school," she said. "Some of them glared at me in shock." She frowned. No one had said hello. "I'm pretty sure I saw Clay's mother-in-law." But Hope Talbot had quickly backed up out of the canned goods aisle and taken off. "She avoided me."

He nodded as if he understood. *Hah!*

"Mercy's mother is an interesting woman," he said diplomatically. "She keeps her nose in the air and most people don't take to that."

Elle cocked her eyebrow at his understatement.

"With her nose up so high it makes it hard for her to see the truth sometimes," he continued. "But she means well."

"She means well?" she repeated incredulously. "Hope Talbot hated us Fosters from the moment my brother met her daughter Janna." And now, with Janna dead, Clay had married the other Talbot girl, Mercy. "She must be half-crazed now that Clay and Mercy are married."

"Clay's proved himself. Hope's happy about the new baby coming." His smile went wide and his eyes crinkled at the corners. He was laughing at her for giving a shit about what Hope Talbot thought. Or maybe he was happy about the baby, too. He'd just said he wanted kids someday.

Elle snorted and backed away from the Hope Talbot conversation. Also, she needed to quit thinking about Logan as a family man.

"I've got to leave for my appointment," Logan said as he rinsed his hands in the kitchen sink. She didn't know where she'd find the hand soap. She dug in the diaper bag and produced a small bottle of hand sanitizer.

Logan used it quickly. "If there's anything else you need help with, give me a call. I left my number on the counter." He pointed to a business card propped up by the sink. Then he left her there to stew and wonder about what would happen next.

As she ate another piece of pizza, she made a mental list of her priorities. The biggest one was finding a job. Ben had paid his child support for the twins on time, but that money had gone for food. She was hoping for a check for Clarissa, but they were small and infrequent.

Now that Daniel's dad had been killed, she wouldn't see another dime from that quarter. Tad had been sketchy about paying Daniel's support, but he'd paid when he could. She'd considered Tad's money a bonus. He'd never worked steadily and never wanted to. It felt ironic that an accident on a job site should have been the end of him. But Tad had been reckless. He should have worn his harness on the scaffold. Since he'd been at fault and hadn't exactly been legal with his employment arrangement, there was no money from insurance.

She blew out a breath and made a mental list of people in Welcome she could hit up for work.

And came up empty.

PROVIDING FOR FOUR children seemed impossible for a woman on her own, Logan decided. Elle had said she had child support, but that had gone for groceries. From his scant knowledge, she'd been on her own for some time. Daniel had been born while she was still a teenager. Jorja looked about eight and Liam seven, judging from their sizes. He'd tried to ask but when it came to simple questions, the middle children were downright rude. Liam had grunted and ignored him, while Jorja had tossed her head and pursed her lips as if daring him to pry them open.

He understood street proofing your kids, but Liam and Jorja clung to their protective shields like warriors.

No doubt Elle Foster had a circus on her hands. A saying popped into his head. *Not my circus, not my monkeys.* Elle's problems weren't his. She didn't want help. She'd made that clear. She was Clay's problem, anyway.

He pulled into the parking area by the sales trailer at Springhill Meadows, a neighborhood his buddy was developing. He was the real estate agent on the project. Houses were selling steadily now and Logan had a small staff here.

Business at his downtown office was also picking up, though he worked alone there. It was quiet and private if things got bad on the family front. If his parents called for help with his brother, Jamie, he could talk freely without anyone overhearing. He missed Mercy, though. She'd understood what he was going through and had been a great help when he'd been called away to help with Jamie.

But here in the sales office for Springhill Meadows what he said and did was for public consumption and he needed to focus on business. He settled behind one of the three desks with a cup of coffee and waited for his clients, the Morrisons. Normally, his staff would handle this, but they were the first buyers in this project and he wanted them happy.

His mind returned to Elle and all those children. Four. Damn.

Logan wanted children. Now that he was thirty and back in Welcome, the desire to recreate the kind of family he'd been adopted into had grown. He wanted to give his children the loving home he'd been blessed with. Unlike his family ties that had been engineered, he wanted a genetic connection, too. The only thing he'd missed out on was seeing a physical resemblance to his parents and his brother.

He'd had a vague hope his previous relationship would be permanent, but returning to Welcome had ended things with Trish. Dealing with Jamie's issues had spooked her. And, as Trish had pointed out, she'd established a great career. She'd had no interest in moving to Welcome to start fresh. In fact, she hadn't had much interest in having a family, either. Once she'd admitted she wanted a high-end condo full of glass and sharp corners with no room for teddy bears and toy boxes, it had been easy to leave her behind.

He had time to find the right woman, he reminded himself. He was only thirty.

Elle was thirty-three and look at all she'd done on the family side of life. While he was building a career, she'd produced four beautiful children and still had a body that could make a man drool.

Clay had asked him to make sure she had everything she needed. Those kids deserved safe bikes to ride. And helmets. They needed helmets, too. He'd talk to Clay about bikes for the middle children.

Elle hadn't wanted him to treat for the pizza, but the order had been his idea. The children had worked hard, were hungry, and deserved a fun meal. Not one of them had asked for the pizza. Elle had trained them well.

A quiet presence loomed over him. He broke his reverie to look up. "Sorry, I was woolgathering. Mr. and Mrs. Morrison," he said, standing and holding out his hand. "Nice to see you again. How can I help you?"

The husband gave him a brief handshake and then shoved his hands into his leather jacket pockets. Logan swore the man fingered his wallet as if frightened he'd have to open it.

Mrs. Morrison offered a soft hand and smiled into his eyes. Then she glanced at her husband. "I want to change my cabinet choices in the kitchen." She took the chair across from him. Her husband sat beside her, looking pained.

"The ones we ordered are fine," he said.

The set of Mrs. Morrison's shoulders changed and a mulish look entered her gaze. "I want to upgrade."

And Logan was caught for the next hour, paving the way toward marital harmony. Before she'd left to return to her Hollywood career, Mercy had handled the Morrisons. She had a knack with people and the Morrisons liked her. Mercy had taken special care of them when she'd learned they were raising their grandchildren. Their needs differed from other buyers in their age group.

Logan settled in to help them make their new choices in cabinetry. "I'm glad you came in now, because the order for your cabinets was about to go in. You've just squeaked in with this change." He gave the husband a steady look.

Mrs. Morrison patted her husband's arm. "See? I told you we had to get over here pronto."

"Good," the older man said with an affectionate, mock-suffering glance at his wife. "We'll make the change, but I want two shelves mounted in the garage." He lowered his reading glasses to give Logan a hard stare.

"Done," Logan said and shook the man's hand. He'd put up the shelves himself if he had to. These days a real estate agent had to be flexible to keep a deal from disappearing.

After their decisions were made, the Morrisons stood to leave. "And how is Mercy feeling?" Mrs. Morrison asked kindly.

"I spoke to her the other day and she said she feels better now than she did at the beginning." Pregnancy was a mystery to him.

Mrs. Morrison smiled as if in fond memory. "Yes, the second trimester is when the morning sickness eases up. At least, it did for me. Not all women are the same, of course." She opened her mouth to say more, but her husband tapped her forearm and she flushed. "You're right," she said to him. "Men aren't interested in pregnancy stories. I hope I run into Mercy again around town and we can have a chat then."

"I'm sure you will," Logan said with a grin. "I'll tell her you send your best."

Mr. Morrison was already out the door and waiting on the stoop. "Er, mind if I ask a question, Mrs. Morrison?"

"June, please. And ask away."

"June," he repeated and blew out a nervous breath. "I know a woman in financial straits. She's a great mom, but her kids are missing some of the equipment that makes childhood fun. Bikes and things."

She cocked an eyebrow. "Is this a girlfriend?"

"No, not at all. She's a woman who needs a bit of help to get back on her feet."

"Does she have family who can help?"

"She does," he admitted with a nod.

"Then leave it to her family. If you're not interested in pursuing a relationship with the woman, you don't want to make her feel indebted." June eyed him curiously.

"Good advice, thanks." Elle's pride wouldn't tolerate charity. She'd made that more than plain.

"Nothing your mother couldn't have told you," June said with curiosity.

Nothing would please his mom more than a new woman for Logan. He shook his head. "My mother would jump to conclusions."

"So have I. If you like this woman, tread carefully with the children." She bit her lip but gave him a smile of encouragement. Her husband rapped his knuckles on the door and then opened it.

"You're not adding more to the cost, are you?"

"No," she responded with a chuckle. "We were talking about children, if you must know."

"Thanks, June." Logan offered his hand and she shook it.

"You've made me curious," she said. "And good luck."

Good people, the Morrisons. Raising their grandchildren took grit, but June and her husband looked unfazed by the change in their lives. Mercy and June had formed a warm friendship and he'd be sure to pass along June's good wishes.

And he'd take her advice about treading carefully. He'd talk to Clay about the bikes and helmets. Surely his buddy would want Elle's children outfitted safely.

But Logan suddenly didn't want the bikes to come from Clay. He wanted to be the one to bring some joy to Elle's prickly, too-cautious children. He couldn't get the image of their happy family group out of his mind. Nothing should interfere with that and if he could enhance their lives, why shouldn't he? School would be out soon and the kids would be hanging around with nothing to do.

What was the harm in providing for a happy, carefree summer?

Chapter Three

"I DON'T HAVE A LEASE agreement with my brother," Elle said, reining in her temper. "And I'm hooked up to his water and electric, which means I don't have a utility bill in my name." Elle drew in a calming breath. All she wanted was to get her children registered at their new school. "I live on the property where I always lived. Where I grew up." School would be out before the end of the month, but she needed them registered to pass into the next grade.

"You still need proof of residency." Denise Jones, the school secretary, set her lips in a smirk that tempted Elle to wipe the contemptuous look off her face.

Just her luck she'd end up on the receiving end of Denise's bullying. She'd always been a bitch; lording it over vulnerable kids at Welcome High. And now she'd turned those natural talents and nastiness into a career by becoming an administrative assistant at the elementary school. She glared at Denise but had to stay calm and try again. "You know me, so why insist on all this identification?"

"Exactly because I do know you," Denise said with a sneer. "I know what kind of person you are and I wouldn't put it past you to—"

"Enough," Elle said, cutting her off. "I'll get a letter from my brother verifying my address."

"Make sure it's notarized." Denise's flat tone put an end to the discussion.

Beside her, Daniel looked tense and seemed about to speak. To stop him, she squeezed his hand. That's all she needed, Daniel starting off on the wrong foot. He was a good student and she'd be damned if her wild reputation would make him foul up now.

31

She smiled sweetly at Denise. "I'll be back with a notarized letter." She took the children's birth certificates and immunization records off the counter and passed them to Daniel. Then she turned the stroller toward the door. At least Jorja and Liam had been in the hall gawking at the school trophy case and had missed the entire exchange. She swiveled her head back to the secretary's wary gaze. "Oh, and Denise?"

"What?" Her beady eyes narrowed in suspicion.

"You've got the remains of your lunch splashed across your saggy boobs."

A minute later Elle walked out of the school with Clarissa babbling in the stroller and Jorja, Liam, and Daniel flanking her. "That woman was a bi—"

"Daniel," she cut him off. "Watch the language. You're right, but that's not the word we use." But it was exactly the right noun. Denise Jones was a bitch with a long memory.

Elle had expected to face some judgment when she returned to Welcome, but her stomach had turned as she'd seen Daniel witness it. The look Denise had given Clarissa had made Daniel's shoulders stiffen as he balled his fists. He loved Clarissa. Daniel knew damn well what Denise had been thinking. Four kids with four different fathers. None of the children looked like the others, especially Clarissa. Her skin and tight black curls made her stand out.

Made her beautiful.

Elle bent over and clucked at the baby to coax a giggle. God, she was sweet. Her heart clenched with love.

She'd be damned if she wandered around Welcome explaining her life and her choices to anyone. *Fuck them all,* she thought, more defiant than she'd been in years.

As she buckled Clarissa into her car seat, she wondered if Logan had had the same thoughts about her that Denise Jones obviously had. Did he see Clarissa as proof of Elle's less-than-wise choices or did he see a baby girl who needed all the love she could get? But Logan had been charmed by the baby, the way most people were.

She kissed the top of Clarissa's forehead and the baby reached for her earring. "No, sweetie," she crooned. "You're not allowed to yank my earring out."

Jorja and Liam burbled and blew raspberries to distract the baby. Elle smiled her thanks. They were great kids; the best children in the world. Again, her heart clenched. Had she done the right thing bringing them to Welcome? Would she end up exposing them to her ancient history? What would they think of her then?

Elle closed the back door and then climbed into the driver's seat. That's what she needed to remember. *She* was driving this rig. *She* was in charge, and no one was going to mess with her children or how they saw themselves. Daniel, the twins, and Clarissa were more than "that Foster trash."

Daniel threw himself into the front passenger seat with a dark scowl on his soon-to-be handsome face. He looked like his father when he scowled and the memory of Tad made her catch her breath.

It saddened her that her first love was gone too young, but he'd never grown up. At least he'd left Daniel in the world, and that was a wonderful thing.

She climbed in behind the wheel and clipped her seatbelt into place. Daniel kept his face turned away. When she went to tug at his earlobe in their version of a mommy kiss, he yanked his ear out of reach. "Fine," she said.

"How long will you put up with this shi—stuff?"

"For as long as it takes to make people forget about me. I'll blend in soon and so will you. You'll get good marks, behave well, and make new friends. The twins will have a birthday party this summer and that'll pave the way for them."

"And Clarissa? How will she blend in?"

"By being as sweet and giggly as she is right now," she said in her don't-push-me voice.

Her belly clenched in shame. Imagine having to call her younger brother just to get her kids registered for school. Humiliation could go eff itself.

LOGAN: "JORJA AND LIAM need bikes. The baby needs a crib."

Clay: "OK, I'll get them when I come home."

Logan: "Already bought the bikes. Tell me what kind of crib to get."

LOGAN'S PHONE RANG. It was Clay. "What the hell? You're poking the dragon if you think Elle will accept bikes from you," he said.

Logan grinned into the phone. Some of it leaked into his voice. "I'll tell her you asked me to get them."

"Let me get this straight," Clay responded. "You went out and bought two bikes for my niece and nephew without consulting my sister, their mother."

"You're laughing. And why are you repeating everything?"

"Because I want Mercy to know. She's itching to grab the phone."

The next voice he heard was Mercy's. "Logan, have you delivered the bikes yet?"

"No," he said. "Before you ask, I had everything a kid could ask for: great parents, a nice home, a brother to hang out with, and friends, family—the whole thing. I look at Elle's kids and see an easy, fun thing to give them. Summer's coming and they should be out on bikes having fun like all the other kids."

"Oh. But why not wait for us to come home? Then Clay can give them to Jorja and Liam without..." She trailed off. "Never mind. This is you, being thoughtful and kind."

"Plus I want to get a crib. Clarissa's sleeping in a playpen."

"We call them play yards."

"Whatever. She still needs a crib."

Mercy gave him the name and model of the one they'd ordered for their baby. He jotted the information down.

"NO WAY," DANIEL SAID as Logan stood in the open door of the house, holding two child-sized biking helmets. "Do you think you can weasel your way in here by sucking up to the twins? You think we haven't seen other guys try it?" His chin jutted and Logan caught a glimpse of the man Daniel would soon become. He should have called first.

"Twins? But your sister's taller and your brother's hair..." Logan trailed off as he read the smirk on Daniel's face. Fine, he'd take the news in stride and move on. "Your bike's too big for them and it needs a lot of work," he pointed out. "They're well past the age to learn to ride. Your mom will be working soon and how will they get to their friends' houses after school?"

Jorja and Liam left whatever they were doing and came to stand behind their older brother to help block the entrance. Three against one. This pack of children was united. They had each other's backs. With Jamie, Logan had been the caretaker, while Jamie had been all risk all the time. "Can one of you get your mother, please?"

Liam careened off down the hall, yelling for his mother. A moment later, he returned with Elle in tow. "He's got helmets," he said and pointed at Logan.

Elle's lovely black eyebrows rose. "They're too small to ride the bike." She didn't make Daniel move out of the way to allow Logan to enter, so he stepped back from the door. She'd have to come outside if she wanted a private conversation.

"I know," he said. Which was exactly his point; they needed bikes that fit them.

She nudged her way through her children and down the steps to the lawn. She smelled of sweet baby lotion or powder. Turning her head toward the children still standing at the door, she said, "Go back to whatever you were doing. Mind Clarissa. I set her down in the hall. I'll handle this." With that, her wolverines abandoned their post and settled back into their burrow. But he noticed it was Daniel who went toward the hall. He heard his voice go high and singsong when he found Clarissa.

"He's great with the baby," he commented. Then he launched into the spiel he'd given the kids about how they'd need to get around on their own. "Living on the outskirts like this, they need bikes."

"Wait, you brought bikes?" Elle's voice rose on each word. Her face turned thunderous.

"Clay agrees and I took a swing by a kids' store and picked up a red one and a blue one. If they don't fit we can exchange them," he said and gave the helmets a shake.

One eyebrow rose as she studied him. "I don't need charity." Her voice was harshly bitter.

"This isn't about you. It's about Jorja and Liam and what's good for them." He shifted his shoulders to loosen them. "And I ordered a crib for Clarissa."

She closed her eyes. "You ordered a..." The words ended with a weak sigh.

"But it won't be in for ten days or so. Maybe more." He gave her his *nicest* nice guy smile. "Bad day?"

Elle wiped shaky fingers across her mouth. "I know how it looks, me coming back to live on my brother's land, in his double-wide, needing *his permission* to get my kids into school." She shook as if throwing off a mantle of shame. Her eyes met his steadily. "But

I've got the bike thing handled. I'm in a swap group for parents of multiples and I've asked for bikes. They'll come along soon enough. And I'll get helmets, too." The last was said wildly as if she was trying to convince herself.

"I see. But new helmets are better." He held up the pair, one blue, and one pink. *Why couldn't he shut the hell up?* It was clear Elle didn't want his help. But an inner voice said she needed it. "They're shiny and fresh with no marks or dings or dirt."

She closed her eyes. When they popped open again, she seemed resolute. "Thanks, but that's not how we live."

"Then you also don't want the brand-new bikes that are still in the SUV?"

"What? No!"

"You could at least walk with me to see them before you make me drag them back to the store."

"That's a bad idea," she said, but she looked tempted.

"I could lie and tell you that your brother requested I pick up the bikes. Would that make this easier?"

"Arrogant asshat," she muttered.

"Not the usual description I get, but I'll take it." He swung the helmets toward her, but she refused to take them. "Look, you said you'll get them bikes eventually. Why not now? If they make friends in school they'll want to ride to their houses or have them out here to ride safely away from traffic."

She looked as if she were squirming with indecision.

"I could have unloaded the bikes and shown them to *the twins* right away, but I didn't. If you say the word I'll take them away again."

ELLE WAS SORELY TEMPTED by the bikes. After the crappy visit to the school and having no luck with a job search, she felt deflated and—dare she think it—like a failure as a mother. "Why would you buy bikes for children you don't know?" she asked Logan.

"All children should have a bike to ride," he said reasonably.

His reasonableness irritated her. "You've already said that," she snapped. It went against the grain to accept the bikes, but the twins had outgrown their first bikes over a year ago and she'd pawned them, like so many other things. Ben leaving them had only been the first of many losses.

She narrowed her eyes at him but she couldn't break his sunny expression. "Daniel will walk them to and from wherever they want to go until I get the bikes from the swap group." Two bikes would take a chunk of money, though, even used. "When I get a job, I'll get them the things they need." Jorja and Liam hadn't asked for bikes. Was it because they understood the answer would be no?

"Pay me back when you're working."

Again, Logan was being reasonable, damn it.

"Show me the bikes." She hadn't forgotten about the crib, but one battle at a time. She set off toward his SUV. He fell into step beside her.

"About a job," Logan said. "I haven't replaced Mercy since she left because I was focused on finding staff for the Springhill Meadows sales office. But I don't have anyone assisting me the way Mercy did."

She held her curiosity in check and said nothing.

"You'd be doing me a favor," he said after a moment. "If you use that I-want-something smile of yours as my assistant, it might work." He eyed her skeptically. "Can you do that?"

She was too curious to be insulted and she knew which smile he was talking about. "You mean this smile?" Sarcasm flared as she flashed him one.

"Exactly." He raised a mocking eyebrow. "Clients will love it."

"And you?"

"That broad, happy, toothy smile makes spiders crawl down my back. I can't tell what you're after, but it's something."

She snorted. "You charmer, you. What would I have to do?" They stopped at the rear of his SUV and she glimpsed handlebars in the back. Her heart picked up speed. The twins would love new bikes and what would it hurt if they got them earlier than she'd planned?

At her question, Logan hung his head. When he looked up at her again, she read doubt in his face. He wasn't certain he could trust her. Nothing she said would reassure him. He'd have to judge for himself. She held her breath.

"There are times I have to take off and I need someone reliable to take my calls. I'm trying to build my client list for resale homes as well as handling new construction sales out at Springhill Meadows."

"And Mercy covered for you?" Her sister-in-law had hidden talents. "She took care of your clients?"

"Mercy sold the very first house at the subdivision. She's great at holding people's hands and finding ways around the obstacles put up by reluctant buyers. She can read people."

"I see. And sometimes you have to leave clients in the lurch?"

"Thankfully, not yet, but I'm afraid it might come to that and it'll kill my business." He nodded. "It's family stuff."

When he didn't say any more she assumed he expected her to ask Mercy what the family problems were. And if he didn't expect her to ask Mercy, he was crazy.

"The kids should be in school by Wednesday at the latest," she said, "but you haven't mentioned the pay or the hours. I don't have daycare lined up." In truth, she'd been hoping to piggyback onto whatever daycare arrangement her brother had for Dilly, his four-year-old daughter. Since Mercy's career was taking off, Elle assumed a nanny could stretch to take care of Clarissa. She'd chip in to pay for the extra child but it would be a big help to have the baby so close to home.

Logan told her the pay per hour, and while it was good, it was also part time to start and she wasn't sure she had the skills to do it. "I don't have a lot of office experience."

"What work have you done?"

"Warehouse for a while. I can drive a forklift. I've worked as a security guard at a mall and most recently as a flagger on road construction." She'd worked hard at all her jobs and fit in with the other, mostly male, employees. She could handle raunchy humor, swearing, misogynistic jokes, and even some light grab-ass, but she absolutely refused to get involved with anyone at work. There'd been times when that decision had cost her job. She looked carefully at Logan.

"We can talk more when you have daycare. I'd need you available at a moment's notice and I can't see how that will work as things are."

She nodded. He was right. Clarissa needed to be happily settled before Elle could commit to a part-time, on-call job. She needed guaranteed wages. "And the bikes? How much were they?"

He shrugged. "They were on sale. I saved a bundle." He handed her the helmets and this time she took them.

"I'll take the bikes when I have a job."

"But they're here now. You don't know when you'll find work."

Anger boiled up from her belly. "You think I can't provide for them."

"I *think* anyone would weigh their purchases carefully if they had four children. And twins complicate the budget."

Her anger went from boil to simmer at his explanation. "That's true. The twins grow at different rates and Jorja won't share clothes anymore." When her daughter was younger it didn't matter if she wore boys' jeans or T-shirts, but at seven she was larger than Liam and also desperately aware of what the other girls wore. "God help me when she hits puberty." The last was said more to herself.

He stood silently and no matter how deeply she looked into his eyes, she saw no judgment. Her anger drifted away, like mist burning off in the sun. "You keep the helmets until I get the bikes. I'll call you. And thanks, it was thoughtful." And considerate. Damn. He really was a good guy.

"If you find daycare for Clarissa, let me know. We can try the job if you want."

She'd have to hit the thrift store for some office-type clothes. Another expense she didn't need right now. "I expect I'll find something with more regular hours."

"I'm sure you will." He reached for the helmets and she avoided brushing his fingers as she handed them back.

"HI, MERCY, IT'S ELLE." She let the words hang out there like the Jolly Roger. Would her sister-in-law see Elle like the skull and crossbones? Did she consider Elle poisonous? She hoped not. She had no beef with Mercy. It had been Janna Talbot she'd had cause to hate. The memory of the bar brawl with Janna hung ghostly in the back of her mind.

But Janna was dead and Mercy had taken her place in Clay's life and had become the mother that Janna never could. For that, Elle was grateful. Dilly deserved a good mom. All children did. She blew the ghostly memory away and focused on the here and now.

"Elle," Mercy said. "It's nice to hear from you. Did Clay leave his phone turned off or something?" Her curious tone held no censure for Elle's lack of contact.

A twinge of guilt sparked to life. She hadn't been welcoming to Mercy and she felt the twinge deepen to a twist in her gut for her thoughtlessness. But the past had a way of choking the hope of a future. She should know, half the town held old grudges and expected her to be the same girl she was before she left.

"I'm sorry I haven't been friendly, Mercy. No excuses. I hope we can start fresh from here." When she asked her questions it would sound as if the only reason she was apologizing was that she wanted something. "The past with your sister and me was complicated, but that's no reason to—"

"Okay," Mercy interjected. "From here on in, we move forward."

Elle smiled and put it into her voice. "Thanks." She waited for a breath and then started. "I'm curious about a couple of things and you're the one with the answers."

"About the house?"

"About Logan Hughes."

"Really? Oh, Dilly needs me for a second. Hold on." And she set the phone down while she tended to the little girl.

Dilly giggled in the background. Mercy was good with her. Elle heard it in the way she spoke to their niece. Technically, Dilly was Mercy's daughter now, but the blood relationship was aunt and niece. It cheered Elle that Dilly was in loving hands. Janna had been a drunken, neglectful woman with a mean streak. It was weird how Clay had missed the resemblance to their mother, but he'd been young and wanted the excitement Janna ignited. If love was blind, then sex made men stupid.

But it was clear Mercy was the opposite of her sister and Clay had got it right this time. He'd fallen hard for the golden-girl Mercy in spite of his history with the Talbot family.

Funny how she and Mercy Talbot, of all people, had both come back broke within months of each other. Elle had hardly been aware of Mercy back in school, other than her being Janna's sister. She shook her head to clear her negative feelings for Janna. They had no place in her dealings with Mercy.

Mercy came back to the phone. "Sorry, she needed me."

"No problem. I get it." Elle warmed her voice. "Children come first."

"Thanks. We're trying to get her to understand about not interrupting when we're talking but being quiet while we're on the phone is a different thing altogether." Mercy laughed and Elle chuckled with her.

"Logan mentioned the work you did for him when you first returned to Welcome. We talked about me taking the job."

"I assumed he'd filled the spot by now."

"I know he needs flexibility and that's a problem for me." Elle explained about not having anyone to leave Clarissa with if she was called into work. "Do you know anyone who might take her on short notice?"

"No, sorry. My mom watches Dilly when we need a sitter," Mercy said, "but she's busy with her acting classes and rehearsals these days. If I were home I'd take Clarissa for you, but my schedule can be erratic. I'm not even sure when we'll be back this time."

"It must be nice to have a mother to lean on."

"Having Hope Talbot for a mom is a double-edged sword." Mercy chuckled good-naturedly.

"Before we married," Mercy said, "my parents had Dilly on the days that Clay worked. But my mom made my return to Welcome a challenge in many ways."

"Can you recommend anyone else? Do you have old friends in town?" She refused to give up entirely, but this was a longshot.

"No. I can't think of anyone," Mercy said. "To be honest, the good people of Welcome weren't exactly welcoming to me."

"I get why no one's been nice to me, but what the hell did you do?" Elle blurted, confused.

"Not me so much as my mother. She's been prickly with most people for a lot of years." She laughed. "Not to mention how judgmental she is."

"Yeah, she ran off at first glance when she saw me in the canned-goods aisle. Took off like a rocket with a full payload."

"I'd like to apologize for my mom, but apologies never worked when I applied for jobs around town. People have long memories and deep grudges in Welcome." She sounded sympathetic.

Elle's belly clenched. Returning to Welcome was the worst idea she'd ever had.

"I took a shot with Logan that paid off," Mercy was saying. A smile seeped into her sister-in-law's voice. Logan had come to Mercy's rescue, just the way he said he had. The way he was trying to come to Elle's.

Well, Elle didn't need a rescue. She needed work. Still, Logan had roused her curiosity.

"What is it that takes Logan away from the office? He was vague about that and hinted that I should ask you." Logan was smart enough to know she'd ask Mercy. That way he wouldn't have to explain. Sometimes the heavy lifting in life was best left to others, especially when it hurt to talk about it.

"It's happening less often now, but his brother, Jamie, has been in rehab for a while. He's had a couple of relapses and Logan's the one who tracks him down and sorts things out."

"Oh. I see." She tried not to think pitying thoughts, but her heart softened just the same. Logan didn't need or want her pity. He was doing what he had to do for family.

She got it.

"Thanks for telling me. I'll keep this to myself." After that, the conversation moved to how her children were faring with the move and how nasty Denise had been at the school.

"I remember Denise Jones," Mercy said. "She has a lot in common with my mother in the attitude department. I can see how your meeting went sour. I'll get the letter affirming your address as soon as Clay comes home. We'll have it notarized and couriered to you immediately. You should have it tomorrow."

"Great. Thanks, Mercy. That's one thing off my list."

"What's next on your list? Maybe I can help with that, too."

First Clay offered her a place to live, and then Logan helped her hump furniture and tried to give her a job and bikes for her children. And now Mercy would get her children registered in school. What had happened to the take-charge parent she used to be? She didn't like the person she'd become: needy, dependent.

Lonely.

She'd never been lonely before. But returning to Welcome had brought up old memories and emotions she had never expected to face again.

But she had to. For the children's sake. And if she needed help, she'd set aside her ego and take what she was offered. "Logan showed up with bikes for my twins. Do you know anything about that?"

"He told Clay he'd bought them."

"After the fact?"

"Yes."

Elle wanted to groan with frustration. "He can't just buy my kids bikes. I'm not a charity case."

"I'm sure he doesn't think that. Logan's a genuinely nice person."

Elle humphed. "I'm paying for them just as soon as I get a job. The crib, too."

"No. The crib's from us. Our welcome-home gift."

"He didn't tell me that."

"We'd be happy to cover the cost of the bikes as well," Mercy offered.

"No, thanks. I told Logan I'd repay him and I will." It was bad enough that Logan saw her as needy and broke. "But I appreciate the crib. Logan says it will take a few days to be delivered."

"Good, it's settled then."

"I need a job," Elle said, "but without daycare, I can't take the job Logan offered. And it's only part time. I'm screwed." Her mind raced and defeat seemed inevitable.

"I may be able to help with the job," Mercy said, with a lilt in her voice. "I just thought of it! And with luck, you can take Clarissa to work with you."

Chapter Four

"WHAT KIND OF JOB WOULD allow me to take Clarissa to work?" Elle asked Mercy. She'd about given up hope for a job through friends or family. But Mercy just may have thought of a good possibility.

"Do you remember Karen Bowler who runs the dog rescue?"

"Of course, she's our neighbor. Had a daughter, Brianna. She and her parents bred poodles when we were kids." *And she was my friend when I needed one most.*

"She's having knee-replacement surgery after putting it off for too long. She'll need help with the dogs. Since I've come back to work, I've hit up friends with connections and the rescue is swimming in donations. I volunteered to help at the kennels when I needed to do something with my time and no one had a job for me. But now Karen could afford to pay you, at least during her recovery. It's something until you find daycare and better pay."

"What would I have to do?" She had visions of handling donations and keeping books and her head swam. She wasn't great with numbers.

She heard a slight hesitation on Mercy's end and then a sigh. "There's a catch."

"What?"

"It involves a lot of shoveling." A suspiciously soft chuckle came from Mercy.

"Let's be clear. Do you mean dog shit?" But Elle knew, she *knew*.

"First, you shovel food into their bowls," Mercy said, her voice a light and airy near-laughter sound. "And then, later, you shovel poop out of their kennels."

Mercy's revenge must taste sweet, after all, Elle had whupped her sister in a bar. "I'll do it. But where will Clarissa be while I'm dealing with pooping dogs?"

"In the house with Karen."

"Oh, no. No way. If Karen's recovering from surgery she won't be able to chase after a baby. Clarissa crawls everywhere." The second job she had to turn down. "There's no point discussing this any further." Even though Karen was a friend, it felt awkward to go begging. Even this conversation made her edgy and uncomfortable. Everything in Elle rebelled at the idea of playing on her old friendship with Karen.

"Go see Karen," Mercy responded. "Take Clarissa with you and something will work out. I'll call Karen right now." Her cajoling tone continued. "Oh, if she's taciturn, please give her a pass. She's in a lot of pain."

Elle winced in sympathy for her old friend. With Karen in pain, she'd need a pair of willing hands. Maybe she was lonely, too. Brianna had moved away permanently when she went to college and this could count as a small measure of payback for all Karen did for Elle back in the day.

"Clarissa's ready for her nap now and I want Karen to see her at her happiest. I'll go over in a couple of hours." She locked away the deepest memories of what had driven her to seek solace with Karen all those years ago. Sometimes recalling the past hurt. "Thanks for thinking of this, Mercy. But I don't hold out a lot of hope that things will work."

After they said goodbye, Elle stuffed her phone into her pocket.

Elle didn't want to get her hopes up about a permanent job with the rescue. However, Elle let a seed of hope grow about a fresh start with Mercy. Elle felt a stronger connection to Mercy than she'd expected. A bridge toward a friendly future had been crossed.

The two women had Dilly and Clay in common and had similar challenges when they came back home. Mercy should have had people falling over themselves to help her out, but she'd been left high and dry.

Logan Hughes, the man who seemed to be always in Elle's thoughts, had been willing to help both Mercy and Elle. Maybe he had a soft spot for damsels in distress. Or maybe he was always fishing for vulnerable women. Or maybe he was just that nice.

Maybe. But knowing Logan had been there for Mercy made Elle feel less special.

The other thing she and Mercy had in common was having grown up with difficult mothers. They were each doing their best to mother differently. It shocked her that the beautiful, poised, and talented Mercy Talbot had a mother who wasn't Carol Brady perfect. Several of her assumptions blew apart. *Wow. Just, wow.*

The baby fussed, needing her nap. After changing Clarissa's diaper, Elle moved the play yard from the living area into the bedroom the girls shared. She pasted on a sunny smile and picked her up. "There's my sleepy girl," she crooned. Eyes drooped, a thumb went into a mouth and Clarissa slid into her nap. She'd need a crib soon. This play yard wasn't sturdy enough, big enough, or permanent enough.

Okay, so maybe she'd take the crib without quibbling because it was a gift from her brother and his wife, but she would definitely reimburse Logan for the bikes.

THREE HOURS LATER, Elle waited at Karen Bowler's back screen door. When Karen pushed the door open, she opened her arms and Elle stepped into them just as she had so many times as a child. She juggled Clarissa on her hip and leaned in close. "You even smell the same," she whispered against the older woman's cheek. Her hair had gone iron-gray and her cheeks bore signs of age and too much sun, but her eyes lit with happiness.

"Elle, it's so good to see you." Her gaze swept over the baby and she smiled in sweet welcome. Clarissa gave her a drooly smile and clapped her hands.

At last here was someone who was glad she'd returned. The warmth of Karen's welcome had Elle dabbing at her wet eyes. "I'm sorry I didn't stop by as soon as I got home."

Karen *tsked*. "Don't fret. I've heard how busy you are with your family." She raised her eyebrows and Elle flushed. The older woman backed up to take a seat at the kitchen table.

"Yes, four children keep me running." Elle set Clarissa down and took a seat across from her old friend. The baby immediately rose to hold on to Karen's knees.

Karen was in obvious pain, her back had stooped a little, but her old neighbor was happy to see her. Elle pushed past her reluctance to ask for help, but this was Karen and she'd understand.

Half an hour later, Karen seemed thrilled at the idea of having Clarissa with her while Elle worked her shift in the kennels. Elle had busied herself making coffee while Karen cooed at the baby. She returned to the conversation haphazardly. "The pay's not great," Karen said, "but since we have regular cash flow from donors now, we can give you six hours a day." She crooned the words at Clarissa. "How would that be?"

"I can manage on that," Elle responded quickly. "Clay's letting me live in the new double-wide rent free."

Karen's gaze narrowed on Elle and the crooning tone left the room. "You own half that property. And Clay would never expect you to pay rent."

Elle grimaced. "I hate needing help, Karen. Hate it."

"You and Clay paid a high price to have the right to live on that land. It's yours now. Wipe the past away by making new memories.

You have a future here, Elle. I know you never expected to return. But you're here now."

Elle gulped and nodded, but firmed her lips to keep from whining like a child.

"Make the best of it," Karen advised her. "This is trite, but it's true: the best revenge is to live well and you and your kids can do that."

"You're right. I should quit thinking about the past and look ahead." Once she got on her feet she'd arrange payments for the cost of the double-wide, but the land was hers. "Six hours a day would work fine. I'll start after my older ones leave for school and Clarissa's ready for her first nap. She can have it here if that's okay." She'd drag the play yard over every morning.

"Great. That'll give me an excuse to clean up Brianna's old crib. I'm hoping to have reason to use it someday for grandkids, but so far, she's had nothing but hard times from men." Karen gave her a broad smile and slipped a knee brace onto her leg. "This thing's been helpful but I'm looking forward to the surgery. They say a knee replacement changes your life. Well, I'm ready."

"What about after your surgery? How will you manage with the baby if I'm out in the kennels?"

Karen waved a hand in dismissal and rose to her feet. "Come on out here and I'll show you." She moved stiffly but that was to be expected. She led Elle through the house to the front screened-in porch.

"This is like a big playpen," Karen said. "I usually sit here for my evening television." Karen patted a lounger. "We can set up a toy box and I'll be fine to watch her play. She can't get into any trouble in here as long as we close the door so she can't escape. If you come in for lunch to feed us it'll work. They say I'll be on my feet soon anyway."

Elle was only half-convinced but kept her concerns to herself. She'd have to check on them more often than Karen envisioned, but she was willing to give it a try.

The baby reached for Karen to take her and the older woman took all of a second to grab her out of Elle's arms. Clarissa cooed and clapped her pudgy hands on the older woman's cheeks. Then she planted a kiss on Karen and Elle could swear her friend blinked back tears. "Oh, it's been a long time since I've had a sweet baby kiss."

Karen looked at her over the baby's head. "Let me do this, Elle. Things are tough for you right now and you're fretting about needing help. But this is what neighbors are for. Lending a hand."

And there it was: the reminder of the times she and Clay had to run to Karen for respite from the fighting at home. No one else in town would have taken them in, given them chocolate milk and homemade cookies, and a place to sleep for the night. She and Clay slept end-to-end on a long sofa in Karen's living room. They'd be gone at first light, returning home before their parents would wake from their stupor. Then they'd get ready for school.

She and Clay never talked about their childhoods with each other. No need. Karen was thoughtful to avoid a direct reference to those bad days. But looking at her now with her iron-gray hair and bad knees and kind eyes, Elle remembered her soft hugs and gentle pats when they were needed.

"I can't think of anyone I'd rather leave Clarissa with than you." She sighed and skimmed her hand down Karen's arm where she held a bouncy baby in a firm but gentle grip. "Thanks for all you've done."

Karen nodded and looked at the baby. "That's no problem," she said in a happy voice. "No problem to see to this little dumpling." Then she blew bubbles at Clarissa, who giggled and clapped her hands on Karen's cheeks again.

Chapter Five

TWO DAYS LATER ELLE served up the last bowl of kibble to a couple of newcomers to the kennels. The pups had been found with their dead mother at the side of the road. The mother had succumbed to injuries before a driver noticed them huddling next to her. The driver had brought them to the rescue right away.

Nicola Thornton, Clay's new partner in his clinic, had checked them over. Healthy and apparently uninjured, the pups were plain brown mongrels. They'd recently weaned and they loved their puppy kibble. She crooned and stroked their silky ears. She rose to her feet and left the kennel, careful to latch the gate behind her. "You're so cute someone will take you home soon. Bet on it," she said, still crooning.

A sharp call from the house made her drop her food scoop and bucket and run for the back door. She barreled inside with her breath held. "Clarissa," she called. "Karen?" She ran for the front of the house. A screaming cry carried through the house like a siren.

When Elle reached the living room, Karen was on her knees, her face ashen and moist from pain. Clarissa wailed from under an end table. She'd crawled under just fine, but hadn't figured out that she needed to lower her head to crawl back out. Another blood-chilling scream erupted.

"She's okay, she just needs help," Karen said between gasps. "I wanted to give her more room to explore and she went for it." She tried to laugh, but it came out a pale imitation. "She got bored with the screened-in porch," she explained. "Stupid of me to let her out without you being here. I should have known better."

"That's okay, sweet girl," Elle muttered to Clarissa. She reached under the table, gently pushed Clarissa's head lower, and pulled her out from under the table. "There, there." She kissed the baby's sweaty forehead and set her down on the richly patterned rug. "Here you are, safe and sound."

She helped Karen to her feet and into an armchair. "I'm sorry," Karen said. "I thought I could handle this, but she's too quick. I'd forgotten how fast a baby can crawl." She grimaced in pain.

Elle nodded. "She's faster every day and more determined to get where she wants to go. She'll be toddling soon, too." She couldn't settle with Clarissa being watched by a woman who wasn't fast enough to save her from harm. And the surgery for Karen's knee loomed like an ax about to fall.

"She's pulling herself up and walking around the furniture," Karen said with a nod. "You're concerned." She massaged both knees. "I understand. I wish I was in better shape to chase a crawling baby, but when she starts to walk, she'll be too fast for me."

Elle patted Karen's shoulder. "We tried." She lifted Clarissa and bussed her cheek. "But I'll have to find another job and daycare."

Karen accepted Elle's decision with a small smile. "I'll pay you for the time you've put in." She shuffled toward the desk she had tucked in a corner of her living room.

"Thanks, I'll take it." Elle wanted to say no to the pay, but she needed the money. She waited while Karen wrote a check. After she read it, her pride kicked in. "This is too much."

"If I could do more, I would. Honestly, I don't know how you've managed thus far." Karen looked sorrowfully at her.

Elle'd sold most of her furniture, the five-year-old SUV Ben had left her with, and anything else of value, but Karen didn't need to know the details. Elle didn't miss any of that stuff anyway. She had her kids and that was everything.

"We get by," she admitted. "Some weeks are better than others." But bravado and nerve could only take a family so far. She'd come home to regroup and give the kids a stable life again. Since Ben left, life felt precarious.

She'd struggled with the decision to come back to town, but living on the property she shared with Clay was her best option. Still, it seemed like going backward, not forward. How could she find a future when she'd returned to her past?

"I wish I knew someone offering daycare, but all my friends are busy chasing grandchildren. None of them has the energy to take on another child. Maybe I could check with Brianna's friends. The few who still live here, that is." Karen pursed her lips as she thought.

"Don't worry about it," Elle replied, appreciating her friend's concern. If Brianna's friends were like Denise Jones, they wouldn't help out anyway. "I'll find someone."

"How are you getting on with Mercy?" Karen asked.

"So far we haven't seen each other. I wasn't able to come to the wedding." She felt bad about bailing on the wedding but that was when Clarissa came and Elle couldn't leave. "We've talked on the phone a couple of times, though. Clay and Mercy will be home by the weekend. We'll get caught up then." It was Wednesday and the children had been in school since Monday.

Karen grunted. "Don't judge Mercy by her sister or her mother. She's not like Janna or Hope. Not by a long shot."

"I've picked up on that." Karen seemed to need more assurance, so Elle continued. "Mercy's good with Dilly and Clay sounds happier than he ever has." She cocked her head. "Is he happier?" Karen would know, really know, Clay's heart. They had a bond that had only grown deeper as Clay had matured.

"He's settled and happy and is looking forward to a future with the woman he loves. A woman who loves Clay's daughter like her own."

Karen's reply eased Elle's mind and confirmed the vibes she'd been picking up.

"Her mom's still a tyrant." She hadn't forgotten how quickly Hope Talbot had distanced herself in the grocery store.

"Hope Talbot's a piece of work, but she's coming around. She loves Dilly, too, but she has a strange way of showing it. They had a hell of a time convincing her to let the child be herself, rather than forcing her to be a copy of Mercy."

Clay hadn't mentioned much but her niece had been unhappy and let the world know in the only way a three year old could: with temper tantrums. "Things are better now?"

"Miles better. Hope's come around about Dilly and is more relaxed than I've ever seen her."

"Sometimes I wonder if my mom would've changed if she'd been given more time." The murmured thought had come out of nowhere. Elle never thought of her mother anymore, especially in a nostalgic, yearning sense. Must be because she'd come home to Welcome and their property. Her cheeks heated that she'd reveal all this to Karen.

Karen shook her head sadly. "Not likely. Your mom lived her life her way. Take what comfort you can from that."

"Her way. Right." Her way had been a damn shitty way to live and raise children.

JAMIE WAS KILLING THEIR mother. Logan was convinced his brother's problems were sapping the life out of her. Logan fell back into his office desk chair, weary beyond belief. Another night of cruising the streets searching for Jamie had turned up nothing of use. This time, he'd vanished into some hellhole where he could use without interruption, without consequence, without caring that those who loved him cried.

Bastard.

He set his head into his hands, rubbing his thumb heels into his eyes. Their dad had washed his hands of Jamie and, if not for their mother, Logan probably would, too. But Jamie, true to his addiction, manipulated their mom into giving him money, time, and love.

Whenever Jamie tried rehab, their mother got her hopes up. She hadn't accepted yet that Jamie liked taking a break from his street life. Rehab was akin to a vacation from Jamie's reality; a place where he could go, get clean, rest, and recuperate all for the price of a few lies and convenient half-truths. *"Things will be better this time, Mom. This time, it'll take. This place has a better program. This time they'll help me."* Bullshit. So much bullshit. Jamie had never once taken responsibility for his recovery or said that he'd do the work. It was always someone else's responsibility to get him clean.

Part of him knew that Jamie was caught in a web he might never get out of, but another, darker part of him hated his brother. God, what a mess.

Logan and Jamie were adopted at the same time. But Jamie had come from an addict mother and Logan suspected he'd been born predisposed. He remembered the night his little brother had discovered booze and drugs. He'd never been happier. *As if he'd found something that had been missing his whole life.*

His office door opened. He straightened so whoever entered wouldn't see how beaten he felt. Elle Foster stood spotlighted by the sun lighting her face from the window at his back. He returned to his slump when he saw her. "Elle, what can I do for you?" Dimly, he realized she'd come alone. No children crowded his entrance and there was no stroller taking up space.

Not a kid in sight. A rare moment. Her expression was wary, almost defiant. She needed something, he guessed. "Come in and take a seat." He waved her toward the chairs on the other side of his desk, but she ignored the invitation and hung back by the door.

"You can tell me more about the job Mercy did for you."

"I heard you were working out at Bowler's Rescue. That didn't pan out?" Mercy had told him how physically exhausting it had been. Not to mention the emotional drain that came with the dogs' stories.

"No, it didn't." She closed the door behind her and stood with her back to it, her hands presumably clutching the knob. He frowned because she didn't want to be here. Which was fine with him, all he wanted was to crawl over to the cot he had in the corner and fall into it. "What's happened?" she asked. "You look like hell."

"Thanks," he drawled. In the interests of speeding up this visit, he said, "I'm exhausted after chasing down my brother all night."

"Did you find him?" she asked with a tilt of her head.

"No."

"Sorry. That's rough." Her eyes assessed him, but he was too tired to care if he measured up to whatever yardstick she used.

"Yeah," he quipped. "I'm supposed to be here, alert, awake, and ready to roll." He smashed his palms into his eye sockets again. "As you can see, I'm bagged. All I want is to pass out on that cot over there."

She followed his gaze to the bamboo dressing screen he used to hide his private corner. She nodded. "It's behind the screen?"

"Got it in one."

"You want me to take your calls? I could stay while you nap."

"Where's Clarissa?" He checked the time. "Is Daniel home from school?"

"Got it in one." Her gaze flattened. "I understand I'm not the ideal candidate, but I'm a fast learner. How hard can it be to answer a damn phone!"

He leaned back in his seat. "For one thing, you need a pleasant tone of voice. To be honest, you don't seem capable of producing one unless you're talking to your kids."

Her brows arched. She looked at the ceiling and tilted her head this way and that as she worked out what he'd said. "Got it." She gave him her widest, most inviting smile yet and said cheerily, "Mr. Hughes, I'm grateful for this opportunity. I want to get out of my forklift-driving and construction-flag person profession and move into professional telephone answering."

He barked a laugh and then another one. He shook his head. "Charming. Is this how you get most of your jobs or am I the only prospective employer to get the real you?"

She shook her head and bit back a smile. "You're the only one who's ever gotten me." She stepped closer and he saw she was serious under the smile. "You..."—she flushed—"Never mind."

"What about daycare?" he asked.

"I haven't exactly worked out all the details, but now that I see this place, I'm wondering if I could bring her here with me? Since you don't need me at that sales trailer, I'd be here most of the time, right?"

"With a baby?"

"Just until I find someone to take her full-time." She hesitated. "Mercy's coming home in a couple of days, maybe..." She trailed off.

"You'd leave her with Mercy?"

Elle hitched her shoulder. "I haven't asked yet. I wanted to see what you needed from me first."

What he needed. *Christ.* How about comfort for a start? How about sex? How about a conversation that didn't revolve around his godforsaken brother or house prices or the too-slow housing market or mortgages?

His thoughts gave him a start. Had he thought about sex with Elle Foster? And right on the heels of that thought came another. Hell, yeah, he wanted sex with Elle.

He smiled like the good guy everyone believed him to be. "I need help, Elle." He sighed deeply. "But until we know Mercy can take Clarissa for the meantime, I don't see how this can work." Plus he wasn't convinced she could actually handle the phone calls. Her pleasant demeanor could only last so long. "Could you pretend that whenever the phone rings, it's one of your kids?"

"I can," she said easily. She moved closer and took a visitor's chair. Once seated, she smiled in a more natural way. His breath caught at the lightness of her expression. This was Elle Foster exposed; the real woman under her tough exterior. The Elle her children saw all the time.

"I'm not sure why I'm surly," she confessed. "Maybe it's because I'm back in Welcome. There's something about this place that brings out the worst in me." Her eyes warmed as she gazed at him. He needed her warmth and slowly, deliberately, Logan leaned back before he showed his interest. It wouldn't do to frighten her off.

Chapter Six

ELLE SYMPATHIZED WITH Logan as she sat facing him in his office. He looked like hell. Exhaustion haunted his eyes, his cheeks looked drawn, and his shoulders slumped. She recognized the signs of useless worry and hopelessness because she'd grown up with both. "I could call Mercy right now," she offered, "and check to see if she'd be agreeable to watching the baby when she comes home. She and I have become closer the last few days and I know she'd be great with the baby. I hear her dealing with Dilly all the time." She drew in a deep breath, unable to stop her wild thoughts from spewing out into the air between them. "I'll keep looking for daycare, but I'm not sure how long Mercy will be home and—"

Logan put up a hand to stop her. She closed her run-on mouth and held her breath. "We just spoke and she's taking a break from filming for the rest of her pregnancy. So she'll be home for long enough for you to find daycare."

"Oh," she said, "that's great. Not sure she'll be up for this, but it's worth asking her." Suddenly, hitting up her new sister-in-law for baby detail seemed too big a favor. What was she thinking? She would put Mercy on the spot and make her feel obligated by family ties to take the baby. "It's still a shock that my brother married a movie star." A successful star who didn't have a nanny. A small-town girl from Welcome who'd come home broke and washed up only to be swept back into a shining career.

Mercy had won acting awards, had directors fighting over her, and had fallen in love with Clay, the former bad-boy-turned-town-vet. Hard to credit any of it. And here Elle was, asking this rising star to wipe Clarissa's nose and change her diapers. "Will she hate that I'm asking?"

Logan shook his head. "No, not Mercy."

"But she's a big star." The foolishness of this idea grew mountainous. Her belly flopped. "I can't ask." She made to rise. "I'll find another job." But her prospects in Welcome seemed pitifully thin.

"Wait. If you believe Mercy will have her nose in the air, think again. She's not like her mother."

"That's what Karen Bowler said. She told me not to confuse Mercy with Hope or Janna." Their conversations had been friendly and fun over the last couple of days, but that hardly constituted a deep and lasting friendship. Elle had no right to ask Mercy to have her back.

Logan nodded. "She's not like either of them. Just give her a chance. Mercy's no pushover. If she can't do it, she'll say so."

She wondered if Logan had a thing for her sister-in-law. It wouldn't surprise her if he did. They were in school together and, from what she'd gathered, Logan had been friendly with Mercy from the day she returned to Welcome. She wondered what Clay thought about Logan and Mercy being on such friendly terms.

"I'll tell her there's no pressure and if she says no, then there will be no hard feelings." Elle pulled out her phone to make the call. She didn't have a lot of minutes left, so she hesitated. Logan watched her a moment and then, without saying a word, passed her his office landline.

She muttered her thanks and with some relief, shoved her phone back into her pocket.

"Mercy's number is three on speed dial."

Surprised, she cocked her eyebrow at him. Her sister-in-law was number three. Presumably, her spot was right behind his parents' and his brother's. Did that mean no girlfriend?

"Okay." She used speed dial and Mercy answered on the second ring.

"Mercy Talbot."

"Hi, Mercy, it's Elle."

"Wow, lots of phone calls this week," Mercy said with a smile in her voice. "Wait. This is Logan's office number. Are you there?"

"We're talking about the job you left." She blew out a breath, but Logan smiled and nodded and she drew strength from his encouragement. "The thing is I still don't have daycare." She quickly told Mercy about Karen not being fast enough to handle Clarissa. "I had to give up the job at the kennels today."

"I'll watch her," Mercy offered quickly. "You can drop her with me whenever you need to be at the office. Or if she's napping Dilly and I can walk out to your place."

"Really?" She hadn't had to ask. Amazing. "Mercy, I can't thank you enough."

"We're family now, Elle. What's good for you is good for all of us." She chuckled in a friendly, interested way. "Besides, it'll be a bit of practice for when Baby Whosits gets here."

"Baby Whosits?"

"Dilly thinks it's a fun name."

Clay and Mercy had decided not to learn the baby's gender before arrival. Elle had to admit it was fun to go back and forth about what they were having. A movement from across the desk caught her eye.

"Logan's reaching for the phone, I'll pass it over." She couldn't believe her luck. Mercy really wasn't like her uptight mother or her hell-raising sister. Or Elle's idea of a movie star. Mercy was down-to-earth and put family first.

"Mercy, I'll need Elle in the office for regular hours, after all, not just casually."

Her breath caught at the news. What would Mercy say to regular daycare hours? "We'll need daycare on a daily basis until Elle can find a regular spot for the baby." He nodded and gave Elle a thumbs-up, but she shook her head. He couldn't decide all this for her. And where did he get off saying *we'll* need daycare? They weren't a team.

But regular hours would mean a bigger paycheck and she couldn't say no to this opportunity. Logan's shoulders sagged lower as he listened to her sister-in-law. The man was bone weary and overburdened.

She set aside her concerns when she saw Logan frown harder. When he raised his eyes to hers, they were dark. Sorrow etched his face. "Yes, he's missing again. I'm beat and need her in the office, but not at the sales trailer." This had to be about his brother. Compassion rose at sight of the pain in his gaze. "You'd be helping us both out if you could take Clarissa full time."

She softened when he used the baby's name. He'd brought out brand new bikes and helmets for Liam and Jorja just because he thought they needed them. He'd ordered a crib after asking Mercy what kind to get. Had she ever run into a man as thoughtful and kind as Logan Hughes? No one came to mind. Not even Clay, who, as good a brother as he was, hadn't asked what she needed for the children. Now that she had a full-time job, she could accept the bikes from Logan and have them paid for sooner than she'd hoped.

"Yes," Logan was saying. "He's relapsed. We'll talk when you get home this weekend." He held out the phone to Elle again. She took it.

"Elle," Mercy said. "I would have offered full-time care the first time we spoke, but I didn't think you'd trust me with the baby." The hesitation in Mercy's voice warmed Elle. "Dilly will love having her in the house."

"Thanks. Of course I trust you. Clarissa's not a china doll. She's just fast and curious. We'll talk more when you get home. Do you need me to do anything for you? Buy some milk, bread, eggs? I'd be happy to have some fresh food in the fridge."

"I'll shop online and have the food delivered to your place if that's okay."

"Of course. Tell them Daniel will sign as long as they deliver after he's home from school." She hesitated. "Mercy, thanks again. I owe you."

"No, you don't. We'll be raising our children together, Elle and this makes for a good start."

They were doing this. Being family. Being friends. It was a new situation for Elle and she wasn't sure how to feel. But warm-and-gooey covered it. She hung up, blinked, and looked at Logan, her new employer.

She handed Logan his phone. "Thanks." She kept saying that word. "I haven't thanked so many people for so many things in years." Probably her last wedding, she thought. Her final wedding, she reminded herself as she looked away from Logan's probing gaze. "What? Have I got a smudge on my face or something?" She brought up her tough-girl voice and hoped to put him off.

No such luck. "You make it seem as if no one's ever offered you a hand up."

She snorted. "I'll be here at nine a.m. Is that early enough?"

He nodded. "See you then." He stood and eyed the corner longingly. He obviously needed to catch a few zees.

She stood to leave but the phone rang, catching her halfway out of her chair. He turned to reach for it, but she lifted the receiver first. "Good afternoon, Hughes Realty." She made her voice nice and syrupy.

"Logan Hughes there?"

"He's stepped out of the office. He should be back in an hour. If you leave your name and number, he'll call you back as soon as he can." She jotted down the information and remembered to keep a smile in her voice. "Thanks for calling Hughes Realty. Logan will return your call ASAP." She hung up the phone and looked at him. Her nerves went taut. "Well?"

"You sounded great," he replied. A tinge of relief colored his words. He'd doubted her.

No wonder, because she'd doubted herself. She glanced down at the scrap of paper in her hand. "He wants to list his house for sale." Oh, God, she should have passed the phone over to him. "I'm sorry. What if he finds another agent before you call him back?"

He stepped over and took the note, brushing her fingers with his. A tingle ran through her fingers where they touched. He looked at the note. "Unlikely. I've met with this couple before. They were renovating and painting before listing the property."

She nodded numbly. It was important that she do a good job. "Can I screw up so badly that your business can go belly up?" From the looks of things, he barely kept the lights on in this office. Self-doubt blasted her and she wasn't used to it. "Whether or not I was good at my job didn't matter much at my other places of work."

Logan chuckled. "You can't screw up that badly. Most of my work is done from my car and my phone. I need an office, sure, but clients don't usually come in. I go to them."

Elle nodded. She generally bit into challenges, chewed them up, and spit them out. Her return to town had spooked her in ways she'd only begun to understand. She used to be a confident, take-no-crap girl. Where was the Foster girl everyone in Welcome remembered? It seemed so hard to be the parent she needed to be; the woman she needed to be.

"It's tough for me to depend on my little brother for a place to live. Like killer tough," Humiliation ate at her. She felt her hands twisting around each other and she looked down. Wringing. She'd been unconsciously wringing her hands.

The way her mother had when life had punched her in the gut.

Logan pulled her back into the present by setting his hands on her shoulders. He looked quizzically at her as if he knew she was lost in her worries. She raised her chin and looked him in the eye and said nothing. His hands were warm where they touched. Warm and gentle.

"It's an hour," he said as if he hadn't just pulled her back from the brink of a meltdown. "Thanks for giving me the time. That was quick thinking," he assured her. "I'll take my nap and call him back. Then I'll take the paperwork over to their house for their signatures. No problem." He squeezed her shoulders lightly. "You did great." With that, he turned and headed for the corner. "Now I need to sleep. Will you stay until I get up? If the phone rings again, I'd like you to take the call." She watched as he fell onto the cot and pulled the pillow over his head.

She stood and watched him for a minute. When he didn't budge again, a warm sympathy invaded. He needed her. She was doing him a favor by being here. She'd given him this hour to rest and he appreciated it.

Taking Logan's chair, she mentally practiced her happy voice. When the phone rang again she took another message. This one wasn't nearly as exciting as a man looking to list a house with Logan, but still, buying office toner must be important. As soon as she learned what toner was, she'd order some.

SATURDAY MORNING IN Clay's great room looked like a scene out of a Norman Rockwell painting. Jorja and Liam were building a fortress out of blocks on the rug in front of the fireplace. Daniel was reading a story to Dilly and Clarissa played patty-cake with Clay on the floor. All this left Elle alone with Mercy for a few moments of quiet chatting over steaming mugs of coffee at the dining table. "It's not often I get to sit quietly and talk to another adult," Elle mused aloud.

"I guess we shouldn't wander too far off topic then," Mercy said with an innocent look in her big, blue eyes. She was sitting farther away from the table now to give her expanded belly more room. Her skin gleamed with good health and her eyes shone with happiness.

Elle had already figured out that her wide innocent eyes meant her sister-in-law wanted details. "What do you want to know?" Elle braced for the typical questions. Like Clarissa's father's name. She could stick to the truth and say she didn't know, but that would only lead to more questions that weren't anyone's business.

"How were the first couple of days working with Logan?"

Elle frowned, taken aback. "Why?"

"He's a nice, single guy. One of the good ones." Mercy raised an eyebrow in question.

"No doubt." Elle blew out a breath. "Logan's younger than I am, in more ways than just years. My life's been a grinder that chewed me up and spit me out along with all these children. He's never been married, has no children, and has had most things in life go his way. I doubt Logan's ever made one bad decision in his life." And then there was the biggie. "Plus, I never, ever date anyone I work with. Ever."

"That sounds definite." Mercy slid a bran muffin stuffed with raisins, seeds, and walnuts across the table to her.

"My last romance started at work. That led to marriage, and look where that got me: jobless, with two more children, and an ex with another kid on the way. Ben took up with a young woman barely out of high school, got her pregnant, and left us. Best I can figure he sees the workplace as a hunting ground for his next conquest. But Ben has a squirmy conscience, so he marries the women before moving on to the next convenient woman he works with."

"Slimeball."

"I have a knack for attracting them. I'm also totally blind when it comes to slime. I swore off men after Ben left. I've been on my own ever since."

Mercy made a sympathetic sound in her throat and looked at the baby. "Not completely on your own, obviously."

She cast a glance over her shoulder and saw her brother cuddling Clarissa and accepting sloppy kisses. "Clarissa is a sweet gift. The last baby I'll ever have."

Chapter Seven

"THE LAST BABY I'LL ever have." Elle was speaking, Logan realized as he slipped inside the open door to Clay's dining area. Mercy and Elle sat at the table with coffee and muffins. He hadn't meant to eavesdrop, but he hadn't wanted to interrupt them, either. The news that Elle didn't want more children shouldn't surprise him, given her circumstances, but he felt a quiet disappointment, just the same. A wonderful mother, Elle's children were blessed to have her.

"Logan," Mercy said, "we were just talking about you." She rose and gave him a hug. He hugged her back but his eyes wandered to Elle's. She wiggled a couple of fingers at him in greeting.

"Oh, no," he said. "My two assistants are comparing notes. I hope you haven't scared Elle off, Mercy. She's been helpful these last two days."

His comment seemed to please her because she gave him one of her natural, easy smiles. Slowly, he was seeing the real Elle under the gruff face she gave the world. Familiarity brought privileges, he supposed.

After he complimented Mercy on how well and happy she looked, he accepted a mug of coffee from Elle, who'd remembered how he liked it. "Thanks," he said.

She set the mug on the table in front of him. Her action meant he missed the warm brush of her fingers. He frowned. The touch of fingers was a small thing for her to avoid, but he felt the coolness in the gesture.

Clay came over to the table with the baby on his hip. Clarissa cooed at Logan and he cooed back. When she reached out toward him, Clay handed the little beauty off to him. She felt warm and soft and had more weight to her than he expected. "She's grown since I first met her," he said to no one in particular. Her brown eyes lit up and her chin looked wet from drool. "Are you getting more teeth, little lady?" He lifted his lips to show her his teeth. She poked them and they laughed together.

Mercy rose. "I'll make more coffee."

Clay bade her to sit. "My turn," he said and set about making another pot while the conversation and children's voices rose and fell in the great room.

Logan blew bubbles at the baby and she clapped her hands on his cheeks. She inspected his entire face and leaned in. When she bit gently on his chin, Logan laughed, startling her. Her eyes widened in shock and then she looked for Elle and leaned toward her. "I scared her," he said. "Sorry, sweetcakes, I didn't mean to."

Elle rose and came to his side of the table to take the baby. She looked into his eyes and smiled warmly. "She's ready for a nap, anyway."

"Put her in the crib upstairs," Mercy said. "We've got the nursery ready."

"Great, thanks." Elle turned and left. The sway of her hips was gentle, her legs long and lean, and her hair shone in a long fall to her shoulders. She was one hell of a woman.

He wanted a woman like Elle; confident, strong, beautiful, and a wonderful mother.

He looked forward to the day he'd hold a baby of his own. He wanted, more than anything, to look into eyes that were like his. He wanted to see a child grow from his seed and be all that he or she could be. He'd never considered life in those terms before, but as he watched Elle go up the stairs and cross the upper hall to a bedroom door, he knew exactly what he wanted.

But Elle Foster was not the woman to give it to him.

The quiet disappointment he'd felt at her comment made sense now.

Whatever attraction he felt for Elle would not lead to what he wanted. Best to let it go and move on.

The arrival of more visitors broke him from his thoughts. Hope and Nate Talbot walked in the same door he had. No one ever used the front door and walked around to the sliders at the back of the house off the eating area. Friends and family felt comfortable wandering into their yard and checking to see if they were in the great room.

Hope, a tall, cool blonde, set a plate of brownies on the table and then hugged Mercy, telling her how fresh and happy she looked. When she spied the children in front of the fireplace, she froze. "Are these Elle's children? With Dilly?"

"Yes," Clay said. "Daniel, Jorja and Liam, please come and meet Mercy's mom and dad." Dilly ran to sit with her grandfather. Nate gathered her into his lap.

As the introductions were made, Daniel eyed the brownies Hope had brought. Liam elbowed Jorja and pointed them out to her. They all silently pleaded with their eyes until Hope lifted the plate toward them. "Take one each and please eat them outside. They're gooey."

"Wow!" Liam huffed loudly and reached for the largest one. Jorja snatched hers and Daniel looked as if he'd like to refuse but in the end, he licked his lips and helped himself. While he ushered the younger children, including Dilly, out to the deck, he looked back into the room. His gaze sought Hope's. "Thank you," he said.

"You'd think they never got treats," Hope commented in a chilly voice.

"They're rare, Hope," Clay said in a quelling tone.

"They grabbed at them like starving animals." She firmed her lips.

This was Hope Talbot in her comfort zone; disapproval in her voice and holier-than-thou on her face. It was no wonder Mercy had run into people unwilling to show her any kindness, especially if they believed Mercy was like her mother.

Elle glided down the stairs after putting the baby down for her nap. Even from across the room, she looked closed off. If she'd heard Hope's comments then Logan couldn't blame her for her aloof attitude. He hadn't seen this particular expression since he'd first offered his help on the day she moved in. "Hello," she said coolly, looking as if she'd prefer to walk over burning coals than talk to Mercy's parents.

But they were all family now and she was stuck. Logan gave her a reassuring smile and watched Elle slide into her seat. She caught his look and a flicker of gratitude came and went, doused by the intimidating glare Hope gave the group.

"How long will you and the children visit?" Hope asked.

Elle narrowed her gaze and set it squarely on Hope. "As soon as my man gets out of prison, we're out of here. Mexico last he told me. He's got business there." The lie dripped sarcasm, all of it lost on the thunderstruck Hope. "These child pornography charges are a setup." Elle turned the screw. "Yep. A setup."

Hope gasped, her husband looked at the floor to hide a grin, Clay broke into a chuckle and Mercy slapped the table with her palm as her wild laughter broke over the group. "Stop!" She managed between belly-rolling laughs. "Do you want this baby to come early?" She wiped her eyes to stem her tears.

Logan gave Elle a high-five and shared a long look with her. Her blue eyes shone. Admiration filled him as Hope Talbot struggled with the crazy reaction.

"I fail to see the humor," she snapped. "Sarcasm is the worst kind of—the lowest form of—well, if you can't give a decent answer, then I believe we'll be on our way." She rose to her feet, clapped her hand on Nate's shoulder to stop his deep chuckles and squeezed him until her knuckles went white.

Hope glared at Clay. "I asked you months ago if having your sister and her children here would be a good influence on Dilly. I can see now that you don't care what being around her aunt will do to my granddaughter."

Nate rose to his feet. "Our granddaughter," he said to his wife. Then he turned to Elle. "You're a breath of fresh air, young lady. Welcome home." He stuck out his hand across the kitchen table and Elle took it and gave it one good shake.

"Thank you, Mr. Talbot."

Clay and Mercy rose as one and wore identical frowns. "Our daughter," they said in tandem.

Mercy rubbed her basketball-sized belly. "Elle is a wonderful mother and her children are exemplary. Dilly loves having them here and so do we." She wrapped her arm around Elle's shoulder and stood united with her sister-in-law, who looked dumbfounded by Mercy's vote of confidence.

Hope took a step back in shock and glared at her husband as if he'd turned traitor.

Logan loved the show of support. The Foster kids had always had each other's backs and it was plain that same attitude extended to Mercy, even against her own mother.

Hope stormed out of the house with Nate reluctantly following. With one more glance back over his shoulder, he spoke. "Sorry, I have to leave. She's my ride." With a jaunty wave, the older man left, leaving the rest of the adults to look around the table at each other.

One more burst of laughter erupted and then Mercy spoke. "She'll be fine. In a couple of days, she'll call as if nothing happened and she'll treat you with more respect," she said to Elle.

Elle shrugged. "I don't care what she thinks of me as long she leaves my children alone."

Clay nodded. "She will. I'll see to it." Mercy patted his arm.

Logan looked outside and saw Hope and Nate talk with Dilly for a moment, bend to give her a kiss and move off toward the driveway at the side of the house. The Talbots were gone, leaving the group closer and united around Elle.

"Thanks, everyone," she said quietly, looking a tad wild in the eyes. "Sometimes I can't control my mouth and stuff pops out." Elle looked sheepish, but Logan was proud of her for putting the run on Hope.

He gave Elle an encouraging grin. "I came over to deliver the bikes for Jorja and Liam. Shall we?"

ELLE WARMED AT THE solidarity her brother and Mercy had shown against Hope Talbot. And now Logan looked at her with appreciation. Not for her looks this time, but for how she'd put Mercy's nasty-mouthed mother in her place. No one, but no one, was allowed to make her children feel less than. And Logan agreed. His agreement sat in his eyes, his smile, and in the way he touched the small of her back as he ushered her outside to watch him deliver the bikes. Mercy and Clay followed behind.

"I'm having Logan hold back some of my pay until the bikes and helmets are paid for," she explained to Clay. "And I'll do the same with the crib. With a glance at Mercy, she continued: "It's not charity."

Clay frowned. "The crib is a welcome-home gift and you'll accept it, or else." He gave her a playful shove on her shoulder.

Elle rolled her eyes. "That's what Mercy said, too. Thank you, it's a lovely gesture."

Mercy gave her a sweet smile. "It was Logan's idea. He asked about a crib when he told us about the bikes."

Kind, generous, and thoughtful. She suspected this was the surface layer of Logan's depths. He had a lot more to show her and she looked forward to figuring him out. Because she wanted to dissect him, so she could understand him and put him into a familiar box. The man-box labeled: "don't touch."

The men in that box were losers, or dangerous, or threatening. He'd be the first nice guy in there. But she was determined to stuff him in and never look at him again.

"He argued with me about docking my pay, but I can out-stubborn any man," she responded. "Ask Clay, he'll tell you."

Her brother raised his hands. "She's the queen of stubborn. Logan didn't stand a chance."

The man in question stood out of earshot because he'd called all the children together and had them join him at the back of his SUV. There, he opened the back and lifted out first one, then the other of the bikes. Daniel's face fell into a thunderous frown, but Liam and Jorja looked ecstatic. They jumped around and screamed and giggled and then screamed some more.

"Mom, what the hell?" It was Daniel, looking choked. Pride and anger made him stiff.

"Daniel, come with me, please," Elle said in her do-it-now voice.

With a glare at the oblivious Logan, Daniel loped across the driveway and lawn to join her. She walked briskly with him toward the ring of trees that separated the homes. As they moved away from the others, her son wound himself up. "What does he want with us? Why would he give the twins bikes?"

"He's a nice guy," she said, keeping her voice level. "Logan helped Mercy out when she came back to Welcome. He gave her a job. The same job I have now, so he's my boss." She sighed at the mutiny she read in her son's face. She softened her tone. "Mercy's known him most of her life. Clay remembers him from school, too."

Daniel stopped walking and glared at her. "So you take their word for it that he's not some weirdo?"

That stopped her. She faced him square-on. "I've watched him when he's with you kids. It's not *children* he's interested in." He never looked at the kids with anything other than normal, healthy interaction. And when she was watching him, he watched her. It was her that his eyes warmed for; her body he glanced at when he didn't think she saw.

A disgustingly eager thrill rolled through her as she admitted how much she liked him watching her. Dangerous ground. The sooner she could thrust him into that don't-touch-man-box she'd reserved for him, the better.

What made a man like Logan tick? His type was a variant on the male species she was familiar with. Logan was gentle, attractive, and straightforward; nothing like the bad boys she knew. She'd been fathered by a bad boy, raised by a bad boy, been made pregnant by her bad boy teenage boyfriend. Then, just to put a finer point on all her crappy choices, she married a bad boy and been left again.

She reminded herself *again* that she was ill-prepared to deal with a man like Logan. But that didn't mean he was a danger to her children. She watched Daniel as his mind worked. He questioned her judgment more often, wanted to lead and expected her to follow sometimes. She couldn't allow him to make decisions that affected the family. Not yet.

"You think it's better that he's using us to get to you?" Daniel demanded. He turned and watched Logan as he bent to adjust the seat height for Jorja. "Because that's what he wants."

"Well, he won't get to me, will he?" Her statement rang true as far as it went. She wouldn't let Logan get to her through her kids. "These days I'm off the dating market, and he knows I don't date co-workers, especially not my boss. He can't hit on an employee. That's harassment and he's not stupid enough to get sued."

Daniel snorted in disbelief. He had an innate understanding of man/woman dynamics and while she doubted he had much experience with girls, he was on the cusp of manhood. She wondered for a brief moment if he'd walk the bad-boy line or not. She hoped not. "Don't grow up too fast, Daniel. My heart won't take it."

"Don't change the subject."

"There are other reasons for Logan not to hit on me. I'm Clay's sister and Mercy's sister-in-law. They're his friends and messing with me will mess with that." Logan Hughes was a respectable man and a *respectful* man. There were boundaries he'd never cross and the ones she'd laid out for Daniel were some of them. "Plus, I'm not interested," she said with emphasis.

She fought off a band of sadness that wrapped itself around her chest. "And he wants kids of his own, so that's the end of that."

Daniel took off across the lawn again. "And you won't have more children. Not for him or anyone, right?"

"No way. No how." She laughed at the thought. "I'm way past that," she vowed between chuckles.

"Okay, then." He shrugged as if a load had slid off his shoulders. "I guess he's all right. But if I see anything I don't like about him, he's toast."

She grabbed his head and drew him close to ruffle his hair. "Damn straight."

Chapter Eight

PRIDE. LOGAN UNDERSTOOD it and recognized it in Daniel. The teen hated that his mother had agreed to keep the bikes for his little brother and sister. But it wasn't Daniel's call to decide and that bit him in the butt as well. Fourteen was a hard year for boys. Half-grown, half his body a man's while the other half stretched to get to full height. And the thoughts about sex were all-consuming. Logan would not want to be fourteen again for anything.

Elle accepting the bikes was making Daniel's pride ache. He didn't seem to care that she'd be paying for them in installments.

Elle already made a difference in Logan's workday. And once office hours were over she happily took calls if he had to forward them. He even suspected her welcoming tone of voice was easier now. He certainly hadn't had any complaints.

Their system for the job was far from perfect because he wasn't sure when his parents would need help with Jamie or if the after-hours calls would come at a quiet time for Elle. There were a lot of ifs and buts and maybes when dealing with his brother. Add Elle's children to consider and things could get bumpy. But he and Elle were determined to make it work for everyone. He was happy to have her to fall back on.

He unloaded both bikes from the back of his SUV and Jorja and Liam squealed when they saw them. Clay jogged over immediately to help set the seats at the right height. Logan tried not to watch Elle and Daniel as they walked away.

Maybe he didn't watch them, but he couldn't stop wondering what they were saying. Daniel carried tension in every line of his body as he stalked beside his mother. Elle had passed along her pride and stubborn nature to her firstborn. She moved with her usual grace so Logan assumed this wasn't a full-blown argument.

Clay stood shoulder to shoulder with Logan as the children sat on their bikes for the first time. While Mercy pulled Dilly's balance bike out of the shed and put her helmet on her, Clay spoke. "Daniel will come around."

Logan eyed his friend. "Not sure that he should. Elle's a beautiful woman and it does her proud that her son's protective."

"She has me for protection. Besides, the day my sister needs protecting is the day pigs will fly."

Logan didn't agree. "It seems to me that she's already needed protection a time or two. She's been left with children to raise on her own. More than once."

"Point taken." Clay gave him a piercing look. "She's given her heart too often. I doubt there's anything left for anyone but her kids." A warning to back off or to be careful, Logan couldn't tell which.

"I admire her for keeping them all. My birth mother gave me up as soon as she could," Logan admitted. "When I was a kid my parents told me she'd been widowed and couldn't afford to keep me. But then I overheard them tell Jamie the same thing. I guess they didn't want us to feel unwanted." As Jamie's descent into drugs began, his mother had confessed to him that she'd lied about Jamie's parents. He'd been born to an addict mother who never named a father. When he got through high school without anything more troubling than typical experimentation with pot and booze, they'd considered the most dangerous years behind them.

But it wasn't illegal drugs that ensnared him. Jamie's poison had been prescribed by a doctor. No one had seen his addiction coming.

Clay shifted and drew Logan out of his memories. "You bought the bikes to save Elle the expense. That's all?"

"And to give them a happy summer. That's what my parents gave me and my brother. Having their own bikes will give them freedom and access to friends."

Clay stared at him as if he were a germ in a slide under a microscope. "You're serious."

"It's not that hard to understand. Kids cost a lot to bring up and they shouldn't suffer for want of the simple things that make childhood great. Having your own bike is one of those things."

Clay nodded. "Elle and I didn't have happy summers. But I'm damned sure Dilly will. So, yeah, I get why you want the twins to have a good time. I do, too." He slapped Logan's shoulder. "I'll help Daniel get his bike into shape."

"Thanks. He for damn sure won't take help from me. Make sure to check the tires, oil the chain, tighten the bolts, and adjust the seat."

"Got it," Clay said with a nod. "It's time I got to know my nephew better anyway."

"You'll make a great role model. Daniel's a smart kid and now's the time to catch his interest in something."

"Best get to it, then." Clay moved off to follow his sister and nephew. "Hey, Daniel, wait up. Let's take a look at your bike. It needs maintenance."

The boy turned and waved. He gave his uncle a tentative smile. "Sure."

Elle turned as well and looked straight at Logan. The smile she gave him was the same one she reserved for her loved ones; devastatingly sweet and natural.

When she returned to the group, leaving Daniel and Clay to deal with the old bike alone, she stood beside Logan. "They had smaller bikes with training wheels before but they outgrew them." She helped both children with their helmet adjustments. Once satisfied with the fit, she let them climb on.

The next hour flew by as both children learned to balance, pedal, and turn on their bikes. Once they reached a competent level, the adults trooped out to the quiet country road to watch them take off. Elle ran into the house to check on the baby and followed the group shortly after. At his quizzical look, she smiled. "She's still asleep. But I'll only stay out here a few minutes." She waved a baby monitor. "I don't have one of these." She cocked an eyebrow at him. "That is not a request for you to buy one. We have a full household and lots of people around to keep an eye on her."

She'd read his mind, but he accepted her refusal of help. She knew best how her family operated.

Jorja and Liam took off with hardly a wobble and headed down the road. "Mission accomplished," he said with a laugh as Liam attempted a "Look, Ma, no hands!" move. Beside him, Elle shuddered.

"My twins taking their lives in their hands. I'm not sure I can watch," she muttered.

"Jorja's much bigger than he is," he noted. Inches taller, Jorja towered over her twin. "At first I assumed she was older." Counting Clarissa's father, Elle had been abandoned three times instead of four.

"You're not surprised they're twins?" she asked. "They look nothing alike, but I swear they were born eleven minutes apart."

Logan nodded. "Daniel told me."

She said no more about her children because Liam's antics took him across the road and into the ditch. Logan got there first, but the boy was already brushing off his jeans and climbing back onto the bike. "There's no stopping him now," Logan said, pleased at Liam's ability to shake off the spill and continue.

His phone vibrated in his pocket and he stepped away to answer the call from his mother. "Hi, what's up?"

"Jamie's in a bad way and says he'll come home."

"Did he give an address?"

"Just directions. I think he's been living outdoors." Her voice caught as she struggled with her emotions. "He sounds sick."

"I'll be right there. Hold on." He disconnected and caught Elle's inquisitive expression.

"I have to go get Jamie. He says he wants to come home." But he knew it would only last a few days and he'd be gone again. Something of his defeat must have shown in his face because Elle stepped nearer and touched his sleeve.

"Go. See to your family. And take care of yourself, too. I'll handle the calls and now that Mercy and Clay are here I can even go into the office if you need me to."

"Thanks." He had the insane urge to brush his lips across her forehead in a simple goodbye, but he pulled back before making a complete ass of himself.

AT FIVE FIFTEEN P.M. on the next Friday, Elle was at her desk, after having a perfectly normal day when, without warning, Daniel's grandparents walked into Logan Realty. Their arrival shocked Elle into next year.

Daniel Graham Murdoch III and his wife, Susan, stood just inside the door and stared back at her. She'd only seen them a handful of times and hadn't talked with them, so she forgave herself for rising to her feet and feeling the need to flee. But they blocked the only exit so she sank back down to her chair. "What are you doing here?"

Icy dread trickled around her heart and seeped down to her belly. She disguised a shudder by straightening a file on the desk. She was alone here so had no witness to the mess of nasty she felt certain would unfold. And it *would* get nasty. The Murdochs hated her. Hell, they'd hated their son, Tad. They'd also refused to acknowledge

Daniel. "What do you want?" she demanded when they ignored her first question. "You showing up here can't be a coincidence. You're here to see me and I want to know why."

Tad's father, looking gray-skinned and old, frowned at her. He took the middle of the office, turning his head this way and that in blatant disapproval. She could read his thoughts as he surveyed the room. Pitiful. Penny ante. Insignificant.

He telegraphed his hateful thoughts the way he always had. In the same way that had made Tad the messed-up man he was. Tad's father lowered his brows and wrinkled his nose as if the room stunk.

The old man dismissed the office surroundings and turned his steel-gray eyes on her. "You've kept him from us for his entire life. It's time to quit this nonsense and let us have him."

"That's funny, because I remember things differently. I remember wanting to be part of your family, needing help with my first baby." She threw Mrs. Murdoch an arch look. "God knows my own mother wasn't there for me. But did you want to be involved? No."

Mrs. Murdoch opened her mouth to speak but the old man chopped the air with his hand to silence her. It worked and Susan Murdoch subsided into her role as timid appendage.

Oh, how Elle wanted to tell the old bastard where to go, but she had to step lightly. The Murdochs were dangerous as vipers and cunning. Tad hadn't stood a chance in that family. Old pity rose for Tad, but she had to shake it off. Pitying Tad had made a mess of her younger self. That girl didn't exist now and she'd best remember pitying Tad had brought chaos.

"What's taken you this long to come for him? We've been in Welcome for almost a month. Never mind that he's fourteen years old and you've never once asked to meet him. Never mind that you still won't use his name."

A gasp came from the unfortunate Mrs. Murdoch, who stepped around her husband to take her stand in front of the desk. She'd been quiet throughout Tad's life. A pushover, Tad had said when trying to explain life in the Murdoch dynasty. "Please, let's not get off on the wrong foot," Susan Murdoch said softly. Shockingly, she gave her husband the cold shoulder and leaned ever-so-slightly over the desk.

Closer, her soft brown eyes, so much like Tad's in his happy moments, looked hopeful. "Might we see Daniel? From a distance, at first, if that works for you."

"Don't be ridiculous, Susan," Graham interjected. "We won't beg. We won't kowtow. We demand access to our only son's only son."

"Get. Out." The blast of Arctic chill should have frozen them solid.

Old Man Murdoch may have held sway over his wife and son, but Elle would be damned if he rolled over her.

Mrs. Murdoch's eyes widened, but her husband took a threatening step toward the desk. Elle rose to her feet.

"Back off," she said. "I've never cared much for bullies," she added. "You push me and I'll tell Daniel exactly what kind of man you are." She slanted a glance at Susan, including her in the threat.

What she saw shocked her more than anything the old man could say. Susan surreptitiously slipped a folded piece of paper, about an inch square, onto the desk and turned toward her husband. "Please take me home, Graham. We've upset Elle and that was not our intention."

"We'll be back," the old man snarled as he took his wife's suggestion, but not her arm, and headed for the door. Susan followed him meekly, but Elle saw her shoulders square as they walked out.

The unassuming Mrs. Murdoch looked battle-ready.

After they left, Elle sank into the chair again. When she picked up the scrap of paper, her hands trembled. Shock, she realized, not fear. Never fear.

She unfolded the perfectly squared note. She read the words printed in a fine hand and then memorized the number under the words. Returning to Welcome had been a mistake, she could see that now.

But she'd never run from mistakes before and saw no reason to start.

The office door opened again and Logan walked in. "You're still here. I thought you'd have closed up by now. Shouldn't you be on your way home?"

"I— she caught her breath—I just had a fright is all. I'm leaving now." She swept the note into the trash bin under his desk.

"A fright? Did someone come in and scare you?" His face darkened with worry and suspicion as he swept the room with his gaze. When his gold-brown eyes settled back on hers, he stepped toward her. "Who frightened you?"

"Nobody important. I can handle them. I'm not easily cowed." With that said she snatched up her purse and left the office.

Chapter Nine

LOGAN STARED AFTER Elle when she sailed out of the office, her face ashen with high spots of color in her cheeks. He couldn't tell if she was angry or scared. Maybe both. He moved to the far side of his desk and looked into the trash. On top sat an open square of white paper she hadn't wanted him to notice. He picked it out of the receptacle and read it.

"Please. PLEASE let's talk. Call me tonight at nine. He'll be out."

Below the pleading words, written in a feminine hand was a phone number. Logan immediately checked the internet for the address attached to the number and found that it belonged to the most powerful family in town, the Murdochs.

Tad Murdoch was Daniel's father. Tad was short for tadpole, everyone knew it. Logan remembered thinking it was a ridiculous name for a guy on the cusp of adulthood. Tad insisted on people using the nickname because he never wanted to grow up and never wanted to be like his old man.

Logan fought for the memory to surface. Right after high school, and a spectacularly bad year of rebellion, Tad had left town for a while, a year, maybe. Then he'd returned and grown morose and vicious. His father had all but disowned him and his mother had suffered in silence.

Tad had died a few months ago, around the time Logan had heard that Elle planned to return to Welcome and needed to stay on the Foster property. With Tad's death, had the Murdochs cut off child support? Had they forced her return to Welcome? From what he recalled, Old Man Murdoch was a bastard and in the end, Tad had been more like him than he'd wanted to be.

Mrs. Murdoch must be reaching out to Elle about Daniel. Logan wanted to ask, but he doubted Elle would welcome his questions. In the past week, he'd given Elle time to settle into the office routine without interference. He had a tendency to hover when he thought someone needed help and Elle would hate that. She didn't need witnesses if she made beginner mistakes.

But from the stricken look on her face, Elle needed a friend right now. An impartial friend. Clay would be her brother and bring his baggage about Tad into the conversation and Mercy would back Elle up unconditionally. But Logan could see both sides of this family issue.

He checked his messages, found nothing urgent and pulled out his business check register. He'd wanted to set Elle up for direct deposit, but she still didn't have a bank account in town. He slipped the check into an envelope and headed out the door for the Foster place.

He parked on the road in front of Clay's place and sent Elle a text.

Logan: "I'm in Clay's driveway. Good time to deliver your paycheck?"

Elle: "Always a good time for $$"

Elle stood just inside the door of her house watching as Logan parked. Daniel stood behind her, frowning as usual. She still wore her office attire: a short black skirt and a pretty, silky top. Her other outfit consisted of a pair of flowy pants and a lightweight purple sweater. Both sets of clothes were emblazoned on his brain. She looked fresh, and bright, and interested when she was at work. She had no trouble using a pleasant tone of voice, either.

Progress.

He had no idea if what she wore was in style, but on her the outfits were devastating. And one of the main reasons he'd lingered in the bakery instead of returning to the office after his meeting this afternoon. He'd needed distance today and he'd been surprised to see her still in the office.

In spite of needing distance from her, here he sat, at her place. He put his window down as she approached.

"Thanks," she said. "I was rattled and forgot it was payday."

He held out the envelope and she took it, careful to avoid his fingers. "What spooked you?" he asked, curious to see if she'd talk about the Murdochs without being prodded. "Can you tell me now?"

Her eyes shifted skyward as she considered confiding. "Daniel's grandparents want to see him." She lowered her face and stared into his eyes, a mother bear afraid for her cub. He wanted to step out of the car and drag her into his arms for a hug, damn it. "They want to be part of his life." She focused on him again, her incredible blue eyes dark with worry. "They only want him now because his father died."

"Tad Murdoch died a few months back."

"Yes." She watched him as suspicion rose in her face. "His full name was Graham Daniel Murdoch IV."

He drew his head back in surprise. "You didn't name—"

"Tad said we'd get support money if we hit hard times," she blurted and rubbed her arms as if she were chilled. She probably was. The Murdochs had ice in their veins. She looked at her feet to shield her face. It wasn't like Elle to hide. "We were kids, scared and on our own. I agreed Daniel would be the fifth because I wanted a relationship with his family." She snorted. "That's how young I was. I believed Tad's family cared. My own never gave a shit." She lifted a shoulder and dropped it again. "Except for Clay. But he'd hooked up with Janna Talbot by then and Tad and I took off."

He drank in every word, surprised that she'd share this much. She must be deeply rattled to confess all this history in one go. He had to tread carefully. "Why did they come today?" he asked softly.

"Why not reach out when Tad died?" Or when the baby had been born, for that matter.

"I'm not sure. Until an hour ago they'd rarely spoken to me. They voiced their disapproval through Tad, and after Tad left me and came home I didn't hear any more from them. I was on my own with Daniel." Her voice had hardened by the end.

The Murdochs had abandoned their grandson once their son had returned to Welcome. He couldn't make sense of it. He'd come to offer another perspective and now had no words to offer. She stepped back from the car door, a silent invitation to climb out. Relieved she wanted to talk, he joined her. "We'll go for a walk," he said, with a significant glance at Daniel who glowered at them from the open door. "Does he know?"

"Not yet."

In a nervous gesture, she unclipped her hair and sent a cascade of dark waves to her shoulders. She turned away and headed off across the property, leaving Logan to follow. Tucking the folded envelope into her bra strap, she tossed the hair clip to Daniel as she strode past. "We're taking a walk," she said to her son. She led the way through the cedars to Clay's backyard.

Once out of earshot of the house, Elle relaxed. Her shoulders no longer looked like squared blocks of tension and her expression had moved from hard and angry to confused.

Logan kept his hands in his pockets while they crossed the lawn away from the driveway. "Let's check on Karen Bowler," Elle suggested. "She had her knee surgery the other day."

"Sure thing." The short walk would give them more than enough time to talk. The Murdochs had opened a can of worms by confronting Elle. Clearly, she had old wounds that he hoped hadn't festered. "You don't seem bitter about the way Tad's parents treated you."

"Whatever bitterness I held died a long time ago. Today I'm more worried about my son and how he'll take this sudden interest.
"

"Maybe the Murdochs are sorry for abandoning you and Daniel," he suggested.

"I doubt they've ever had regrets about anything. Especially the old man. They have a lot of business enterprises and no one to mold into their idea of a businessman. Tad never wanted to do the work needed to take over." She said it simply. "He had no ambition. Tad worked as little as he could. He held seasonal jobs. They didn't last long because he wouldn't show up the day after payday. He liked to party."

"You sound accepting. Didn't you expect him to be a provider? A father Daniel could depend on?"

She snorted, stopped walking and looked up at him, her eyes solemn. "I was just happy he didn't smack us around. He was good to Daniel, in his way. He'd send checks when he could, which wasn't often. He'd visit a few times a year."

"And when you married the twins' father?"

"Ben. His name is Ben." She stared at the sky for a long moment. When she looked at him again, she blinked. "Tad was okay with me marrying him and he cared enough to ask what kind of stepdad Ben would be."

"Did Ben party?"

"No. He was in a program and stuck to the twelve steps. He never faltered in that way, but Ben had a habit of dating women at work. They were easy." Her voice turned bitter. "I took a long time to see it."

He couldn't think of anything to say except the obvious. "He's an asshole."

"Got it in one. But he's a sober asshole, which means he can't blame the mess he made on booze."

It was Logan's turn to snort.

They walked in silence for a time and Logan didn't press for more about her ex-husband. Ben was a loser and had proved it by throwing away Elle and his twins. As they neared the fence that divided the two properties, he returned to the original conversation. "You believe Tad's parents want to groom Daniel to take over their business interests. That doesn't sound like much of a disaster to me." He couldn't see anything wrong with wanting to leave a business to a younger generation. "That's what families do. They pass along what they've worked for. Did they say that?"

"No. It's a guess," she muttered, sounding mulish. "But what other reason could there be? They haven't suddenly developed love for a boy they don't know."

"No matter their motivation, think what it would mean for Daniel. College, a ready-made career, and all that Murdoch money."

She studied her feet as she walked. "They'd take him from me. Take him away from Jorja and Liam, too. That's not right, no matter how you look at it."

Taking his cue from her, he walked without looking at her and talked without emotion. "He's old enough to decide for himself and no matter what they do, he'll remember all the years they ignored him. Give him credit for being the smart kid you've raised."

Instead of being angry, she sighed and stopped walking. She looked up at him, her eyes narrowed. "They'd probably get him into an Ivy League school."

Logan nodded and said nothing. She turned her eyes skyward and blew out a breath that sounded oddly like acceptance. "I could never do that for him. With just me, he'll need to work his way through college. And maybe he won't go if it's too tough," Her tone softened as the words came, taking on a dreamy quality. She sighed.

"From what I've seen of Daniel, he'd want to go straight to work to help you out," Logan said. "He could skip college even if you want him to go."

She bit her lower lip and nodded. "It was a miracle Doc Rimmel took an interest in helping Clay get through veterinarian school. Without his help, Clay would probably be driving a truck like our father."

"You won't find out what plan they have for Daniel unless you open the door. Call her tonight," he said. "See what she has to say."

She tilted her head and her gaze turned hard. Under the glare, he read a twinkle of humor. "You dug through the trash to read my super-secret note."

"It was sitting right on top. There was no digging involved."

"You knew before you came out here who'd upset me."

"Yep."

"You came to offer your opinion on something that's none of your business."

He put up his hands. "Shoot me. I give a damn."

She chuckled. "You believe I owe them something?" Her tone went cool and her eyes stilled.

"You don't owe them a fucking thing. But we're not talking about you and them. We're concerned with Daniel's future here. You could be closing a door before looking through it."

"Concerned, huh?" She looked at him with curiosity and he realized his mistake. He had no right to be concerned about Daniel.

"Aren't *you*? Concerned, I mean?" he prodded.

She climbed the split-rail fence that separated the Bowler and Foster properties. Once on the other side, she put her hands on her hips and shook her head. "I never considered Daniel being involved in the Murdoch businesses."

"But he's a Murdoch."

"I should have changed his name when I married Ben."

"Did he want to adopt Daniel?" She ignored his question and marched off toward the distant kennels. With her back straight and her strong strides, she looked every bit the tough girl she used to be. But he smiled because he'd made her think hard and that was all he'd wanted.

For now.

BRIANNA BOWLER ANSWERED her mother's door when Elle knocked. With her auburn hair and wide, bright-blue eyes, she'd grown into a beautiful woman. For a split second, they stared, and then fell into each other's arms. "Brianna," Elle said, choked with joy at seeing her again.

"Elle!" Briana drew Elle into a warm hug and squeezed her hard. "How are you?" During the hug, Brianna pulled her into the kitchen. "Mom," she called. "Elle's here."

Something warm and gooey opened inside Elle at the sight and feel of her old friend. Brianna was younger, around Logan's age, and had followed Elle around whenever Elle showed up at the Bowlers' place. When Brianna got old enough, she'd stand at the fence between their properties and call out Elle's name.

Karen had forbidden the young girl from climbing the fence onto the Foster property. Good thing. Elle had had enough to deal with protecting her kid brother. Shielding a neighbor child would have been an added stress.

As it was, Brianna had easy memories of their rambles through the woods when Elle heard the girl call. Their nature walks had been a welcome relief from being home and Brianna had been spared the tension in the Foster home.

"Brianna," Logan said in his deep, smooth voice. "Nice to see you again. You look great." He stood close behind Elle and the heat of him at her back warmed her through.

"Logan Hughes?" Another warm hug was offered and he took it. Brianna's eyes went from one to the other of them in appraisal.

"Logan's my boss," Elle said in a flat tone. "He was delivering my first paycheck and wanted to see how your mom's surgery went."

"It went fine. Textbook. She's in the sunroom. Come on through," Brianna said and led the way.

Karen stood when everyone trooped into the room. "Ta-da! See, I'm on my feet already," she said before she sat back down.

Half an hour later, it became obvious that Brianna was eyeing Logan like a woman on a mission. That was a good thing, Elle told herself. Logan and Brianna shared news about old friends from school and established that they were both single. They even liked the same television shows and binged watched when they found new ones.

Logan looked at her. "Do you have any favorite shows?"

"No. I'm too wiped at the end of the day to veg in front of the TV. I'm lucky if I can outlast Daniel."

"Me, I like those channels that show the oldies," Karen said from her lounger. "But I'm with Elle on the binges. Two episodes at a time, tops."

Karen rode the fast track to recovery and now that Elle had seen her old friend, she felt relieved. "Are you visiting, Brianna?" she asked Karen's daughter. "Or are you moving back to Welcome permanently?"

"That depends," she said with a quick glance at Logan. "I want to be here until Mom can get around well enough on her own. I'll oversee the rescue for her. There's nothing waiting for me in Seattle. I quit my job when they refused me leave to come help here."

Logan looked interested. "What kind of work do you do? Maybe I know of someone who's looking."

Which was what he'd asked Elle. She kept her face impassive, but inside, she couldn't deny feeling a twinge. Here was the proof she needed. Logan Hughes was a nice guy and kind to everyone.

"I'm in administration. I offered to work from here as much as I could, but my bosses didn't go for it. I might try my hand at virtual assisting." She gave a weak smile. "But for now I'm helping here." She stood beside her mother's chair and patted Karen's shoulder.

Karen smiled up at her daughter. "It's wonderful to have my girl home again."

A pinch near Elle's heart signaled her usual response to mother-daughter love. She never shared that closeness with her mother, but she was damn sure she'd have it with Jorja. They were close in a way that was different from the boys.

"I have to get to the bank before it closes," she said to Karen. "I'm glad you're already up and walking."

"Please kiss Clarissa for me. You've got a real sweetie there."

"Thanks, Karen."

Logan trailed her out of the house. On the back stoop, she said, "Don't leave on my account. Why not stay and catch up with Brianna?"

"We're having coffee tomorrow." He shrugged as if it were no big deal.

Half of her wished that was true. The other half wanted to spit nails.

Chapter Ten

HALFWAY HOME AFTER visiting with Karen and Brianna Bowler Logan got a text from Elle. He used voice activation to listen. The automated voice sounded cold and deadly in its computer-generated monotone.

Elle: "I need you at the credit union. Hurry before I kill someone."

Logan: "On the way. Hold your fire."

He pulled a U-turn when it was safe and headed for the credit union a couple blocks down from the office. Main Street was suffering its usual mini-rush at the end of the workday. Take-out meals were being picked up, people were picking up their children from a downtown daycare center and still others were running errands. Cars backed out of their parking spots as if no other cars were on the road. Logan needed all his focus to avoid a fender bender. He saw Elle long before he could get to her.

She stood stiffly by the front door of the square brick building when he arrived. Even from inside his vehicle, he could see her fuming. He parked and climbed out of his car. As he neared he saw that her face was blotchy, her eyes damp, and she had her hands clenched at her sides. "They won't let me open an account and take my money out right away," she blurted when he got close enough to hear. She shook her head. Other people had heard her and glanced her way.

She glared back.

He reached her side and clasped her elbow gently in reassurance. "Why not?" he asked in a low voice to calm her.

Her shoulders sagged, the fight gone out of her. "They said they want to hold it for a few days. To make sure the check will clear." She lowered her voice. "It's Craig Davis being a prick like he always was."

"What the hell?" Obviously Logan's check would clear. Davis knew damn well it would. Anger rose fast and hot at the insult.

The two of them intent and staring at each other were causing a scene on the sidewalk. All eyes were on Logan and Elle. Damn. He leaned close to her to shield her from curious stares. He forced three deep breaths in and out. When he'd calmed a bit he nodded. "What exactly did he say?" He kept his voice low and nodded to a passerby.

She stared at the sky for a long moment. "It's another piece of bullshit to deal with. But I need groceries and the check place down the block charges too much. I want a bank account, damn it."

"What did he say?" he repeated firmly to get her to focus on a solution, rather than the obstacle.

"Davis didn't want me opening the account just to take out the full amount of the check. He wants me to leave a balance." She bit her lip and her gaze hit the ground. "But I won't be able to do that with every check. Sometimes my account balance will be zero." She shuffled as if embarrassed.

Logan left her there and stormed the doors only to see Craig Davis watching avidly from behind the counter. "Craig." The guy had always been an asshole. Nothing new there.

"Logan." His gaze darted back and forth from Logan to where Elle stood outside. From here she looked ragged and alone.

But she wasn't ragged or alone. She was smart, determined, and had family and Logan at her back.

"My employee needs to open an account with her paycheck. What's the holdup?"

The asshole turned his flat expression Logan's way. "Our policy is to be certain a check's good before we cash it in full with a brand-new account. Who's to say Elle Foster isn't passing bad checks? Or that she didn't steal one from you."

"I'm to say." Logan stared him down. "I just told you she's my employee." Craig must be aware that Logan used the credit union to conduct business. Logan didn't keep all his accounts here, but Craig didn't know *that*.

"Send her in," Davis said. He made to leave and snapped his fingers at a teller to get her attention. "We'll deal with it."

Logan spoke before the other man could step away. "You handle this personally," he demanded. "With an apology."

Craig halted mid-turn. He scrunched his nose as if he'd smelled something brown and disgusting. Logan wanted to punch the look off his face, but settled for cocking an eyebrow at him. "I'll handle it," Craig muttered. "But it's not my place to apologize for this institution's policies." His narrow chin rose.

Logan turned to face the door and gave the watchful Elle a quick nod. She arrived at his side with her eyes aflame with a mixture of anger, relief, and triumph, but her downturned lips said she was furious. "I'll meet you for a coffee at the bakery when you're done." He smiled to put her at ease. "Since you've been paid, it's your treat," he said to give her back her pride.

"You got it," she said with a brusque nod before turning her baleful gaze on Craig's. "Let's try this again."

Twenty minutes later, Logan still steamed in the back booth of the bakery; his coffee forgotten, his cheese scone sat intact. Is this what she'd had to deal with since returning to Welcome? She'd mentioned needing a letter from her brother to get her children into school and now this. No wonder she was stubborn and on edge. Everywhere she turned people put up obstacles or the system beat her down. Where was the help for people who were trying to better their lives?

By the time she slid into the bench opposite him, he wanted to take action. "I'm calling the president of the credit union. She should be informed about how prospective clients are treated."

"Like she'd care." Elle touched the side of his still-full coffee mug. "You've gone cold." She popped back up out of her seat and went to the counter to order him another coffee. When she turned to come back, two steaming mugs in hand, she grinned. "My treat."

She placed his fresh mug down in front of him. "Everything's sorted out now. I'll leave twenty bucks in the account so that idiot Craig won't be written up for breaking the rules and I'll have my bank account." She rolled her eyes. "This is probably a good thing anyway. Maybe next time I can leave another twenty bucks in there."

He couldn't see how she could shave any money out of her budget, but she was used to living close to the wire. "I hate to dock your pay while you're short of cash."

"And I'd hate to return the bikes to you." Her level stare said she'd do it if she had to.

"Stubborn woman."

She cocked an eyebrow. "Surprised?"

"Not in the least."

She patted his hand on the tabletop. Her touch felt cool and impersonal, while he'd prefer hot and willing. He shut down the thought. "You forget that I'm not paying rent. I can manage as long as no unexpected expenses crop up."

"What have you decided to do about the Murdochs?"

"I'll speak to her tonight and see what she has to say," she responded in a considering tone. "It's interesting that she doesn't want her husband to know about the call."

He tilted his head. "People have secrets. Maybe she wants to protect Daniel from the old man."

Her eyes widened as she lifted her lips into a wan smile. "She never stepped in to protect Tad. She may have regrets about that now."

"Tad died just before I came back to Welcome," he said. "I heard his father collapsed at the funeral and his mother wasn't seen outside the house for weeks afterward."

"Humph. They never gave a damn about him when he was alive. He was never good enough for the Murdoch name and when I came along they did everything they could to break us up." She smiled grimly. "Maybe if they'd left us alone we'd have drifted apart like teenagers do. But once he saw how much they hated me, Tad wanted me even more."

"And now they want to meet Daniel," he said drily.

THE TWINS WERE TUCKED into bed, Daniel was busy with a final project for school, and Clarissa was sound asleep when Elle made the call to Susan Murdoch. The phone was answered after one ring. "I'm calling out of respect for Tad," Elle said, before giving the person who answered a chance to say hello. "I owe him that much."

"We'd like to meet Daniel," she said softly.

"I understand that," Elle responded in a dry tone. "But why? What could you possibly have to say to him after all these years?"

She heard a soft huffing sound and then an indrawn breath. "I'd like to apologize to him. To offer him support with his education." A pause came that Elle refused to break. After a long moment, Susan's voice came again. "I want to know my only grandson."

"This is because Tad's dead." Sugarcoating this wouldn't make it go down any easier.

"Yes. Because my son is gone and my husband is ill."

"He looked hale and hearty to me today," Elle snapped. "As obnoxious as ever, too."

Another long pause. Elle was about to ask if Susan was still there when the older woman spoke again. "It's not a physical illness."

This time Elle was the one to pause. She considered the words. "Are you telling me he's facing memory loss?"

"A form of dementia that will steal him away. We're not sure how long he'll be capable of living normally. How long he'll remember me."

She got it now. Mrs. Murdoch wanted Daniel so she wouldn't be alone. "You want my son as a replacement for yours. For company?" She should get a dog, Elle thought, but that would be too cruel to say. A waffle of sympathy wormed its way through her chest and cooled her annoyance.

"We should talk in person. Could we do that, please?" Susan's voice went ragged and Elle didn't want to make her plead.

"Over lunch tomorrow," she replied. "If I'm not tied up with work, I can meet with you in the bakery at noonish."

"I'll be there at eleven forty-five and stay until you arrive. Any time will be fine."

Elle hung up before she said anything more. She had a lot to process and Mrs. Murdoch had been candid. Kicking a woman when she was down didn't sit well. Susan had enough to deal with. And from the sounds of it, she'd sit in the bakery and wait all day if necessary.

The truth was Elle couldn't prevent the Murdochs from seeing Daniel. They could watch him from a distance at any time. They could manufacture a chance meeting or go to the school directly. Elle was sure Denise Jones would allow them to meet Daniel if they asked. That woman would do anything to get under Elle's skin.

And then there was Daniel. He might want to meet Tad's parents. Over the years, he'd asked a few questions but she'd managed to put off giving him any direct answers. Instead, she'd discussed the pitfalls of teen pregnancy and the collateral damage. She had no idea if she'd been right to segue into lectures, but so far, he hadn't pushed back.

Ultimately, at fourteen, he should have the choice of meeting his grandparents or not. This should be his decision, not hers. Logan had given her good advice. Her emotions around their treatment of Tad and how they'd abandoned her and Daniel needed to be set aside. Bitterness never did anyone any good.

However, the dementia the Murdochs faced was not her concern and she refused to feel pity.

But with Tad gone perhaps Daniel could finally get some of his questions answered. He deserved to have the chance to get the information direct from the source and not filtered through whatever bitterness and regret she may feel over ancient history.

She left her bedroom and found Daniel watching television in the living room. "Homework all done?"

"Yeah." He turned off the television and eyed her suspiciously. He'd fed everyone while she'd been at the bank and then having coffee with Logan. And he'd put the twins to bed while she'd been hiding in her room gearing herself up for the phone call. Daniel must have figured something was going on; he was a perceptive kid.

He was her rock, but sometimes she worried Daniel had taken on too much for a kid his age. Her son deserved more carefree days in his life. He deserved to enjoy his teens and do what other fourteen year olds did.

Elle settled in beside him on the old couch. When she sat too close he edged away, but she smiled and leaned in to brush his shoulder with hers. "What?" he asked.

"I have something to tell you and you need to give it some consideration before responding."

"What?" He eyed her warily.

"Your dad's parents, the Murdochs, would like to meet you."

His neck stiffened as he drew back. "Since when?"

"They came to see me at the office today and I just got off the phone with your grandmother." It felt strange to use that word to describe Susan Murdoch.

"Why now? I thought they hated us."

"That's what your father said, but after talking with Susan, I'd say it's worth listening to them. You can judge for yourself if you want to spend more time with them." She didn't want to badmouth Tad, but he'd been a bitter man. He'd expected to spend the Murdoch fortune without working for it. When they hadn't supported him or his decisions, he'd hated them. To the Murdochs, she and Daniel had been part of Tad's poor choices. But now it was up to Elle, Daniel, and the Murdochs to move forward if they chose.

She cupped Daniel's head and drew him close so she could kiss the top of his head. He actually settled against her that way and for a moment he seemed like the sweet, loving boy he'd been at four. She sighed and he allowed the snuggle, but only for a moment.

Four, after all, was a long time ago.

MRS. MURDOCH ANSWERED on the first ring again. "Murdoch residence," she said.

"You can see him on Sunday morning," Elle said without a greeting. "Alone. He doesn't want to see your husband." This way they wouldn't have to meet at the bakery tomorrow. The less time spent with Tad's mother the better. She held the phone out for Daniel to listen, too.

"Where?"

"Somewhere quiet. He refuses to be seen with you. He only wants to see you at first, not your husband." Daniel had insisted and he deserved some control over the situation.

One sharp intake of breath gave away Susan's shock. "Fine. Would your place of work be all right? It looks very quiet in there."

Elle narrowed her eyes at the remark. Yes, the office was quiet, but things would pick up soon.

Daniel nodded, putting an end to Elle's rising temper. This call was about Daniel.

"If the office is empty at eleven o'clock, we'll see you then. If not, you'll come here." Elle said and Daniel nodded again. Then she hung up.

Chapter Eleven

ON SATURDAY MORNING after a couple of meetings at Springhill Meadows, Logan decided to swing by and check to see if Elle needed help putting the baby's crib together. Clay was probably helping, but he hoped his buddy could go for a run. As he slowed to turn into the driveway, another car approached in the drive. He stopped and waved them out. As the car rounded his, he saw two women inside.

One looked to be early forties while the other looked young enough to be in high school. A baby sat in the back but he couldn't see more than a head of dark curls. Judging from the smiles and hand movements the women were talking excitedly. They looked happy and focused on each other. He didn't recognize them, so maybe they were friends of Mercy's from Hollywood.

He passed by the big house and slowly drove the extra yards to Elle's section of the property. But when he pulled in to park by Elle's home, the door hung open and Jorja and Liam sat on the steps. Jorja's hands covered her face, but Liam's was wet with unchecked tears. *What the hell?*

Dark foreboding pulled him from the car. On closer inspection, he saw neither twin was injured. In a clear bid for privacy, Jorja and Liam turned their faces away as Logan walked through the open door to the house.

Inside, he found Daniel stony faced with his shoulders squared and his back straight. He stood still, his face haunted, in the middle of the living room. A children's show danced across the television screen but the sound had been muted. A large flat rectangular box sat propped by the kitchen counter. The crib had been delivered on schedule.

Logan looked from the box to Daniel. The kid looked like he needed to punch something.

"Go for a run," Logan suggested. "Burn it off." Whatever 'it' was. "A run always helps me."

"She's in her room," Daniel said and pushed by him. It looked like the kid might take his advice. Daniel loped outside and took off up the driveway as if police dogs were on his tail.

A sudden silence filled the house until he heard the twins sniffle on the stoop. He leaned out the door. "Are you two okay? Not hurt anywhere?" But he'd already seen that they weren't hurt; not physically anyway.

They shook their heads no but didn't explain what was going on. Then he realized he couldn't hear Clarissa's happy babble. *Christ. Was she sick?*

He strode down the short hall and found Elle curled in the fetal position on her bed. No baby here, either.

The double bed took up most of the space in Elle's room. With nowhere else to sit Logan eased down beside her. The mattress dipped under his weight, causing her to roll toward him. "Elle," he coaxed softly. "Come here." He tugged on her shoulders and drew her close. A sense of doom curled like black fog around them.

She came without resistance, which frightened him more. *What the hell had happened?* She sobbed brokenly against his neck.

"Where's Clarissa?" Dread seeped, sticky and cold through his vitals.

"She came," Elle said in a broken whisper as if he wasn't there. "I knew it would happen someday, but not yet. Not today." More sobs.

Confused, Logan still couldn't hear the baby. "Where's Clarissa, Elle?" Where was that sunny smile, the welcoming giggles, the girl he'd given his heart to at first sight?

And then he knew. He set aside his denial of the awful truth. Someone had come for her. Someone had taken that sweet girl. "Who?" His voice sounded harsh but he couldn't soften it when his heart choked his throat. He wanted to *shake* the answer out of her. But, God, if he did that, she might break into pieces. And maybe he would, too. "Who? Damn it, Elle. Who took her?"

Elle drew in a harsh, bleeding breath but shook her head as if she'd said all she could manage.

His brain turned sharp and thoughts shot clear and true from every direction. "We have to get her back. Wherever she is, we'll find her and get her. The sooner we start looking the greater chance we have of finding her." The baby's happy, toothy grin danced in his mind. He could feel the pat of her little hands on his cheeks. His heart tore. "I'll call the police." He smoothed his shirt pocket and felt the reassuring rectangle of his phone. But Elle would have called by now. The cops should be swarming the place looking for—

Elle looked up at him then, ravaged and startled as if she'd just seen him. "I know where she is and she's never coming home."

Her lips moved and sound came out but he couldn't process what she offered. The clear thoughts he'd had scattered and his head filled with unformed sound. A scream inside his mind, maybe. Yes, a silent scream.

Cold anger broke through. "Her father? Did her father come here and steal her? We'll call the police. They'll get her back. He can't come here out of the blue and take her. There are laws."

Elle shook her head. "No, not her father. I don't know who he is."

He slumped and blew out a breath. "A one-night stand," he said simply. Elle had needed someone and she'd taken comfort. And Clarissa, that bundle of happy, had been the result. "Whoever he is probably won't care if we come for her. We'll pay him. I have some money." He'd do anything. He loved that pumpkin.

"Her mother came for her. And her grandmother, too."

"But you're—" *Those women in the car.* The happy, smiling, *fucking*, women had come and taken Clarissa away. "You're not Clarissa's mother." The words came out flat as the idea took hold.

She rocked like a child to comfort herself.

"Why would *you* have her? How did you let this happen?" How could she let him fall in love with a child that wasn't hers? How could she hand back a baby she loved? They *all* loved?

Elle wiped her damp face in his shirt, too overcome to answer him. She didn't need his recrimination. "Oh, Elle. What happened?" Whatever this was couldn't be fixed, not by him. Maybe not by anyone.

After a time which could have been ten seconds or ten minutes, Elle controlled her deepest sobs. "It's okay," he murmured against Elle's hair as he held her carefully. She was broken, dark with sorrow, and needed his comfort, not his questions. Most of his questions wouldn't have answers anyway.

"I worked with a college student who found herself pregnant. She was a sweet girl from a conservative family. I told her to be honest with them, to ask for their support. She took my advice and I believed she'd be fine. They were church-going people. Decent people."

Her breath went ragged again and he feared she'd lost her control. "But when—but when she told them the baby would be mixed race, her dad flew into a rage. Her mother turned to stone and said she'd never accept the baby. That their friends wouldn't accept the baby."

From what he'd seen that had changed. "So you took Clarissa?"

She nodded. "She begged me. It was only supposed to be for a short time. She was convinced once the baby came that they'd want to help, but they cut her out of their lives throughout her pregnancy. She said it would be a couple of weeks. She tried to reconcile with them." He could see why Elle had helped. As the time had stretched into months, the pumpkin had stolen their hearts. Including his.

"The father?"

"He's still in college, trying hard to stay focused and determined to marry her and raise Clarissa. He's a strong young man who loves them both." She wailed, long and hard into his shoulder. "He went to her parents and faced them like a man. He proved himself over the last couple of months. He went to their home every day and after a few weeks they let him in. He wore them down. Her father has apologized to them both and accepted him. Her mother came with her today and when Clarissa smiled at her grandmother, I could see the love bloom, right there in her face. And they took her." Her voice ghosted away as if she had no more heart to speak.

All Logan could think of was how Clarissa's sweet smile had encouraged him closer that day when Elle and her tribe were moving in. Without Clarissa's welcome, he wasn't sure he'd have braved Elle's snark.

Dear God, she was taken and will never come home again. He sagged against Elle as the truth swept over him.

Lips pressed against his neck and Elle drew his head down to hers. He tilted, she stretched up, and a kiss took his breath. It started as comfort, a meeting of mouths in a desperate bid for sanity in an insane situation. Tears blended on their lips as loss consumed him. "Elle," he whispered.

"It hurts," she said. "They'll never bring her back to us."

He followed her down to the bed.

THE NEXT MORNING LOGAN rose from a night full of nightmares, each one progressively worse. They started with him losing Clarissa in a swirl of fog that burned his skin. And they ended with his brother Jamie wandering the world like a wraith, dead but breathing. Breathing raggedly and laughing maniacally. Logan shuddered awake and stumbled out of bed.

In his early nightmares, Logan had been helpless to save Clarissa and by the second Jamie nightmare, he'd been ready to crawl into the grave marked with his brother's name. He'd wanted to plain give up.

His help had never helped anyone. Never would help anyone. He'd be better off never helping anyone again. He sagged against the sink in his bathroom, braced his hands on the wall and stared into the mirror.

Who the hell was this guy? No white knight. No generous benefactor. No savior. No help at all.

Clarissa was gone, Elle was a wreck, his mother was stressing into an early grave, and Jamie didn't give a damn.

His stubble made him look unkempt and damn if he didn't see a couple of silver threads in his hair. Splashing his face with water didn't help.

Should he have stayed with Elle? Given her the comfort she'd needed? She'd been broken. Needy. But the kids had needed someone, too and Elle hadn't been capable.

The hardest thing he'd ever done was pull back from Elle's need. His desire had nearly overwhelmed him, but sex with Elle in that condition would've been selfish and probably done more harm than good.

He'd been hammer hard and ready, but if he were honest, he didn't want to begin anything serious with Elle when she felt vulnerable and not fully engaged. He wanted Elle in a way he'd never wanted anyone else, but the stupidity of his want made him wince. The whole thing was impossible. Stupid.

Logan wanted children of his own. He wanted more than anything to see his genes in another person's face. That would not happen with Elle. She wouldn't go down that road again and he couldn't blame her.

Elle Foster needed to focus on the children she already had. She wanted to build a stable life for them and bringing a man into that mix could make them unstable, especially after losing Clarissa.

Yesterday, Elle had kissed Logan desperately, clinging and hot and oh-so-sweetly. He shivered at the memory of her, soft and warm in his arms, her lips coaxing. But he'd been needed outside the bedroom too and he'd left her bed before things got too hot. With his last shred of control, Logan had remembered the twins' tears. They needed an adult and Elle had been too distraught.

So he'd left Elle's bed and walked into the living room. He found Jorja and Liam. They'd been staring at the empty play yard, Jorja hugging a stuffed turtle, while Liam had looked explosively angry. Logan couldn't blame the boy. He set his palm on Liam's shoulder. "I feel the same way," he said softly. Both children had leaned against him and allowed a gentle hug. "Is Daniel still on his run?"

Jorja nodded. Liam swiped his sleeve across his nose.

At fourteen, Daniel must have felt a terrible blend of emotions. Logan hoped guilt wasn't one of them. There was nothing Daniel could have done to keep Clarissa from being taken. But boys could twist events in ways that made them the bad guy. He'd talk to Clay about Daniel because he was certain Daniel wouldn't want any advice from Logan.

The twins gathered the baby's toys and the few clothes that the baby-stealing women had left behind while Logan had closed up the play yard. After a quick call to the other house, Clay had come for the twins, his eyes stricken with grief. "I'll see my sister when she's ready. Jorja and Liam will sleep at our place tonight."

Logan settled in to wait for Daniel. "Come with me," he said when the teenager had returned from his run, sweaty and spent. The anger had dissipated, his body drooped with exhaustion. "We need to clear this stuff out of the house. Your mom has enough to deal with."

Daniel nodded and off they went to the thrift store to donate what they could, then to the dump to toss what needed tossing, and, finally, to the baby store to return the crib.

People should never have to return a crib; should never have to explain why there would be no baby sleeping in it.

The man in the mirror stared back at him, red-eyed and ruined. Logan rubbed his eyes and ran his hand around his stubbly chin, but he didn't have the heart or energy to shave. At the baby store, he'd thought he'd lose control of his emotions, but Daniel had been watching him. Logan had bucked up and got through the return procedure.

The kid must think him a wuss. No points there. No teenage boy wanted to stand in a baby store with a grown man near tears.

His phone rang, pulling him away from his dejected thoughts. He looked at the screen. His mom. She never called this early. Shit. Must be more crap with his brother. He forced a calm tone into his voice. "Mom, how are you?"

"Done."

"What do you mean?"

"It's time and I'm ready." She sighed. "Jamie called so I know where he is. Can you come with us?"

His father must be going, too. If his dad wanted to engage with Jamie then this was serious. "Of course. I'll get ready and be right over."

He reached for his shaver and then set it back down. He tried, but he couldn't find the energy to give a damn. He had no idea what he and his parents were in for, but it wouldn't be pretty. He was glad his mom hadn't elaborated about her plan, but he hadn't heard that determined tone in years.

His mother meant business when she used that tone and nothing, but nothing would sway her from her course. A part of him rejoiced, but the other caretaking part worried that Jamie might shatter.

FIFTEEN MINUTES LATER, Logan pulled into his parents' driveway. Their neat three bedroom bungalow had been a haven in his childhood. As he climbed out the sun broke through the clouds and birdsong erupted in celebration. He loved this house, this neighborhood.

He and Jamie had been blessed with the best parents two boys could have. Vacations included road trips to national monuments, theme parks, homemade pie, and lots of support. Later, when they were older, they all headed to sunny beaches for spring break. And laughs. The Hughes family laughed a lot in those days.

But when Jamie had been injured in college everything had changed. First came concern over the injury, but after he'd healed, the real problem had been revealed. Painkillers had stolen his brother, had stolen his parents' son.

As Logan parked, his parents stepped out their front door looking determined. His mother's face had the expression that matched her tone on the phone. The set face he hadn't seen since he'd stumbled home drunk from a sweet-sixteen party at a neighbor's house. That look had ended the drinking games for Logan.

Something cold ran through his chest. Jamie was in deep shit.

His father looked grim and carried a grocery store bag. When he turned to lock the front door, Logan noticed a stoop in his back. Nearing seventy-three, Dad looked weary from the strain of Jamie's addiction.

He took his wife's arm and they walked together with determined strides to Logan's car. Dad helped her into the front passenger seat and closed her door. She turned her face to the side window, her shoulders straight and chin set. His parents were older than his friends' folks. They'd tried for years to have babies of their own, but nothing had worked.

After years passed with no luck, they'd settled on adoption and once they were in, they went all the way and took the two boys at the same time. There was barely nine months between Jamie and Logan, but it might as well be a century. Logan hadn't had anything in common with his brother for years except these two people who were aging before his eyes.

His dad's hair had thinned to nearly bald, his shoulders stooped and he had trouble with his knees. His mother had lines down her cheeks that Logan swore hadn't been there last Sunday. She'd been complaining lately that her night vision was shot and she'd booked cataract surgery.

Once his father settled in the car he spoke. "Downtown. Jamie's in the park by the picnic area."

With a nod, Logan backed out of the drive and headed downtown. As they passed Clay's veterinary clinic on the corner of Main and Elm, he cleared his throat. "What's the plan?"

"I'll say what I have to say and we leave him there," his mother said softly, firmly. "We can't continue this way and it's time Jamie knew it." She kept her face turned to the side window.

His father said nothing. Presumably, he'd come along to provide support.

When they pulled into the picnic area, they saw Jamie sitting atop a table beside a trickling brook. He looked like death. Jamie's face was colorless, his hair matted. His knees were wider than his calves and his shoulders bony.

Their mother's sharp inhale told of pain and loss. Still, she climbed out of the SUV with her back straight and shoulders squared. She headed straight for her son without waiting for Logan or her husband. This would be over quickly.

By the time Logan caught up with her, she had a cell phone in her hand. She offered it to Jamie. "What's this for?" he asked sourly. His eyes searched their mother's and then he darted a glance to Logan.

"So you can stay in touch." Amazingly, her voice was strong and firm.

"What does that mean? You're taking me to rehab." He scrubbed his head and looked ready to smile, but when their mother shook her head, Jamie balked. "Look," he said. "Mommy, it'll be different this time, I swear. They'll help me. They'll make me straight." His wheedling tone grated on Logan's last nerve.

Mommy. Jesus, did he think he could still manipulate her?

"They would if you let them," she replied. "If you work at it. But you haven't really worked at getting better."

"What?" Jamie reared his head back as if she'd slapped him. Maybe she should have.

"Take the phone, Jamie." Mom set it on the table. "Or not. But we're not giving you any money, or taking you to rehab until you accept responsibility for your recovery."

"But I want to go," he used his whiniest voice, and Mom stiffened at the sound.

Logan spoke. "No wonder Dad wrote you off years ago. Christ, Jamie, grow some balls."

His brother ignored him and focused his reddened, weepy eyes on their mom.

His father stood beside Logan. "That's enough, Logan. Jamie will either apply himself to recovery or he won't."

Logan stood strong. His dad placed the bag he'd brought on the table next to the phone. "Here," he said with a brief glance at Jamie.

"Here's a set of fresh clothes, soap, a razor, and toothbrush. You'll find your favorite candy bars, too. If you want breakfast, we'll bring you some from a drive through. But we're done with the rest of it."

Logan gently clasped his mom's elbow to support her, but she shrugged him off. Instead of giving in, she kissed Jamie's cheek and turned and headed back toward the car. His father followed while Jamie sputtered in disbelief. After a moment, his brother turned his gaze on Logan.

"Bro, you gotta help me out. A few bucks. I feel like shit, man. I'm gonna lose it if they don't help me. Just this one time."

"Call them once in a while to tell them you're still alive." This was harder than he'd thought. "You know where the shelter is and what services they offer. Clean up and get help." He turned to leave but then turned back to face his brother. Jamie looked stunned and horrified as if he'd been abandoned. "There's no money left to pay for expensive programs. You've wiped them out. They love you, Jamie, but they can't watch you kill yourself."

"You talked her into this," Jamie shot the accusation at him.

"No, not me. Your false promises brought this on," Logan said sadly. He reached out to touch Jamie's arm, but his brother stumbled out of reach. "Jamie, I don't want to leave things like this. You need to know that I miss my brother. I miss the family we used to be. If you miss that, too, you'll take the steps."

"Fuck you!" Clearly, the shock had worn off and the addict inside his brother roared. "Fuck you all! I don't need you," he yelled to their retreating parents. "I don't need your fucking money or your love."

Jamie's voice carried through the park and followed Logan back to the car.

His mother sat ashen-faced in the front seat while his father let tears roll down his cheeks unchecked.

Logan climbed in, checked to see that his mother had remembered to buckle up and said, "He has to help himself now."

"He will," his mother responded. "My boy is stronger than he looks."

Logan hoped like hell that was true. His phone vibrated with a text from Elle. "I have to take this," he said, wondering if Elle would let him near her again. Had he disappointed her by leaving her wanting or did she believe him a wuss the way Daniel must?

LOGAN'S KISSES STAYED with Elle for far too long; through the night and into the next morning. Elle had brushed her teeth three times, gargled and showered, but she swore she still tasted the press of Logan's lips and the salt of his tears. Logan Hughes had cried with her, had held her and kissed her, and walked out on her when she'd have grabbed for more.

Thank God he'd walked away. Logan was strong, so strong, even in the face of disaster. She walked into the living room and saw empty space where Clarissa's play yard had been. Her toys were gone, too. The baby's grandmother had insisted that Clarissa needed brand new toys and had left the yard sale finds behind.

"Where's all her stuff?" she asked Daniel, who was supervising breakfast. She should have risen earlier, but she hadn't wanted to face the day. Later, she'd tell Daniel how much she appreciated him.

"Logan took it. Said you shouldn't have to deal with disposing of her gear." Daniel stared into his bowl of cereal and nudged Jorja to keep eating. She complied but Liam popped out his lower lip and shoved his bowl away. "Jorja and Liam left with Clay," Daniel explained. "I went with Logan to the thrift store and the dump with her stuff. We took the crib back to the store." He shoved the heels of his thumbs into his eyes.

She dragged a mug out of a cupboard and poured herself a coffee. Thank God for sons who could make a damn fine brew. "Liam and Jorja, you'll need to stay with Clay and Mercy again until Daniel and I get back," she said. "We have an errand that'll take a while." The thought of meeting with Susan Murdoch after losing Clarissa sent cold little cat feet down her spine.

Daniel shrugged. "I guess," he muttered at the reminder of his meeting.

"I hate this town," she said as she tipped her mug to her mouth for her next drink. She drained the coffee in a couple of swallows and reached for another jolt. She felt like hell had swallowed her, found her distasteful and puked her back up. "You should shower and put on your clean jeans. And your best T-shirt." *Please God, one without a stupid slogan on it.* But she knew better than to make the request.

She ate a piece of dry toast quickly and went to dress. Without thinking she sent Logan a text.

Elle: "Will the office be empty today?"

Logan: "Yes. Why?"

Elle: "Neutral ground. Taking D to meet Mrs. M there."

Logan: "Want me there?"

Warmth bloomed. He'd be by her side if she needed him. She wanted to say yes, but in the end, gave him the most correct response. After yesterday and the way she'd clung like a baby, she had to be realistic. Logan had left her alone so he could deal with her children when she hadn't been functional. He'd been the strong one, but she had to get back on track. Now. Tempted to say yes, she forced herself to do the right thing.

Elle: "No, I can handle it."

Logan: "Fuck that. I'll be in the bakery. Show up or you're fired."

She actually chuckled. First at the surprising F-bomb and then at the way he assumed she'd need him regardless of what she'd said. The man was dangerous and it was no laughing matter.

Daniel took longer than she did to get ready. He'd begun to take longer showers lately, and more care with his hair. She should buy stock in a hair-products company. When he appeared, reeking of too much body spray, he held out his arms for pseudo-inspection because he damn well wouldn't take off his father's T-shirt. It read: "Life's a bitch and then you die."

She closed her eyes. Just what Susan Murdoch needed to see, Tad's motto. Elle's ex had always called his mother The Bitch. Elle squared her eyes with Daniel's. "Are you sure you want to rub her nose in his death?"

"It's the last gift he gave me."

"Okay," she sighed and kissed the twins. Jorja's wide blue eyes looked worried but Liam bounded out the door and ran through the cedars toward Clay's house.

"Will Daniel come back with you?" Jorja asked.

"Of course I will," he replied with a ruffle on her head. "I'm not going anywhere. Not ever." The last was said fiercely as if he wanted to imprint the words in his little sister's mind.

"You said that someday Clarissa's mommy would come for her, but that was a long time ago and I..." Her voice trailed away. Elle hugged her close and tight and whispered all her love, all the comfort she could manage.

"We'll never forget her. And her mommy said she'll send us pictures and we'll be able to have video chats with Clarissa and everything."

Behind her, Daniel snorted. At Elle's sharp look, he patted Jorja's head. "We'll still love her and she'll *always* be our baby," he announced fiercely.

"Okay." Jorja nodded, but her seven-year-old mind seemed to be joining the prevarication. It saddened Elle to realize that her little girl was as prepared as an adult to lie to herself to get through the pain. A bit of innocence lost. "But we still have Dilly, right?"

"We do. She'll always be your cousin and when Auntie Mercy has her baby, that will be another cousin."

"A brand new one." Jorja's eyes lit.

"As new as they get," Elle agreed. She couldn't wait to hold the newborn, to breathe that lovely scent again.

The twins trooped out together and crossed the lawn to their aunt and uncle's house. Time with Dilly would help ease their morning.

Once in the car, Daniel wanted to talk. "Logan's all right," he said out of the blue. "When we took the crib back the lady asked why we were returning it. It looked like Logan might bawl right there in front of her."

Her heart pinched because she hadn't prepared Logan for this loss. "He assumed she was ours. I never told him she wasn't." Her stubborn inner bitch had refused to share anything with Logan, until last night when Elle had all but collapsed into him. But he hadn't taken the bait and she wasn't sure how to feel about that. Relieved? No. Grateful? Maybe she should be grateful. Disappointed? Her body had been.

"Clarissa liked him," Daniel broke into her selfish, selfish thoughts.

"Yes, she liked him," she agreed with a sigh. There'd been no end to the flirting between Logan and the baby. Clarissa lit up at first sight of Logan and he never tired of peek-a-boo.

And still, his kisses lingered.

Chapter Twelve

SUSAN MURDOCH STOOD five feet two inches and had all the presence of a small, gray mouse. It wasn't her lack of stature that made her seem mousy. Her demeanor smacked of living in corners, hoping not to be seen, scurrying about her day.

All of that was true, Elle decided. But not today.

Today, Susan Murdoch had walked into Hughes Realty with her shoulders squared and took Daniel on without flinching. He towered over her but Susan deflected the power of his looming presence by taking a seat. She patted the other chair for him. "Sit, please." Her voice was soft, her eyes avidly interested.

Daniel sat.

"That T-shirt belonged to your father," she said. "Thank you for wearing it."

Daniel responded by pursing his lips and staring at the floor.

Susan gave him a tentative smile and shot another wobbly one toward Elle. "I'm glad you had a relationship with him. He never talked about visiting you."

Elle gave her points for persistence.

"My father didn't see us much." Daniel flashed Elle a frown. Clearly, his grandmother had surprised him. He eased back into his seat and waited for the next salvo.

"Your father told us that your mother kept you apart, but I always wondered if we'd been told the whole story." She assessed Elle with a curious eye. Elle slowly shook her head in denial. *Tad, you lying bastard. I wanted to know your parents.*

Susan acknowledged the shake of Elle's head with a slight nod. "No matter now," Susan said with a wave of her hand. "From here on I'd like us to move forward and share in your future."

"What about the old man?" Daniel's voice cracked overloud in the still office. "I don't see *him* asking for me."

"He was here," Elle with a nod. "But Susan wanted a less-tense meeting." She eyed her son, who nodded in understanding.

"Your grandfather is a hard man, that's true." Her mother-in-law sighed. "But, he did his best. He told me many times that Tad wouldn't have survived the childhood he'd had to suffer. My father-in-law was violent with his family. With Graham especially."

"He thought if he didn't *beat* Tad he was better?" Elle broke in. "That if he only bullied and verbally abused his son it made him a better father than his own?"

Susan winced at the graphic depiction of their private affairs. "And a better husband," she replied. "He never raised a hand to me or Tad. You probably won't believe this but my husband can be quite kind at times. Even tender." She lifted one shoulder. "Sometimes I wonder if that kindness was what made his father hate him."

Elle looked at Daniel, saw his face go white but she couldn't discern his reaction. Shock, likely. Tad had never said anything about his family's history. He only ever complained about Graham and Susan. She understood, of course. Maybe Tad never really knew what his father had gone through. Families kept their secrets.

When no one responded to her explanation, Susan cleared her throat. "Yes, well. I suppose you want to know why I'm here alone. Aside from wanting less tension."

Daniel shrugged. His pale face now sported high spots of color over his cheekbones.

"You gave me the impression your husband isn't well," Elle prompted.

"Graham's been diagnosed with dementia. It's early days yet, but he gets confused by new situations and needs routine in order to stay calm. We've brought in an old friend to help so Graham's comfortable when I leave the house. But I've curtailed my social engagements accordingly."

Elle took that to mean Susan would be housebound with him soon, her life derailed.

Daniel's face turned thunderous. "You worry about *him* being comfortable when you never stood up for my father?"

Elle shook her head at him, but it was too late, he'd said it and maybe Susan needed to hear it. Tad had been broken early in his life. Something about his wan smiles and wide, hurt eyes had made Elle want to heal him. She closed her eyes. Pity. She'd felt pity for Tad and ended up with Daniel as a result.

Susan swung her gaze to meet Daniel's. She blinked back tears and Elle gave her credit for reining them in. "Some dementia patients turn violent," she explained. "If Graham mimics his father's behavior I won't be able to keep him with me. Things will only get worse. The time may come when my husband has to go into care. But not yet." She waited with her chin tilted up proudly. Susan Murdoch was mousy no more.

She'd taken charge and she'd make certain everyone knew it. Her gaze swept Daniel from the top of his head to his toes. "From what I see, you're halfway grown into a wonderful man, capable of having a loving family. I'd like to see all that happen for you. Don't think I don't understand that all these things are because of who raised you. Your mother's done a fine job. I've seen you with your little sister and brother and the baby." Susan's gaze flew to Elle's and back to Daniel. "You'll make a fine father someday and you *will* break the cycle."

"Don't talk about Clarissa and the twins," Daniel blurted. "Don't say anything about anybody in my family." He sounded cold and harsh. But losing Clarissa had brought on the hard tone. No matter how often they'd told themselves that Clarissa wasn't permanent they'd all fallen in love with her. Even Logan. Daniel was heartbroken and didn't need the reminder of his loss, not from a grandmother he didn't know.

"All right, I won't," she agreed. "I apologize for commenting on things I have no right to speak of."

Daniel grunted.

Elle eased back into her chair and Susan gathered her thoughts. Then she brightened. "Do you have any questions about your father? He loved you very much." She clasped her hands in front of her and Elle noticed a tremble she attempted to hide.

Elle doubted Tad had ever loved her, but he had cared for Daniel even if his efforts fell short sometimes. Turns out, Tad hadn't had much of an example set for him.

As for Susan's recollections, people often used selective memory when recalling the behavior of the dead, especially a grieving mother. Elle couldn't fault Susan for giving Tad the benefit of the doubt.

Daniel shifted in his seat and Elle read a silent plea in his eyes. Her son wanted to be free to ask whatever he wanted without Elle in the room. "This is my cue to leave so you can talk privately. I'll be downstairs in the bakery when you want me." She directed the last at Daniel. When she rose, the older woman stood with her.

As Elle rounded the desk, Susan offered her hand and Elle took it. "Thank you, Elle. You have no idea what this means to me."

Elle didn't want to be judged for her behavior when she lived in Welcome as a girl and Susan didn't want judgment for her past transgressions either. "It's a fresh start," Elle said. "There's a lot of that going around."

ELLE FOUND LOGAN IN the back booth again. It was becoming their favorite table, it seemed. He watched her approach, his hands loosely linked on the tabletop. "You look like hell," she said as she got near enough to read despair in every line of his face. She wasn't the only one who had family angst to deal with. "What happened?" she asked as she slid in opposite him.

He dragged his hands back under the table. Too bad, because she wanted to cover his hands with hers, just as a show of support, of course. "My parents handed out some tough love and it didn't go well," he said through tight lips. He'd clearly been through a battle and after yesterday's loss of Clarissa; he didn't need any more emotional upheaval.

She held up a hand to forestall him asking anything. "I'm not ready to talk about Daniel and me meeting with Susan."

"Okay."

"Or about, you know, yesterday in my room."

"Okay."

No way would Elle dissect the kissing and crying and hugging and desired-denied time. A public booth in the Welcome Bakery and Café was no place to discuss private moments of weakness and need.

"I also don't need to hear sympathetic murmurings about Clarissa being taken home." Home, where her mother lived and her father wanted her. Home, where she'd have a loving family, brought together by the shared love of a sweet baby girl.

"Okay."

Logan was being quite reasonable and it was starting to tick her off. "You're being very agreeable," she said in a fit of pique.

"Clarissa's gone home where she belongs," he said, echoing her thoughts.

After months apart Clarissa was with her mother, father, and grandparents. "We'll never be part of her life again." Tears welled, but Elle refused to let them fall, so they hung on her eyelashes instead. Acceptance was a bitter pill.

Logan tilted his head and his eyes softened in sympathy. His expression brought her back to the matter at hand. She mentally dusted off her rarely-used compassion and offered it. "Tough love never goes well at first blush. That's why they call it tough. It's hard for everyone."

He rose, effectively ending the conversation. "Coffee and cheese scone?" A perfect avoidance technique she often used herself; when you hate where the conversation's going talk about food.

"You know me so well," she said. He ghosted a smile for her and her heart squeezed to see the pain behind it.

"When I come back you can tell me how it went upstairs."

She snorted. Logan's broad back sagged as he stood at the glass case checking out the baked goods. From here he looked worn and tired. If she could offer comfort, she would but she was fresh out. After losing the baby and now being terrified she'd lose Daniel, too, she had nothing left to give. Zippo. Zilch. Zero.

He placed their order and brought their coffees first then returned to get the plates. "Here you go. This will help with whatever fresh hell Mrs. Murdoch has inflicted on you." He slid into the booth opposite her, his gaze compassionate. Or maybe pity filled his gaze. If that were true, she didn't want it.

"We're both messed up right now." She didn't want to relive the events in the office; they were too fresh and painful. "I don't want to talk about Daniel and the Murdochs."

"Who better to talk to? People who live in a happy, sunny, too-smiley-for-shit place don't want to hear from those of us living in the dark." He sounded matter-of-fact about this morsel of life truth.

"A surprisingly gloomy comment from a man who's usually pretty happy," she commented drily. He shrugged.

"In general I am a happy guy. I don't look at life like it's a big, stinking pile. But sometimes, that's what we're handed, and that's where we're both living right now, in the middle of big, stinking piles."

She couldn't think of a thing to say to counter that, so she didn't try. Instead, she bit into her scone. The flavor burst on her tongue. Buttery goodness. Cheesy tang. Delicious decadence. "Oh, yeah, baby, yeah..." She moaned around the pastry, her eyes closed.

"Careful, you'll give a man hope."

She popped her eyes open. He'd said it casually, but his gaze heated and turned seductive. What if he'd meant it? What if Logan hoped there might be something between them? Maybe they shared a crush or a sense of humor or a crappy pile of family stuff. Shared something more than the desperate need she'd shown him yesterday. He'd been right and honorable to leave her and see to the children.

Honorable. Hm. Not many men would've left her that way. Most men would have taken what she offered without a care for her true feelings.

In the end, she ignored his comment and polished off her scone without looking at him. Looking at him might hurt. "I was hungrier than I thought," she said when she swallowed her last bite. "I demolished it."

Logan leaned back and pressed his palms into the edge of the table. "I need a shower, a shave, and sleep."

"And a haircut."

He chuckled and released the table. "Probably."

"It's curling at the tips of your ears." He had reddish waves that caught the light and gave his hair a coppery shine. And then he flushed. "I made you blush," she said, surprised. "I didn't think a grown man would blush about his hair."

He laughed at that. "It's not what you're saying that's got my blood up." Logan's steady, focused look made time slow and gave her goosebumps.

"Then what?" She shouldn't have asked. Shouldn't have encouraged this flirting, but it was too late for shouldn't haves. They were in it. And a small female part of her rejoiced. To tell that small female part to shut the hell up she reminded herself she didn't date at work.

Didn't date, period.

Didn't.

Her phone buzzed with a text. "It's Daniel."

Daniel: "I'm going to their house. Be home later."

She sagged into her seat and closed her eyes, and tried to keep her lip from trembling.

"What's happened?" Logan asked.

"The Murdochs have him. Daniel's gone to their house. I assume Susan's taking him to meet the old man."

"It's natural that they'd want to get to know him now that you live close by." But Logan's tone lacked conviction.

"His grandfather is in the early stages of dementia, which means there's some pressure time-wise."

He nodded. "Are you okay with this?"

"Hell, no, I'm not okay. But Daniel's okay and that's all that matters. They can do a lot for him that I'll never be able to do. College, for one; leave him a fortune, for another."

"Mercenary, but accurate," he said softly. Then she remembered that he'd been the one to point out the mercenary advantages in the first place.

She smiled at him. "Money talks," she said. "What happened with your brother?"

He shifted and raised his eyes to the ceiling. "My mom gave Jamie a phone and told him to call if he was ready to work to get straight. The work part has been tough for him," he explained. "She didn't give him money and she didn't want him to come home. Even my father went with us to back her up."

"I take it Jamie was surprised?"

"Appalled. Offended. Whiny. Belligerent. You name it."

She opened her mouth to speak, but he shook his head. She subsided and let him talk.

"The addiction has done all the talking, not Jamie, but this is killing our mom. For my parents, this was an act of desperation. But we've tried everything else and nothing's helped."

"You're worried this won't help either."

He nodded. She slipped her hand across the table to cover his. "You can't go on this way. Your parents need to have their lives back. Jamie's addiction has been controlling all of you, not just him."

He raised his eyes to meet hers. Heat blazed across the table, sudden as forked lightning. "I want to go upstairs and hammer the hell out of that cot. With you."

That female side of her that she'd tried to shut up screamed in her head, but she couldn't, wouldn't tell it to stop.

"Me, too," she said and slid out of the booth. Without looking at him again she walked with certain steps to the exit. Her world had fallen apart and she needed something to ease the loss. She couldn't drink the pain away or use drugs to ease the ache.

But she could have sex without hurting anyone. A respite from her responsibilities, a rest, a moment to catch her breath; that was all she wanted.

The touch of Logan's hand on the small of her back startled her. She glanced up and felt the world slide and tip into an abyss. She fell along with him, the two of them alone down the low, slow path to oblivion.

The kind she hadn't had in ages. She tilted the corner of her lips up and he, large and focused, urged her through the door. Outside in the bracing breeze, one second of clear thinking hit. She had to set ground rules. "One time, Logan. No repeats."

He responded by opening the door to the stairway that would take them to the office and that squeaky, too-narrow cot. He ushered her inside. "One time," he said. "But I want you twice."

Oh. The female at her center sang hallelujah.

"You're a damn good negotiator." Twice. Perfect.

As she neared the top of the stairs her feet picked up the pace, through no instruction from her. Logan hustled up right behind her, heating her, rushing her.

Wanting her.

He was younger. He was her boss.

And he was the kindest, most generous man she'd ever known.

He was hurting and maybe a bit scared of what might come for Jamie and his parents.

Logan deserved this respite, too. She was happy she could offer it. When she turned at the top of the staircase and held out her hand he took it. Her belly clenched at his touch. So simple, this holding hands thing. Their fingers entwined and Logan pulled her along the hallway to the office door.

"I have no appointments scheduled until this evening."

"I'll call Mercy and see if she can keep the twins until supper." That shouldn't be a problem.

"Text her."

"Yes, that's better." She wouldn't get caught in a conversation and give herself time to change her mind; because she really, really, didn't want to change her mind. Logan unlocked the office and stepped inside, tugging her in behind him. The smart side of her didn't protest, just followed the female side right into trouble.

Chapter Thirteen

LOGAN KICKED HIS OFFICE door shut behind Elle and backed her against it in one motion. He pressed her back to the door and turned the lock. Hughes Realty was closed for business. Her eyes widened at the *snick* of the lock but the welcome in her eyes blazed high.

"Send the text," he demanded. For this short time, he didn't want Elle thinking about anyone but him, not even her children. This time belonged to them. He was so aroused he could hammer nails and he needed oblivion.

"After this first time," she murmured. Her voice turned soft and husky, her brilliant-blue eyes moist, and then her lips parted in invitation. "Show me what you've got."

With the gauntlet thrown he had no choice but to pick it up. He braced his forearms on either side of her head and shifted his lower body away from hers. He wanted nothing to confuse her, not his stiff rod, not the feel of her breasts against his chest, nothing. And especially not the way he left her hanging yesterday.

He moved in and took her mouth. *So soft. So yielding.* She moaned at first taste, the sound opening her lips ever so slightly. It was all the opening Logan needed. He slid his tongue against hers. Slowly. Had he ever had a kiss this sweet? Her mouth was so often sharp; her words like little slicing blades, but kissing her caused flutters of need in his gut. Her soft lips accepted his as if she'd been made for him.

He let her tongue invade him until she slid her hands to the back of his head and held him in place. *Not enough.* He needed to feel more of her so he rubbed his chest against her nipples. Hard, delicious points poked him as he deepened their kiss. When she moaned again, he slammed his hips against her and pressed.

"Oh," she said and pressed back in the sweetest invitation.

"I like that. Do you?" He couldn't help but grin into her slumberous, needy eyes.

"Yes." She sighed against his lips. "Do it some more."

He obliged her with another full-body press. Her arms tightened around his neck. Maybe Elle would regret this later, but later wasn't now and they both needed a break from their personal hells. And then she reached for the buttons on his shirt. He shuddered as her knuckles grazed his over-sensitized skin. "Go easy. It's been awhile." He tilted his head back and suppressed a groan.

Pitiful. Just the touch of her knuckles could send him over the edge.

She snorted. "A while? Try going without for years. Now that's a dry spell."

But he was already working the button of her jeans and the moment he had room he delved and felt wet heat. Her head slammed the door as she reared back at his first invasive touch, but she chuckled and ended with a sigh. Her eyes drooped. "That's nice, very nice," she said with a hitch in her voice.

"I thought your mouth was soft," he crooned against her neck. "But here, you're velvet."

"You're not as nice as you seem, Logan Hughes. Underneath all that kindness and generosity, you're a pirate raider."

He chuckled. "Got it in one." He stroked her deeply, letting his fingertip delve inside. Not too far though. He wanted her begging for more.

"A thief. A con artist." Her breath hitched as he plunged farther inside her. "And you've been hiding it all these years."

He laughed deep in his throat. "Nice guys and bad boys have different moves. But we all have the same goal." She stiffened under his hand. Five more strokes and her eyes glazed as her breath caught. He rolled her clitoris with his thumb. She gasped and stuttered out some syllables that made no sense, but he kept working her. Her head tilted to his shoulder as she quivered against his fingers and tipped over the edge in a series of pants and moans and shudders.

Right there on his hand.

Her face flushed a deep pink and she looked stunned by her quick response. She sagged against the door and reached for the tab of his jeans. "That was great," she murmured. In one of the quickest recoveries, he'd ever seen she said, "But I need more."

"Happy to help." He bent and lifted her into his arms. The narrow cot wasn't ideal but since they'd be stacked one on top of the other, they'd make it work. When he got close enough to the rickety bed he tossed her down. She bounced once and laughed, her eyes bright and her smile wide. He shucked his jeans and underwear as he toed off his sneakers. When he straightened, she was tugging off her jeans, too. He helped by grabbing the material at her ankles and giving one long yank.

Suddenly naked from the waist down, they both stared as if neither had seen another naked person before. Her blue eyes assessed him while he stood over her like a raw kid, desperate for relief. But he wasn't a kid and he had to protect them before he lost all reason. He fumbled in his jeans pocket and dug out a condom. While he opened the package and rolled on the protection, he studied her.

Dewy black hair hid her secrets. Tidy and dense, her muff looked lush. And hell, maybe it was true that he'd never seen a woman in her natural state. In her beautiful, sexy, natural state. "You're spectacular," he said, surprised by the growl his voice had become. He cleared his throat, but it was no good, his tongue felt thick with need. His mind, too.

She moved her hands to cover her mons. "It's been so long, I haven't had a reason to—you know—trim the bush." Her flush now was pure embarrassment, not ardor.

"You're wet and glistening and I did that. There's nothing more beautiful." He fell on her like a randy bastard, fast and hard. To Elle, he probably seemed like a kid, but nothing could end this surging need but being with her. In her. And that made him a man and when he felt the soft moistness of the woman she was he wanted to howl.

The cot was narrow, hard, short, and the frame squeaked under his added weight, but she welcomed him. Deftly, she opened her legs and gave him room to settle. Cupped between her thighs, he rested a moment and looked into her blue, blue eyes. "Okay?"

"More than okay." She kissed him then and opened her mouth hungrily. He slid his palms under her shoulders and propped her up to return her kisses. The movement made her hips sink into the cot and he followed eagerly. She shifted again, widening for him. "Please, Logan. Be a nice guy one more time and help a girl out."

With an invitation like that, how could he refuse? "Since you put it that way..." He trailed off as he notched himself inside her. Her eyes opened wide at the intrusion. He stilled, determined not to ram her like an animal.

"Oh." She rolled her hips to ask for more. "Where's the pirate you were by the door?" Her hand moved between them.

"Here," he muttered, nearly overcome. If she wanted a raider, he'd oblige. He slammed into her and pressed hard while she adjusted. He shuddered at the heat of her, the scent of her, and the feel of her tight, warm flesh.

She found his sac and gently squeezed. He groaned and shuddered as Elle's eyes went wide and her mouth went slack as he pressed again.

And then she moved.

SHE'D COME FAST THE first time. Elle figured she'd last a while now. But no. As she held him in her fingers, saw his immediate response, an orgasm rose from her depths. It came over her so quickly she didn't feel it until sparkly light and deep shudders rolled across her body. She broke apart in a dazzling array of glory and womb-deep release. Elle crooned and shuddered, too far gone to feel anything but sweet liquid release. Her muscles melted, her brain fogged and dimly she was aware of Logan, kissing her forehead, her ears and licking something off her cheeks.

Tears. He kissed away tears. *God, she was a mess.* Her chest went tight as she realized he was tending to her, neglecting his own release. For her.

She opened her eyes to see him as he stilled between her thighs. He watched her with full focus. "You need to learn to be selfish sometimes," she offered in a husky, grateful whisper.

"Don't cry," he murmured as he kissed away more salt.

"Don't notice," she said, wishing he hadn't. He agreed with a nod and plunged into her firmly. On the drag out, her nerve endings gloried. Logan pressed deep and hard again and the cot bounced, bringing him in tighter. She wanted to laugh at the creaky, squeaky noises from the cot, but Logan might take it the wrong way. Men's egos were fragile, and her joy might be misunderstood.

She loved that he'd given her this time and attention. Loved that they needed each other in exactly the same way in this moment. Just this once.

Suddenly, he pulled her back from her rambling as he stilled and with a long, low groan, shuddered and fell into climax. She rocked him to prolong the glory and let him settle on her chest when he needed to. She clasped him close and enjoyed the glow for a long, long moment.

"Thank you," she said next to his ear. "I needed that." A soft chuckle escaped her. Joy. She recognized joy. Huh. It had been way too long if it felt rusty.

He raised his head and grinned into her face. "Me, too." He rolled tightly and carried her with him to settle her on top of him. "No room for spooning, but I'm not ready to let you go yet. Stretch out on top."

She did and sank into the hard plains of his chest, the valley of his belly. Their legs entwined; his hairy with knobby knees and hers smooth. "This is nice," she murmured as she closed her eyes for a moment. A mere moment...

Elle woke a few minutes later to the sound of Logan's voice. "Yes, we're at the office and this meeting will take longer than we thought." He must be on the phone. And he must have moved like an eel to get out from under her without waking her. "Thanks, Mercy. I'll tell her," he was saying. "No, Daniel's gone to his grandparents' place." Silence while Mercy must be talking. "Yeah, it's been an interesting day for both of us, but work will take our minds off the family crap. Thanks again." She heard the sound of the phone being dropped into the cradle.

"You made the call for me?" she called from the cot. Their jeans comingled on the floor beside their discarded shoes. He must be half naked by his desk. She found the idea arousing.

He poked his head around the room divider. "I didn't want to disturb your nap. You looked at peace."

She growled low. "I had no idea you were such a good liar. 'Work will take our minds off the family crap.' Logan Hughes, you really are a many-layered man." *Bring your sexy body where I can see it.*

As if he'd heard her thoughts, Logan came to the foot of the cot, his shirt hanging open to reveal slick abs and a flat belly. The delicious man made her want to lick him all over. "When you've got the reputation that I have, people only hear the truth. Perception is everything." A wide smile, all innocence and sunshine broke across his face. "I'm a nice guy, everyone believes that. Tell me, who wouldn't believe a white lie?" The smile widened to salacious and turned her arousal up a notch.

"This power that you have; you only use it for good, right?"

"And very rarely." He blinked and if she hadn't watched closely, she might have missed it. She wanted to ask what he was hiding, but he slid his shirt off and dropped it to sit on top of the rest of their clothes. Her mouth went dry at the sight of Logan fully naked and for the life of her; she couldn't form a coherent thought. "Your turn," he said, with an expectant cock of his eyebrow.

Elle stripped off her shirt and bra lickety-split.

He liked what he saw because his reaction was obvious and instant. "There's only one problem." He shook his head sadly.

She rose to her knees on the squeaky cot. After she clasped him and watched his eyelids sink and his head tilt back, she said, "What could possibly be wrong?"

"No more condoms."

"Are you serious?" Aggravating news. But she didn't feel like dressing and heading out to a store to buy more. Not when they could be here, like this. Taking care of business. "I mean, it's not a problem for me. We can do this instead." And she showed him with her mouth how this time was going to go...

And it did.

He groaned encouragement and when it was her turn to enjoy his attention, Logan showed marvelous generosity in a gentle, loving way. Elle should have known he'd be loving because that's who he was: loving Logan. One day some woman would be loved by this man beyond her wildest dreams. Elle hoped this mystery woman appreciated him. Every single bit of him.

After the stars had come out behind her eyes and her last shudders had died away on his tongue, Elle's tears flowed again. She dabbed her eyes with her fingertips and drew in a deep breath. This time away from the real world, these moments of forgetting the crap her life had become were over and sorrow for the loss gathered like clouds in a summer storm.

Quietly, they dressed. Subdued, they collected their things, smiled wanly at each other and walked out of the office, each of them alone, each of them a little lost, she thought.

But she refused to be sorry for what they'd shared. Refused.

Chapter Fourteen

"MAYBE IF YOU'D BOUGHT these back in the day, you wouldn't be where you are right now." The cashier in the Good Value Foods looked vaguely familiar, but Elle couldn't pull up a name from the hundreds she'd spent years forgetting.

"Oh? And where is that, exactly?" Elle countered the snide remark with her very best don't-mess-with-me tone. She kept her voice soft and low, with just a touch of menace.

The cashier leaned in, her expression avid and her eyes alight with haughty censure. Elle stiffened and waited to hear what came next.

"Four kids with four different men. Seriously, Elle, what were you thinking?"

Instead of punching her in her big, fat mouth, Elle dropped the money for the package of condoms on the cash desk, grabbed the package and stepped away. On the way out the door, she waved the package in the air like a flag. "Thank you," she called out to anyone who'd listen. "I'll put these to good use just as soon as your man gets out of prison." *Yes! That was Marilee Tompkins and her boyfriend was serving time for armed robbery.*

Her old classmates weren't the only ones with long memories. With a self-satisfied smile, Elle made it to her car without looking back. She climbed in, tucked the package into an inside pocket of her purse.

She had not bought these condoms for Logan. Or to use with Logan. But since he'd broken through her defenses, Elle figured there could be another man in her future. Her no dating rule had gone past its best before date. Her days of getting pregnant and left behind were in her past.

Now she could have sex again. Could *date* again. *And why shouldn't I?* Elle loved the feeling of a new relationship. She missed the wide-open possibilities when a man was new and the feelings fresh and unexpected. Those things could be hers again if she lifted her moratorium on dating.

But living in Welcome, where her history followed her like a pall, she'd never find anyone interested in getting to know her today. People here only saw who she had once been, not who she could be, or the person she had become through her life trials.

People were judgey in Welcome. She snorted at the town's misnomer.

Before Logan, she'd been happy enough to be alone, but now—damn him—he'd opened the floodgates and released in her all kinds of wants. Wants she'd shut down ruthlessly for her children's sakes.

As if she'd conjured him from her addled mind, Logan walked to her car across the store's parking lot. Oh, no. Damn it, why now when she'd just embarrassed herself with her childish response to Marilee? Had he seen the whole thing? She rolled down her window and stared straight ahead.

He loomed outside her car like a dark mass that blocked the sun and air. She tried not to look at him, but he leaned down, thrusting his face toward her. "I heard you on the way out the door. What the hell happened?" In her peripheral vision, she saw him shove a package into his jacket pocket.

"The cashier mentioned my children and *all* their fathers. Gave me the benefit of her advice." She looked up at him then and saw a smile crack wide. "You stop laughing."

"I'm not laughing. This is a smile."

"Your eyes are laughing." But he made her feel warm and affectionate as if he liked her. As if—well—that wouldn't—couldn't—happen. Not with him. He wanted his own babies and she was not the woman to give them to him.

To the lovely citizens of Welcome, and to people like Marilee Thompkins a baby with Logan would mean five fathers and she couldn't put Logan through all that gossip and speculation. She was immune, but he had a good guy reputation and he'd never hear the end of the pitying comments and concerned looks. *What would a nice guy like Logan Hughes see in that lowlife trash, Elle Foster.*

No, she couldn't do that to him. "Thanks for the sex. I enjoyed it." She spoke straight into his sexy, good-humored gaze.

His smile went wider. "Glad to be of service, ma'am."

"Shut up." She started her car. "You know it can't happen again."

"We'll see." He turned to leave.

"Wait," Elle called. "I'm serious, Logan. No more."

"I saw what you bought."

"They're not for you."

"Right. You're waiting for that dude to get out of prison." He tossed the comment over his shoulder and kept walking.

He was now too far away to yell at. Man, he could walk fast when he wanted to. His long legs had put real distance between them in seconds.

ON MONDAY MORNING LOGAN walked the half-block to Clay's veterinary clinic. It was his friend's first day back at work after two weeks in LA with Mercy. He couldn't remember a time when Clay had taken that much time off, but his buddy had wanted the alone time with his wife and little girl.

Their budding friendship had had a rocky start. Clay had been leery of Logan's interest in Mercy when he'd offered her a job, but over the past few months, the vet had come to understand that Mercy's heart belonged to him.

Besides, short, dark-haired women snagged Logan's attention. Not that Mercy wasn't a beauty inside and out, but not every man on the planet wanted tall blondes. No, some men wanted women who looked like Elle. Round, full, lush women. His blood heated as he remembered how she'd kissed. How she'd tasted. How she'd moaned and quivered.

It was rare Logan and Clay carved out time for a jog together but they each had a break this morning, so here he was, walking into the clinic, trying to banish thoughts of Elle. Sybil, Clay's receptionist, wore an avid expression and invited him to approach the counter with a wave. Too late, he recalled her love of gossip.

"Hi, Sybil, how's Bud?" Maybe she wanted to list her house for sale instead of gossiping. She and Bud owned a big, rambling two-story and now that their children were married, downsizing could be on her agenda.

"Have a care with Clay today," she said in a quiet voice.

"Oh? Something wrong? It's not Mercy, is it?" Alarm wormed through him.

She shook her head. "It's the other woman in his life. His sister, Elle."

Logan schooled his expression to vague. "Oh?"

"You remember her, right?"

He nodded.

"She was a wild one, and you better believe it. And Clay's upset about what people are saying."

"Oh?" He repeated because Sybil needed no more encouragement. She and her husband, Bud, liked nothing more than keeping tabs on the locals.

"Did you hear she's got a bunch of kids and doesn't even know who the fathers are?"

His gut clenched, but he kept his expression neutral. "I'd lay bets she knows, Sybil. Whether she's saying or not is up to her."

"Well"—she stretched the word for emphasis because she wanted his full attention—"I heard the last one, a baby, was taken by children's services."

He ground his back teeth at the reminder of Clarissa, but Sybil wasn't done yet.

"She had the baby with her when she registered her kids for school." She raised her eyebrows to see if Logan followed the story. "And now the poor little lamb is gone. Pfft! Just like that."

"And Clay's heard all this?"

She nodded. "He's in a mood, I can tell you."

"Can't blame him though, can you?" He narrowed his eyes. "People spread ugly gossip without knowing the facts," Logan responded with a tight leash on his voice. Denise Jones, the school's admin clerk, must be the source. She'd always had a nasty way about her.

"Of course," Sybil soothed. "Some people can't help but embellish their stories. Like the ones who're saying that Elle called children's services to come get the baby because she interfered with her carrying on with a new man."

His head might explode if she said one more thing. "You're saying that Elle Foster sent the baby to foster care so she could date?" It wasn't a question but a blue-steel statement. He stilled as he speared the woman with his eyes.

Sybil shifted, finally uncomfortable with the turn in the conversation. "Well, I'm not saying, but some are."

"Some."

Sybil lowered her voice further to encourage Logan to lean in. He did. "Apparently, there was a scene in the Good Value Foods yesterday. She caused a ruckus while buying a package of—you know—birth-protection products." She dropped her voice to a titillated whisper. "For safe sex."

He reared back and turned away sharply. "Tell Clay I'm outside."

Elle had mentioned incidents in passing. Registering the kids in school had been a trial. Mercy's mother had dodged Elle in the grocery aisle. Hell, he'd seen how Hope had treated Elle at Clay's house. And then to have Daniel's grandparents show up out of the blue. And Clarissa...hell, even he felt the sting of that loss; he couldn't imagine Elle's grief.

And now yesterday's scene from the Good Value with Marilee Tompkins was all over town.

No wonder Elle had needed him yesterday and fallen into his arms. No wonder she'd insisted it was a one-time thing.

And now he had the burden of telling her their condom broke. While a piece of him was more than okay with the idea of a little Elle/Logan creation, she'd be furious. Or scared.

Or she'd make a decision that would break his heart.

Clay stepped outside, dressed for their run. "Let's hit the trail." His face was stone, his eyes hard as diamonds.

On Logan's nod, they headed out in silence.

Five miles, several hills, and a ton of sweat later, they were back without a word spoken. But Logan felt less worried about 'fessing up to Elle and Clay's mouth was no longer set to grimace.

Logan clapped him on the back as they bent over to catch their breaths. "Good run."

"Yep. See ya."

Glad we had this talk, Logan thought with a mirthless chuckle. Sometimes a hard run was all the talk needed.

Chapter Fifteen

ON MONDAY MORNING THE sun shone exquisitely through the three windows that wrapped the living room in the double wide. The dreariness of the early part of June had passed. A long stretch of warm, sunny weather beckoned them toward summer. As Elle poured cereal into bowls for the twins a chime sounded on the laptop.

"Jorja, Liam," Elle said with her heart in her throat. "Your dad wants a video chat." Ben had never wanted to chat this early before. She hoped nothing had gone wrong as she carried the laptop into Jorja's room so the twins could chat privately with their father.

Elle had zilch to say to Ben. She'd said it all when he'd told her about his new baby and how he was leaving her and their family to "do the right thing." She snorted for the millionth time at the phrase.

She set down the laptop on Jorja's pillow and made way for Liam who tore into the room and bounced on his sister's bed. "Dad! Dad!"

"Cereal's ready," she said to no one listening. Both children were too excited to hear anything but their father's melodic bass voice. Ben could do voice-over work if he wanted to. She left the door open a crack because she may not want to talk with Ben directly, but she wasn't above eavesdropping.

Wanting a coffee, she joined Daniel in the kitchen and left the delighted voices of her twins behind her. She planned on one more jolt of jet fuel to get the day started then she'd go back and hang around outside the bedroom to listen.

Except she caught her eldest with half a mug of coffee in his hand. He looked sheepishly at her. "What? I'll be fifteen soon." He may look sheepish but his voice held an edge of defiance.

With a teenager, a mother had to pick her battles. This was not one of those battles. She made sure her shoulders sagged and used her exasperated voice. "Put lots of milk in it and don't have any more today." Her theatrics only made him grin and she grinned back. "Is this your first coffee?" Of course, he'd had sips, but she'd never seen him drink a mugful.

He nodded. "I didn't sleep much." He poured enough milk into the mug to top it off. Half-strength she could bear. Score one for mom. At least he drank it on her terms.

"You have a lot on your mind," she said with a nod toward the sugar bowl. She slid a spoon across the island to him. He turned his nose up at the sugar and tasted his brew.

"Thanks," he muttered and grabbed the spoon to get a heaping spoonful of sugar.

"How did the visit go with Susan and the old man?" she asked.

Daniel shrugged and blew on his sweet, milky drink. Elle suppressed a smile at the motion. "She's nice, I guess," he said in answer, but he kept his enthusiasm tamped down. "Showed me some of dad's trophies and old pictures. I look like him."

"You do. He was handsome." Tad had been every teen girl's fantasy. Broad shouldered with a tapered waist. His hair had a hint of curl when it touched his ears. His dark-blond hair had golden and reddish threads that showed up in the sun. His sad, lonely smile had caught her first. Stupidly, she'd believed she could take his sadness away, that together they could overcome the crappy things that had scarred them. "And your grandfather?" she asked Daniel to get her mind back on track.

"He didn't seem to be losing his marbles, but what do I know? They're both ancient."

She chuckled at that. By her reckoning, the Murdochs were in their mid-sixties. Young for dementia, but she'd heard of earlier cases. She fought a stab of sympathy for Susan. "It's up to you if you want to spend more time with them. No one will force you to do anything you don't want. I won't let that happen."

He snorted and blew on his coffee again. Surely it had cooled by now. "As if I'd let anyone push me around." His voice firmed and she heard his father in the tone.

"And now you sound like Tad. Your father hated being told what to do, too." Tad had put up walls that no one could get through to make him see reason. Stubborn was one thing, blind stupidity another.

"They've got gates, a fancy house, and a barn with a couple of horses." His nonchalant tone failed to hide how impressed he'd been. She was impressed, too. She'd never seen the Murdoch home. Tad had refused to take her there, not even to walk the grounds when they were in high school. He'd said the less she knew about them, the better.

"The Murdochs are wealthy people," she said carefully.

"She said they'd put me through college if I wanted to study business."

Right. Business. The same track they tried to put Tad on. "Did *she* say business or did he?"

He frowned and took a tentative sip of his coffee. He smiled and nodded in response to the taste. "I like it."

"Remember, no more today. See how you feel in half an hour. If you get jittery, you've had too much." She sighed at this rite of passage. Fourteen seemed young for coffee. But she had bigger problems at the moment.

Daniel looked tired and red-eyed from lack of sleep. Milky coffee once in a while after a bad night might be all right. She'd keep a close eye on him.

"I didn't start a daily dose of caffeine until a certain wailing baby made sleep impossible," she said with a smile. "I needed to be up for work." And now, that wailing baby was drinking coffee, too. She didn't usually feel old, but this reminded her of how much of her life had passed. Lots of women were starting families at her age, and here she was, already done. Done and with her eldest sipping caffeine.

Sex with Logan had rattled her more than she'd thought if her mind had skipped to babies.

"Back to your grandmother," she said, to stop her wild mind. "Was she pressuring you to take business?"

"She mentioned college and tuition but *he* said I'd have to study business." Sip number two down.

"So your *grandmother* didn't suggest business?"

He shook his head. "I don't know what I want to study yet. Maybe I'll be a vet like Clay."

Elle smiled. "Maybe. But it's nice to have options." She hoped that with Susan ultimately in charge, Daniel would have the freedom to choose. Her son had a lot to consider in the next couple of years. To suddenly learn he had a different future than the one he'd seen yesterday must be mind-blowing.

"Yeah. I'll have options and it will be my decision," he said with some force. His third sip went down.

"Good. You have time to see what interests you most. Stay open to possibilities."

And with his soft sigh, she saw that he'd been overwhelmed the day before. His world had changed drastically and he had more choices than ever. No wonder he hadn't slept well. She heard a cheer from Jorja's room, signaling that the chat had ended. Ben always bumped a fist to the screen and the three of them yelled boo-yah as a goodbye. Damn, she hadn't had time to go listen in.

Daniel set aside his drink. "That's enough for now."

Elle peered into his mug. "Half a mug half-full of milk is plenty. Remember what I said about the jitters." She took the mug and tossed the remains of the drink into the sink.

He rolled his eyes as if he were immune to caffeine overload.

The conversation with Daniel died just in time because Liam barreled into the room filling the air with excited shouts. Jorja followed quietly behind with an oddly stubborn look on her face.

"Quit screeching," Daniel said. "We can't tell what you're saying."

Jorja spoke up. "Dad wants us to stay with him all summer." Her daughter looked nervously from Elle to Daniel.

Elle felt too stunned to respond, but Daniel was quick.

"What for?" Daniel covered Liam's mouth with his palm to stifle the noise. "Shush, buddy, we can't hear." It worked. Liam shushed, finally seeing his twin's hesitation and everyone else's surprise.

"Dad wants us to meet our new sister," Jorja explained. Angelica was three months old.

Ben and his tart of a wife apparently claimed they wanted the twins to feel part of their new family. Video chats weren't cutting it, Ben had said. Why, oh, why hadn't she eavesdropped? She'd had a feeling something was up when Ben had called early. And damn him for not clearing this with her first.

"How soon?" Daniel asked quietly. Daniel had felt Ben's betrayal deeply when he'd left them and now Daniel hadn't been included in the invitation for family time with his stepdad's new family. But Daniel needed to focus on the time with his grandparents, so Elle figured it evened things out.

"Friday afternoon because school's out then. He wants to spend the whole weekend with us before he goes to work on Monday." Jorja's eyes filled with worry. "I should have called you to come in to talk to him," she said to Elle.

"It's okay." Elle tugged Jorja, her serious, sweet girl, into her arms. "I'd have liked it if your Dad had let me know first, but I guess he wanted to surprise you." Liam's eyes went wide with bubbling excitement. She dragged him close to her other side and ruffled his hair. He'd been missing his father and she didn't have the heart to dampen his spirits.

"You'll have a wonderful summer." Each word felt torn from her throat, but she couldn't fault Ben for wanting the twins. He'd been a caring dad, all things considered, and she'd be petty to keep his children away from their baby sister and father. And their stepmother, she conceded sourly.

Some days she hated being an adult, especially when she wanted to let her inner bitch wreak havoc. But she couldn't do that, not with the twins' hopes flying high.

All three children looked at her expectantly, as if wishing she were a different kind of mother, one who magically understood the right thing to do and say. The weight of raising them alone bore down. She lifted her chin to show them her best imitation of a grown-ass woman. One who held her true emotions in check and locked the door on her inner bitch. She gritted her teeth and caved. "We'll pack your things on Thursday night, that way you're ready as soon as your father comes to get you on Friday."

"Yay!" Liam did a jumping jack to celebrate.

Jorja, her sad-eyed, too-sensitive daughter, hugged Elle hard. "I don't want you to miss us."

"I will miss you, but it'll be okay. Daniel and I will be fine together. And it won't be for long." She smiled at all of them to keep up the pretense. Daniel glanced sharply at her. He'd seen through her. To be expected, she supposed, now that he was adult enough to drink coffee. *Oh, hell. Coffee.*

"Maybe Logan can keep you company," Jorja whispered next to her ear.

"Maybe he can," she said. But he'd best not offer, because Elle wasn't sure she could resist.

AFTER THE CHILDREN left for school, Elle stood in the kitchen in an emotional stupor. Nothing made sense anymore and she couldn't tell exactly when her control had slipped away. She raised her hands in front of her face and stared at them. She had capable hands. They could soothe a child's hurt, earn money, put food on the table, clean the house, and offer comfort. But they couldn't tell her what had happened to her family.

She was losing all of them. Four children taken away in a matter of days. First Clarissa, then Daniel's grandparents had shown up demanding a huge piece of him, and then right on the heels of that devastation, Ben had swooped in with promises of a loving family and sweet new baby and *boom*, Elle was on her own.

Oh, she wanted to cling to her children, to keep them all, to say no to all the people who wanted to take her babies.

But a grown-ass woman didn't keep her children with her out of spite, or fear of loneliness, or any of the myriad ugly emotions running rampant through her heart.

A grown-ass woman, a mother who wanted to set a good example every day, allowed her children to have others who loved them.

She clenched her fingers and felt like punching something, but didn't. No, she didn't. Instead, she kept her cool, collected the dirty plates, cups, and bowls from breakfast and filled the dishwasher. Then she emptied it again.

Elle filled the sink with soapy water and hand-washed everything. She found comfort in the warm water and the mindless chore that took her back to her childhood. The only time she and her mom had talked with any consistency was when they did the dishes together. Those times didn't last long; only until she was seven or eight and deemed old enough to wash up on her own. She'd missed her mom after that, missed sharing this simple task.

But she doubted her mother ever had.

Daniel's coffee mug found its way into her hands. Smiling, she dried the mug and put it away, uncaring that tears washed her cheeks. *Coffee. Already.* Making a big deal out of Daniel enjoying a cup now and then didn't feel right.

Maybe having this taste was the end for a couple of years. Maybe he'd been testing her. Her eldest did that sometimes; pushed for things a little too grown up, pressured her for freedom he knew would make her uncomfortable. If a man was in the house, maybe the push would be against him and not her.

But she was on her own with Daniel and had to let him grow up in increments. He set his bedtime hours now, he chose his clothes, and he'd have a phone if they could afford it. He was angling for permission to get a job, even though they'd agreed on his being sixteen before working. As a mother, she wanted to wrap him in bubble wrap and keep him safe, but as a strong parent, she had to let him go.

She'd talk to Clay and get his opinion. Maybe see if her brother could introduce him to some manly interests, like mechanics or carpentry.

After tidying the kitchen, she showered. With the water sluicing over her, she supposed she should be concerned about seeing Logan after they'd all but destroyed the narrow, flimsy cot in the office, but she didn't have the energy to fret about him. She soaped and lathered and let her mind wander.

Having comfort sex with her boss seemed unimportant when bigger events were upon her. Yesterday's respite had happened. They'd both needed it. Today they'd move on.

She already had.

AFTER A MORNING RUN with Clay and a shower at home, Logan arrived at the office earlier than usual. The run had helped with his concern for Jamie and his parents. But he wasn't sure any amount of running could dampen his feelings for Elle. And he sure as hell couldn't talk to Clay about her.

Yesterday had been a hell of a day all around. First, he'd had to deal with his parents' decision to cut off Jamie's financial support. Thank God his mom and dad had accepted that paying for Jamie's addiction may have done more harm than good. He prayed Jamie saw that his only way out of the hell he'd fallen into was to accept the hard work involved.

In an attempt to keep his mind off Elle, Logan picked up a coffee and bagel from the bakery, walked up the stairs to his office and settled in to check his email and the current listings. A couple of houses had sold in the neighborhood where Mercy's parents lived. No surprise. The area was aging out and large family homes were too big for empty-nesters. The market for condos and three bedroom ranchers had heated up. Maybe his mom and dad could redecorate and bring their place into this millennium and sell. If they downsized they'd have money to travel. Logan wanted to see them have their dream and he felt certain that deep down Jamie wanted that, too.

His parents also dreamed of grandchildren. His mother never mentioned it, but she'd been disappointed when Trish had refused to move to Welcome. That had ended any hope for grandchildren from that quarter. More than anything, Logan wanted to give his mom a grandchild; to have a child who looked back at him with his eyes. Be it a boy or girl, a baby would give the Hughes family new reasons to laugh and to hope again.

He washed the rest of his bagel down with the last of his coffee and set aside his dreams about a non-existent kid. He had to be patient.

He also needed to tell Elle as soon as he could that the condom broke. The office door opened and the woman occupying his mind strode in, coffee in hand.

She gave him a tentative smile. "You're here early." Her glance, as she hung her purse and a lightweight cardigan on the coat rack, turned speculative.

"I went for a run with Clay; felt energized, and thought I'd get a jump on the week." Logan turned his chair sideways and stretched out his legs, crossing his feet at the ankles. He clasped his hands on his belly. "You look upset. Should I apologize for our time here yesterday? I will if you want."

"No, it's not that." She brushed off the sex as if it meant nothing to her. She settled into a chair across from him and lifted the lid off her coffee. "We're adults and behaved with full consent."

"Good, because I'm not sorry about making love." He used the term he preferred and watched her eyes flare. She blinked to hide her reaction.

"But we stick to our agreement, right? No more." She held his gaze steadily. The woman looked rock solid.

He nodded. "No more hot sex on the cot. In fact, I'll remove it. I shouldn't need it anymore."

She tilted her head and assessed him like a housewife with a roast beef. "You got a good night's sleep. I'm glad."

"Big thanks to you." He chuckled. "Also for the first time in months, I didn't get a call to go find Jamie." She'd neatly avoided telling him why she'd looked upset when she'd arrived. After yesterday's conversation in the bakery, he felt they'd crossed a line and should be able to share the good and the bad. Clearly, she didn't agree.

"What's happened to put those thunderclouds in your eyes?" he asked. "News from the Murdochs got you down?"

She closed her eyes, pinched her lips together and shook her head.

He moved quickly and crouched in front of her. He used a fingertip to tilt her face up to see her expression. "What? Tell me. Is it the kids? Are they okay?" He told himself that if there'd been an accident she wouldn't be here.

"The kids are fine. I'm the mess." She shuddered, but put up her hands to stall the hug he wanted to give her. "Don't. Don't offer comfort. I don't need it."

Bullshit. But he respected her wishes and drew back to lean against the desk to wait for her to explain if she wanted to.

ELLE DIDN'T WANT TO tell Logan about Ben and the twins. This news would cement her loser status if he didn't already consider her one. A single mother, battered by her experiences, Elle had no control over her life or the lives of her children. Logan had witnessed all of her crises from the moment she'd returned to town. She'd begged for help for the simplest things since returning to Welcome, and now all of her children had been taken from her in one way or another.

Of course, Daniel would still be around through the summer, but he'd be focused on his future, getting to know his grandparents, and doing what fourteen-year-old boys do: enjoy their freedom. She set her chin in her hand. Maybe he'd learn to ride a horse. The Murdochs had two after all and Susan had been an accomplished equestrienne.

"It's more than Daniel," Logan said. "You accepted the Murdochs yesterday. Is it Clarissa? Is she okay?"

"It's not the baby. I've seen her on my phone and Clarissa's happy and healthy with her parents and grandparents. They offered to let her see me, but I thought she might cry, so I just watched her for a bit." It hurt, but Clarissa had been her giggly self. Still, Logan's caring left her defenseless. He opened her, spread her out for the world to see. She'd been closed tight for so long, she wasn't sure she could handle being laid bare. But she wanted desperately to let him in.

"My ex is taking the twins for the summer. He lives south of Tacoma now with his *new* wife and a *new* baby. Ben wants them to be part of his *new* family." Saying it out loud flayed her and she shuddered again, another sign of weakness.

Logan leaned back, his long legs stretched out, feet braced on the floor. He seemed to vibrate with outrage. Or anger. Or sympathy. She couldn't read him because his face shuttered against her.

Hell, she couldn't understand her own emotions, how could she expect to understand his?

They barely knew each other. Mere weeks were not long enough to know anyone. Hell, you could live with a man for years and not understand him. Logan opened his mouth and closed it. "What?" she prodded. "You have something to say. Say it."

"I don't want to dump this on you, not like this. Not now when you're in the midst of another crisis, but the clock's ticking. We can't run out of time and make this all worse."

Her insides stilled. She heard her breath loud in the room, her pulse pounded. "Spit it out, Logan."

"The condom tore."

Chapter Sixteen

"YOU DIDN'T JUST SAY that," Elle screamed and bolted to her feet in the office. Logan couldn't mean the condom *broke*. Logan stared sorrowfully back at her. He *did* mean that. A horrid, sick feeling washed through her and she covered her mouth with both hands.

She blindly turned to run out the door but found no escape. She fell back into her seat with a thump. "But how?" Her brain stalled. Garbled thoughts drifted but she couldn't grab onto a single one. She dragged in two deep breaths. "Condoms are checked," she gasped out. "*Lives* depend on quality control."

Logan looked stricken and red blotches covered his neck and moved up to his face. Guilt. She saw guilt in the red stain on his cheeks. "How?" she repeated.

He raised his palms. "I'm not sure that it happened inside you. It's possible it snagged on a fingernail as I took it off. But there's no way to be certain, right?" He looked at her as if she were the Goddess of all Prophylactic Knowledge. "It wasn't a gaping hole."

"Where? Where was it?"

"Not at the tip. Closer to the top. A nick, that's all."

"You're minimizing." Probably to make her feel better and while she appreciated the gesture, she didn't feel reassured. "Wait, wait. Wait!" She put up her hands, fingers poker straight. "Let me think."

His desk sported a small paper calendar with the business name emblazoned on the top. *Who uses these anymore?* She did, that's who. Right now. The tangible, paper proof in black and white that she had her dates right.

She grabbed the calendar, tore off the top three months to bring it up to date and ran her finger down the pertinent days. Counted them. Her third shudder in as many minutes. "It's okay." Her voice went hoarse with relief. "The dates are good. I'll be fine."

"Are you sure *we'll* be fine? You wouldn't be in this alone."

His tone said she'd wronged him by assuming she'd be on her own. Elle wanted to crawl into a hole in the ground and pull the sod over top of her. "I suppose you disposed of it?"

He cocked an eyebrow at that. "Wouldn't you?"

She nodded. "It must have been old. What other explanation could there be? We were hot for each other, but far from rough." He'd been perfect. Demanding, hard, but gentle at the right time. Perfect, considering it had been their first and last time.

"I'm sorry for the scare. Trish and I stopped using condoms when we hit a year together. We were clean, safe, and committed. She used birth control and I never tossed out my supply of condoms. Forgot about them until you woke me up." His eyes filled with remorse.

She set aside the fact that he'd been celibate until they'd met. "You didn't tell me yesterday because?"

"I meant to, but by the time I came out of the restroom, you were asleep. After that, we improvised and didn't need one." He frowned deeply. "If I'd checked the expiration date I never would've used it."

She believed him. "And we might not have had yesterday. Regardless, I still don't regret it."

His eyes warmed. "Me, neither." After a moment of mutually shared memories, he sobered. "Do you need to get an emergency pill?" His voice went husky and his eyes darkened. "We'll go right now."

She shook her head. "Believe me, I know my cycle. I've been caught unaware twice before. Quit worrying." The adrenaline rush died off and left her deflated. "Why didn't you say anything after the second time?"

"I figured we'd both had a craptastic day so why add to the misery? And we have time now to discuss it."

"I get it. You had no idea that my morning with the twins would be worse than yesterday with the Murdochs." Her head spun. At least she wasn't angry the way she'd been on the drive to work. Ben should never have asked the twins about the summer without consulting her first. "This scare blew what Ben did right out of the running for worst morning ever."

"Sometime soon, you'll catch a break. No one's luck can be bad forever."

"Actually, I guess I—*we*—did catch a break with my cycle. We should celebrate the win." She gave him a weak smile that he returned. "The time with you was perfect. If you'd told me about the condom, you'd have blown the mood and well, I'd have been right back where I'd started; stressed, scared, and angry."

Those wonderful moments with Logan shone like a beacon and had taken her away from all her problems. Now that Ben had mired her in crap again, Elle was glad to have the soft, glowing memory Logan had given her. "You took all my bad feelings and frustrations away."

"You did that for me, too." His voice went warm and sent gooey, sweet tendrils down her spine.

"But it can't happen again," she said.

"No more hot sex in the office," he swore and placed his palm over his heart. "Now, tell me about your ex and the twins."

"A couple of minutes ago, I didn't want to put all this on you, but now? What the hell. You've seen me in total crisis since the moment you met me. What's one more between friends?"

Logan already knew the basics, so she ended by expressing how ticked off Ben's tactics made her. "Going straight to the kids was wrong. Ben should have discussed the invitation with me first."

"You'd have said yes?"

She wobbled her head like a whiny child. "Of course. But I might have suggested a month rather than the whole summer."

"Do they miss Ben?"

She rolled her shoulders. "Yes. He's their dad. And until he got tangled up with whats-her-name he was pretty good at it." She begrudged him the compliment, but she was only human after all.

"They must miss Clarissa."

Loss rose at the mention of her name. "Of course. We all do." She cut her eyes to his and saw that he felt the loss as well.

"Having a whole summer with this new baby sister sounds like a healing time."

Elle drew in a long, deep breath and blew it out while she wrestled with the three-year-old inside who wanted to throw herself on the floor in a fit of temper. The adult won. "You're always reasonable." At this moment levelheadedness became his least attractive trait, whispered the child inside.

"When do the twins leave?"

"Friday after school."

He looked surprised. "That's quick. Not a lot of time for you to prepare yourself."

Her phone vibrated with a call. She glanced at the screen. "It's Ben. Maybe he's changed his mind." She could hope, but Ben didn't like to disappoint the twins once a plan was set. When she answered, though, he heard Ben's tart of a wife on the phone.

"Elle, it's me, Jodie." Elle made a motion to Logan and then walked toward the room divider for privacy. Once behind the screen she stared at the ruined cot and felt heat creep up her cheeks.

"What do you want?" she asked the tart. "Aside from my husband and now my children." The old Elle, the one who didn't take crap from anyone, roared to life and she felt power build inside. She could put a stop to this right now, with the tart.

"I understand that must be how it seems. But I don't want to *take* them." Her voice sounded wispy and young and maybe even scared. And the tart should be scared.

She was messing with a mother's children, with their hearts, their happiness.

"Don't you *dare* try to take back Ben's invitation." Maybe it seemed counter-productive to warn Jodie off, but her kids had been promised a visit. "Jorja and Liam are *expecting* to spend the summer with you. With Angelica and Ben, their *father*." Anger cleared her mind and narrowed her focus. Glorious, glorious anger.

"I didn't mean this visit," the young voice caught on her words. "I meant that I'd never want to come between you and your children. And I *totally* understand why you think poorly of me. But I'd never disappoint the twins. I want them here as much as Ben does."

"Then what do you want? Why are you calling?" She shot the questions like bullets. "What could you possibly have to say to me?"

The tart held her breath for a couple of beats. "I'm sorry Ben didn't check with you first. I told him to, but you know how he is. He gets an idea and runs with it."

And her ex assumed everyone would go along; more often than not, they did. Too often, Elle had climbed aboard the speeding train that was Ben. Elle sighed. "And?"

"I want to reassure you that I'll be nice to them and be kind. I have a kid brother and sister a bit older than them and Jorja and Liam will have them to play with. They can hang out and go swimming in my parents' pool and stuff."

Elle slowed her mind to take it all in. "You put some thought into this."

"Yes, oh, yes! I really like kids and it'll be fun, I swear."

Jodie was so young that she probably didn't realize that she'd torn apart a family by falling for Ben's seduction. Elle hung her head as another thought crossed her mind. This young, gullible woman had no idea that Ben would break her heart and likely ruin her little family, too. "I'm sure you'll have a wonderful summer." She kept her tone soft. No small feat, considering. "I have beautiful children with open hearts. Please send them back to me in the same condition."

"I will. I promise."

Elle hung up. "Every time I want to let my inner bitch loose, somebody needs me to be a grownup," she said to Logan as she stepped out from behind the screen. "I want to punch somebody's lights out."

The man chuckled, all sexy and low.

She dropped her shoulders and gave them a roll. Then another. "Damn, I hate this town and what it's done to me." She moved toward Logan who straightened away from his perch on the desktop. His face changed to compassionate and it was all she could do to stay clear of his arms.

LOGAN WANTED TO PULL Elle into his arms and hug away the pain in her eyes. But they'd done that yesterday when they'd needed each other, he'd made a promise not to offer hot sex in the office again. Today, all he could offer was encouragement.

The office phone rang and took Elle's attention. For the best, he decided. She needed time to sort her emotions and neither of them needed any more temptation. Besides, he had to write a couple of listings and get them posted. He took pride in his writing skills, worked hard to make his words draw in buyers. A lackluster listing could make a seller leave an agent in the dust. He worked quietly while Elle handled paperwork and answered calls from the staff out at Springhill Meadows.

He made an appointment to show a house and headed for the door with a smile and nod. Elle looked relieved that he'd let their conversation drop. The phone rang again and he stopped in the doorway in case he was needed. Elle answered.

"Hi, Brianna, what can I do for you?" Elle asked and then waved at him. "Yes, he's here."

He took the phone. "Hey, there, Brianna. What's up?"

"Hi, Logan. I'll be in town for errands later. Do you have time for that coffee we talked about?" They'd had to cancel their previous get-together and Logan had forgotten about it.

"How's three o'clock at the bakery downstairs?"

"Perfect. See you then." When he passed Elle the phone to hang up, her gaze slid away from his.

BRIANNA BOWLER WAVED to Logan from the front counter in the bakery. The stools faced the street, perfect for people watching. He stepped into the warm, yeast-scented air and accepted her welcoming hug. She already had a mug of something foamy and hot. "My weakness," she said, "A latte and a blueberry scone."

He went to order and after being served, carried his coffee and cheese scone to sit with her. "This is nice. I like watching the comings and goings sometimes."

"Especially if you're here alone. It's not as obvious that you have no friends to sit with," she said with a wink.

"You were always a joker," he said, remembering the trait fondly. He and Brianna had been on Welcome High's student council together and he'd taken to her soft, self-effacing humor right away.

They shared some gossip and also some real news about each other's lives and passed a lively and fun half-hour together.

Soon it became clear neither felt a zing of interest. They were friends, the way they'd been in school.

"And your mom's recovering from her knee surgery?" he asked.

"Right on schedule," Brianna said, with a smile. "Her physical therapist is pleased. No more pain meds required and she's graduating from a walker to a cane tomorrow." She glanced at the time. "Oh, I'd best get home, the dogs will need to be fed soon and I'm short a volunteer today. We'll all have to do extra."

"Sorry I can't stop by and help, but I have another appointment."

"No problem, we'll be back at full strength in the morning." Brianna rose to leave. "You haven't heard from Jake Morrow, have you?" Another kid from student council.

"He's in town. Never left." He smiled. "So he's why you asked me for coffee?"

A pretty flush spread across her cheeks. "No. I just wondered." She leaned in. "I'm curious. Did he get over it?"

"Would anyone?" They shared a look full of dark, stark memories and then she opened the door and walked out.

Brianna and Jake had been best friends in school until Jake had pushed her into leaving town. Logan wondered, all these years later, why they hadn't been in touch since. If they had, she'd know where Jake was and what he was doing.

Chapter Seventeen

ELLE'S CYCLE DATES were correct, but she refused to play with fire. She'd made enough stupid, hormone-driven decisions to last a lifetime. She gave her name to the receptionist at the women's clinic and took a seat in the waiting room.

Another woman near her age settled in the seat beside her. Shoulder length blond hair, wide brown eyes, and a pert nose seemed like the perfect package. The woman shifted in her seat. "Elle? Elle Foster? How are you?" she said warmly.

Elle slanted the stranger a glance and hesitated. Her warm tone sounded alien after all the censure she'd received from people who remembered her. "Shandy Armstrong?"

"It's Camden now," she said with a grin. "I married and divorced Justin." Her eyes lit joyfully. "But he gave me a son, Josh, so it's all good." She turned toward Elle and looked genuinely happy to chat. "I heard you were back in town. It's great to see you."

Surprised, Elle faced her square-on. Like old friends catching up, she thought. And they had been friendly back in school. But maybe that had been because Shandy had had a crush on Clay at the time. No matter, she'd always liked Shandy. "I returned a couple of weeks ago," she explained. "I have fo—three—children; a son who's fourteen going on thirty and twins, Jorja and Liam, who are seven and a half. The half is important."

"Sounds like my Josh. He'll be ten soon and won't let up about being in the double digits." They shared a chuckle.

Shandy patted her hand where it rested on her knee. "Let's have lunch. Are you free tomorrow?"

As easily as those few words, Elle felt accepted. Warmth bloomed in her chest.

"Lunch? I'd like that." Life had been too hectic for Elle to pursue friendships with women. Add her busy day-to-day life to the drama and dread of the last year and she cheered inside at the invitation. Suddenly Elle had a sister-in-law she liked and a lunch invitation from Shandy. "I'd love to have lunch," she repeated. "I work over the bakery. Could we go there? I have an hour and that's the closest place."

"Their salad and sandwich deals are the best," Shandy said frankly. "I'll text you when I arrive."

They exchanged contact information and then Elle heard her name called for her appointment. Ridiculous how happy she felt. Her mood improved more after her check-up and she walked out with her birth control prescription. Firmly, she reminded herself the prescription wasn't for Logan's benefit.

No more hot sex on the office cot; that's what he'd promised.

She climbed into her car and buckled up.

And then it hit her. He hadn't promised no sex anywhere. Just not in the office.

Behind Logan's good-guy image; his wide, guileless smile and warm, friendly eyes lay the mind of a master at getting what he wanted. Sure, he'd blatantly given the twins the bikes, but Logan also expected her to see through him and had tried to make it seem like Clay's idea. *As if.* And here she'd thought she'd been the one to insist on her pay deductions. That had likely been his plan all along, to make her feel better about accepting the bikes. Also, Logan had busted through Daniel's wariness when they'd returned Clarissa's crib together.

She narrowed her eyes. *Rat. Conniving rat.* Logan Hughes had wooed her, bamboozled her, *and courted* her. Worse, she wasn't sure she could stop him from doing it all again. Maybe she didn't want to. After all, she'd purchased a fresh pack of condoms and now she had a prescription for birth control in her purse. She closed her eyes and rested her forehead on the steering wheel and thought about sex with Logan.

The slow kind.

The hard and fast kind.

The kind people had when they were in a mad fling.

Technically, she'd never had a fling. Her first love with Tad had been fierce and crazy and hormonal. She'd loved Tad with all of her seventeen-year-old heart and soul and her body had followed along in the way of healthy, normal, teenaged bodies. Everything in her life had amplified in the crazy rush of first love.

Hyperbole had reigned. Tad had been her *everything, no one* had loved her the way he did, *no one ever would. EVER.* She recalled the tumult of emotions in a forgiving haze. *Kids, they'd been kids.*

A year later, with Daniel to raise by herself, the magnificent splendor of first love had sagged into the depths of single motherhood. No, she couldn't consider what she'd had with Tad a fling.

And her life with Ben? Not a fling, either. They'd taken things slow at first. She'd been wary of dating a guy at work, but he'd patiently won her over. She saw now that it had been a seduction. Ben was older and she'd wanted a more stable man than Tad had proven to be. Ben had been steadily employed, had been married before and he'd had no qualms about her having Daniel. Ben had wanted her fiercely and she'd fallen for him. Five years later, she'd figured out Ben had a pattern of seducing younger women at work and fathering children. Ben was and probably always would be a serial philanderer and father. Maybe he believed children bound his women to him. She'd tired of sorting through her limited ideas on his psychological make-up months ago.

Ben might be the past, but he had not been a fling.

Now that she'd visited the clinic she felt protected and in control. Logan understood she'd never have more children. A seed sprouted in her mind. That seed grew into a plan and though she searched for a downside, she couldn't find one. A summer fling with Logan, one with a start and end date and no future—what could go wrong?

ON FRIDAY AFTERNOON, Elle drove to the school to pick up Jorja and Liam. The flood of excited, happy children waving report cards, lugging backpacks, and squealing about the end of the school year made her laugh. Until she saw her ex-husband Ben beside his pick-up truck across the street. She hoped she'd have more time to say goodbye.

She should have known he'd show up at the school. He'd texted her about having their stuff in the trunk of her car. He'd planned to swoop in at the school all along.

Ben never liked goodbyes and he probably wanted to avoid hers. He'd likely bounce from foot to foot while she hugged and kissed her babies before they left with him.

Too bad. She'd cuddle them and squeeze them and love them up so hard they'd lose a clothing size.

The twins saw Ben before they saw her. Their faces lit with love and excitement and they ran to the crosswalk, jumping with joy. Ben crossed the road to her babies and began squeezing and loving and cuddling them both. She wanted to snarl and snatch them out of his arms.

Her heart cracked with loss at the sight of her children's happy faces. *They'd be gone two months. A few weeks. A break from their routine. A summer to remember.* She closed her eyes as she repeated the sentences that had got her through the days since Monday's sudden invitation.

With Daniel at the high school, he'd miss seeing the twins off; another reason for Ben to show up here instead of the house later. Elle shook off the hurt and strode over to the lovefest.

"Hey there," she said to the trio.

Ben rose to his feet and faced her. *Rotten SOB.*

"Hey, Elle. Glad you're here. Do you have their gear?" His hazel eyes scanned over her shoulder as he looked for her car. He'd had a haircut and put on a collared shirt and fresh, clean jeans. She caught a whiff of his favorite cologne.

She ignored his question and looked at her babies. Jorja was sprouting but Liam was catching up. "Are you okay?" she asked them, although it was clear they were beside themselves with joy.

Liam squealed and jumped as high as he could. "YES!!"

Jorja tamped back her happiness and her expression gave Elle a start. Her daughter wanted to spare Elle's feelings and lighten her loss by hiding her excitement. She ruffled Jorja's hair and pulled her into a hug. "It's okay," she whispered to her girl. "I'll be fine. I want you to have a wonderful time and give your baby sister tons of kisses and hugs from me, okay?"

Jorja nodded. "Okay."

"Where's your car?" Ben asked impatiently.

Liam pointed to her beater. "There. Do you have our stuff, Mom?"

"What are you doing with that piece of shit? What happened to the car I left you with?"

She frowned at him. Ben never considered what he said before saying it. Words burbled out of him like a drinking fountain with no off-switch.

"This is what I can afford," she said succinctly. She'd had to default on the car he'd left behind and her credit rating had taken a nasty hit. But that had been only one financial setback in an avalanche of setbacks since Ben had left them. She gritted her teeth.

Her ex snorted but didn't look the least bit fazed. Once Jodie had announced her pregnancy, Ben couldn't wait to come to her rescue.

Now, he'd been rewarded with a summer with his children. Bitterness welled, but instead of acting on it, she held the twins' hands and took them to the car for their bags. Inside the trunk were the helmets Logan had provided. "Take these in case you end up riding bikes at Jodie's parents' house."

"They have a pool!" Liam squealed, blinded by all the wonders ahead of him.

Jorja squeezed her hand. "I'll make sure he wears his helmet, Momma."

Ben reached into the trunk and took the tote bags while the twins carried their helmets. He'd insisted they didn't have room at his condo for their bikes, but Jodie had requested the helmets, so Elle had brought them.

"Are your report cards in your backpacks?" she asked.

"Yes, Momma," Jorja said with a sniff. Her lip quivered. "They're okay."

"Don't cry, Jorja. I'll see you soon. Video chat with me when you're ready for bed tonight."

"Okay!" Liam flung his arms around her for a nanosecond and then caught up to Ben, who'd left them to their goodbyes.

Jorja hugged her for ten whole seconds but managed not to cry. "Love you, Momma."

"Forever and ever," she responded. She patted her daughter's shoulder to encourage her to catch up to Ben and Liam. "I'll see you before you know it, and we'll talk tonight."

Ben had been right. A short goodbye was best.

ON FRIDAY AFTERNOON, Logan signed a listing for a rancher in the Talbots' neighborhood. Once the sign went up with his name on it, he expected some queries from neighbors.

He sat in his car out front and called his parents. "Hey, Mom. I'm checking in to see how you're doing."

"We're good. Things are fine. We haven't heard from Jamie and your father says I shouldn't call him." She sounded strong, but he hoped like hell his brother didn't call and catch her in a weak moment.

"Dad's right. It's only been a few days. Jamie needs time to sort his life out on his own."

"It's hard not knowing how he is; if he's eating and safe."

"He must be okay because if he wasn't, he'd call."

"You're right." She sighed. "But this is harder than I expected."

"Tough love is tough on everyone."

"I guess it is," she responded. "I'll keep that in mind. Where did you hear it?"

"A friend told me that the other day." He made a mental note to thank Elle.

Logan had driven by the park where they'd left his brother but he hadn't seen Jamie. He'd either gone to ground or gone for help. Either way, his parents had agreed to leave Jamie to decide his fate. "Jamie will be in touch when he's ready," he assured her.

His mother needn't know that Jamie had turned off his location settings on the phone they'd given him. He'd taken them at their word that he'd be on his own. Logan wasn't sure what to think. Had Jamie gone to the shelter and asked for help?

Maybe the addict inside his brother was finally sick and tired of conning their mother. God, he hoped so.

"Will you be here for dinner?" she asked and brought him back to the conversation.

It was Friday night. He'd called to say he couldn't make it, but she needed him there. "Yes. I'm looking forward to your pot roast."

"Your favorite."

He laughed at the old joke. Pot roast was his dad's favorite and they all knew it.

"See you at six thirty." And now he had a couple hours' worth of work to do at the office. As he drove, he wondered how Elle had coped with saying goodbye to the twins.

If she needed to talk, he'd cancel dinner with his parents to give her the time she needed. His dad said leftovers were as good the second time around anyway.

He walked into the office a few minutes later and found her at his desk. She wore a top he'd never seen before. The color glowed the same cobalt blue as her eyes. Thin straps exposed her shoulders. The neckline drooped and showed off her remarkable cleavage. Distracting, that's what it was. But he couldn't tell her that. Something about sexism or harassment or...something.

"It's time to get you your own desk," he said. He hooked his thumb toward the corner where the cot used to be. To avoid temptation, he'd tossed out the cot days ago. "We have lots of room."

"But this one's by the window," she countered with a steady look. He held her gaze, determined not to let her see he'd noticed her chest.

He cocked an eyebrow. "It's by the window because it's mine." He set his briefcase down. "You look different."

"Different how?"

Sometimes she pushed him with non-answers or answering a question with a question. *Don't mention her physical appearance. Not the top, not how pretty her hair looks with the shiny clips in it, nothing like that.*

"Just different," he answered her. "Not unhappy, I guess." He hung his jacket on the coat rack and waited because she had more to say.

Any minute now.

Still waiting.

He caved. "How did it go with your ex picking up the twins?"

"It happened. It hurt. But I have a date to video chat at bedtime." She looked at the computer screen studiously.

"You've had a rough afternoon," he said as he took three soft steps toward a visitor's chair. Clearly, she needed to talk.

Then, she shuddered and came back to herself. "You've got two messages. Both from the Talbots. One is from Hope and the other is Nate's." She passed him two pink slips of paper by their corners.

"Thanks." He glanced at the notes. Not real messages, just their cell phone numbers. "You'd think they'd coordinate their calls." Or at least say what the calls were about. Maybe she hadn't asked. Not the time to point that out.

She shrugged. "It's Hope Talbot. Who knows why she does anything?"

He nodded. "I'll call Nate first."

"Good choice." She looked at him again with a serious expression. He heard her draw in a long, deep breath as she wound up to speak. "I want to have an affair."

"Excuse me?" He couldn't have heard right.

"With you." She cleared her throat. "For the summer."

He set his cell phone down on the edge of the desk. Nate Talbot could wait. "Come again?" He only asked because he needed a moment to catch his breath and *think*.

"If you're interested, that is. But I think you are. You look at me as if you are." She tilted her head and looked up at him from under her eyebrows.

He raised a hand to stop her from saying more. "You want an affair for the summer. You already see an end date?"

"Yes. When the twins come home, we're done." She sighed and folded her hands on top of the desk, like a schoolteacher listening to excuses about lost homework. "I've never had a fling and I'd like to know what I'm missing."

She went on about her first love Tad and then explained a bunch of stuff about her ex-husband, but he barely listened. He had to wrap his mind around the fact that Elle Foster wanted to sleep with him again. And again. And again. All through the summer.

When she stopped talking and expected a response, he said the worst thing he could have. "What about Daniel?"

Her head snapped back in surprise. "What about him? He won't find out."

Logan fell into a visitor's chair—another action to give himself a moment. "He'd know that we're dating."

"I didn't say dating." She gave him a look that could freeze his parts. "Dating implies this would be public. Affairs are usually secret."

"Only if one of us is married, or at least committed to someone else." He frowned. "But we don't have to hide. Therefore we'd be dating."

"No, we wouldn't," she insisted as if he'd suggested jumping off a cliff into the Pacific. "Affairs are like flings." Again with the teacher's expression. "They're brief and hot and sexy and fun. That's not dating."

"Semantics. Fling, affair, or dating." He wanted to follow her logic but his dick had jumped up and done the Macarena when this conversation started. Right now, he was convinced his little head was doing the talking. Try as he might he couldn't shut the bastard up. He straightened and leaned toward her. "You want secret, hot, sexy, fun for a short time."

She smiled deeply and his heart stuttered in response. "Exactly."

"Most men would climb over this desk right now and take you to the floor." But he wasn't most men and he didn't jump into relationships. He had his own plans for his life and until this conversation, he'd never once considered a fling with a best-before date. "But I won't do that because I have dinner plans I can't break."

Sure, he'd have broken his plans for dinner with his parents if she'd needed to talk, but this? No, he needed time to come at her suggestion with a clear head.

At his over-the-desk and on the floor comment, she flushed from her remarkable cleavage to the roots of her hair. "Fine. I'd say no anyway. We can start our affair on Tuesday. Today isn't a good day." She smiled into his eyes.

"Tuesday," he repeated in a stunned monotone.

Time slowed as she rose to stand. With a pivot, she bent and picked up her purse from the floor beside her chair and gave him a great view of her lush behind. "I doubt you need my help with anything else today, so I'll head home."

"Okay," he muttered. As she crossed the room, he tracked her with his eyes. She opened the office door, stepped into the hall, and closed the door softly behind her.

Chapter Eighteen

THE NEXT MORNING, DEAFENING quiet, deadly stillness and a feeling of utter abandonment brought Elle a nerve-wracking gasp as she rose off her pillow. Nameless fear left her cold and shaking. Her home felt empty, her heart frozen; her children were gone.

The house may be still, but not empty, she realized as she drew in the alluring scent of fresh-brewed coffee. Daniel was still here. Still loved her. Was still her boy.

She peeled herself out of bed and stumbled to the bathroom. After splashing her face with cool water, she padded into the kitchen. "Again with the coffee?" She asked on spying her son with a mug to his face.

"It's been a few days since the last one and I slept like crap last night." He took a big, loud slurp to assert his independence.

She grimaced at his language but knew not to correct a teenager who'd slept like crap last night. Score one for parenting. "Slurping coffee is definitely not cool," she said with a raised eyebrow.

"I'm not sure the twins should have gone," he said in a very adult voice. He watched her pour a cupful of the brew. "Not for the whole summer. It's too long. Who knows what crazy ideas Ben will come up with."

She froze. "What do you mean?" Fourteen was a killer age, too young to know much of life, but still full of child-like logic that made teens seem wiser than their years. She shook her head. "I need to drink this whole mug before we have a serious conversation."

He gave her the look he reserved for the terminally stupid. His chin came up and he looked down his nose at her. His brows smoothed out as if to say she couldn't help being slow to catch on. She ground her back teeth while a persistent drip from the faucet made the house seem that much quieter.

"What if he convinces them to make this permanent?" he blurted into the petrified stillness of the kitchen. "What if he *steals* them? Steals their hearts. He's got a baby to entice them with."

Wise beyond his years. "You're scary, you know that?" But she nibbled her lip and took another sip of coffee while he watched her with steady, too-adult eyes. "Jodie told me she'd never come between me and my children," she explained. "She understands this summer apart will be hard for me. For all of us," she amended.

"You know how Ben is."

She and Jodie had talked about Ben making plans and expecting everyone to follow along. He'd been the one to go directly to Jorja and Liam with this summertime visit. He'd circumvented their custody agreement. She'd have looked like the bad guy if she'd said no and Ben knew it. No one should look like the bad guy. Not with their children. "There's no reason to think this arrangement will become permanent," she said with some hope.

"It better not," Daniel muttered in sullen disagreement.

"Ben isn't a mean person. He's a screw-up with women and temptation. He's not the only man who can't keep it in his pants. The news is full of them."

He shrugged as if the outing of bullies and sexual predators had nothing to do with him. She took the opening to have a real conversation with her budding romance hound. "You see that it's wrong to grab, kiss, grope or otherwise use your strength to coerce a girl, right? You don't get them drunk or slip them drugs."

The horror on his face seemed sufficiently genuine. She may never corner him for this conversation again. She pressed on. "Now that I've explained what not to do, I'll tell you the signs that say a girl is interested."

He perked up and the horror slid away, replaced by nonchalant interest. "What?"

"She'll look at you when no one else is. Her eyes will light up at the sight of you. You may see her more often in the school halls than you used to."

"What?" He looked flummoxed and his cheeks showed red flags.

"Girls can be where you are pretty easily. We don't consider it stalking, but it's definitely cat-and-mouse."

"So if I hang out at the gym and I suddenly start seeing her there all the time?" He looked bright and hopeful. "Anything else?"

Bingo.

"Brush her fingers when you pass her something. Like a pen or notes. If she lets your fingers linger then you can assume she'd like to hold hands. If she pulls her hand away quickly, then back off."

He nodded and his neck reddened. "Holding hands is for losers."

She shook her head. "It's something we all like to do. Remember, girls are people first. Most people like casual touches. They reassure us. So holding hands is a good way to test the waters."

"Okay." His mind turned inward. "Then what?"

"If you were to hold her hand and walk somewhere slightly out of view, like, say the bleachers, or—"

"Behind the slide in the playground?"

"Perfect. It's public, but not in full view of everyone." She had his rapt attention. "You watch her face. If she turns toward you, her eyes happy and focused on you, then ask if you can kiss her."

"Go on!" He blew out a disbelieving huff of air.

"What's wrong with my scenario?"

"That's too easy."

She burst into laughter. "Girls are not that complicated. We like kissing. We like holding hands. We like being with boys who like us." She sobered. "And we really like boys who don't push for more before we're ready."

He stared at her. "I'd never do that."

"The other thing you'll never do is go out unprepared." She held his attention by lowering her voice and using her most serious tone. "If I'm reading you right, there's a girl you like who probably likes you."

The red from his neck rose to his cheeks and to his ears, but he would neither confirm nor deny.

"I'm putting a package of condoms in the medicine cabinet. You will use them and will never, *ever* take chances."

He nodded. "I won't, I swear."

"I love you."

"Yeah." He swung his head and finished his coffee. "Thanks. You don't need to worry about me."

"If I see you with a girl on the street, I'll be cool. I won't wave or cheer or otherwise take any notice." She would, however, press for details as soon as he got home.

He sighed gratefully. "Thanks."

"Okay. But one more thing. If you make me a grandmother before my time, I'll hunt you down and take you out." She walked over and kissed the top of his head. He pulled away and laughed, as he was supposed to.

"But to get back to the twins," she said with a sigh. "Don't forget I have experience adding twins to a family. It's not easy and when they're as active, loud, and in-your-face as Liam and Jorja—well, it's not something Ben will want to live through twice." Daniel had been there when the babies had joined their little family so he remembered the insanity, too. "Besides, Jodie has her hands full with Angelica. Having the twins for the summer is one thing, but permanently is another."

For the first time, she wondered how her ex was coping with this brand-new start. She shuddered. She'd never go back to babyhood again. Of course, she'd helped with Clarissa, but that had been different and necessary.

It didn't matter a whit that she missed the happy squeals and warm, clean baby scent. She wasn't sure she'd ever stop missing those things.

After breakfast, she walked across the backyard to her brother's place for a chat with Mercy. For the past few days, they'd taken to showing up unannounced whenever they felt the urge for adult female company. It felt good to have Mercy to talk with. She had a sophisticated wisdom that Elle lacked. Also, Elle had fun bouncing ideas around with her.

Maybe she should have discussed the affair idea with Mercy before she'd told Logan, but what was done was done. He either wanted a secret summer fling or he didn't.

"NOT TAKING YOUR OFFER is a waste of perfectly good birth control," Mercy said half an hour later after Elle had told her the whole story. She tapped her fingernails on the rim of her coffee mug. "But Logan..." She trailed off.

"You mean he's a good guy and a secret affair isn't his style."

"Sort of." Her sister-in-law pinched her lips together. "Yes, that's true. With Logan, you get what you see. He's the real deal. He's kind, generous, and considerate."

Elle snorted. "There's a different side to him."

Mercy gave a short bark of laughter. "There's the private side I don't want to know. You've slept with him, I haven't."

Elle got suspiciously hot around her neck. She wasn't used to frank girl talk. "He can be sneaky about getting around a woman's defenses. He lies, for one thing."

"Lies? Logan?" Mercy shook her head in full denial. "No way."

"He admitted it. He said no one ever suspects a good guy of lying, but he gets away with lots of things." She set her chin in her hand. "Take the way he promised no more hot sex on the office cot. He didn't say no more hot sex *at all*. He threw in the qualifier and I didn't notice until days later."

"Sneaky," Mercy said sagely. "You do know he's a man like any other. In my experience, they'll say a lot of things to get a woman into bed. Some of it's true, some of it's outrageous, and some is exactly what we want to hear."

Elle smiled. "And if we're charmed, we won't care." She flushed harder. Was she that gullible? Falling into lust had caused a lot of uproar in her life.

"Exactly. The only twist here is that you've been upfront about what you want."

"And when," Elle added. "I don't have blinders on. I swear I don't."

"Have you considered what will happen when it's over? Do you trust Logan will let it go?"

"He'll have to. There's no way I'll give him what he wants. My family's complete, even if I do suddenly have to share my kids with grandparents and ex-husbands."

Dilly chased Ethel, their wiry little terrier, around the table. When Dilly tripped over her own feet, she went down with a giggle and Ethel licked her face. Mercy gave Dilly a quick glance, saw that no harm had been done and returned to focus on Elle without missing a step.

"You've taken to mothering like a pro," Elle commented.

"I've learned a lot in the last year. Clay doubts himself less often, but he never doubts me. Dilly proves all the time how resilient she is." The chase between child and dog began again.

"How are things between Daniel and the Murdochs?" Mercy asked.

Elle left thoughts of Logan and his wish for a family behind. "Daniel doesn't say much, but he sees them all the time so it can't be bad. He's even learned to ride."

"Horses?"

"Yes. But he's also grooming and mucking out stalls, whatever that is." She wrinkled her nose. "When he comes home he stinks like man sweat and that's a good thing. He has a lot of privileges but he's also seeing the work." She wasn't sure Tad had lifted a finger as he'd grown up.

Mercy nodded. "You'll have a lot of free time this summer with Daniel spending long days at the Murdoch estate."

"Exactly. Why can't I have Logan for a time?"

Mercy frowned. "Logan's not a utensil you can pick up and use for a few weeks. He doesn't deserve to be treated as if he's disposable." She got a ping on her phone. She glanced at it, frowned, and then picked it up to read her message. "Sorry, I need to look at this."

After she gave her phone a moment of her attention, she set it face down on the table. "I'm back."

"My being honest and clear about the ending is not treating Logan poorly. He's an adult and can agree or not. If we lay things out and stick to the plan, neither of us will be hurt."

Mercy looked doubtful but gave her a half-smile. "I'm sure you'll have a lovely summer." She raised her palms. "And I swear I won't tell Clay."

"You can't. He'll be weird around Logan and it'll become a problem. They run together sometimes and I'm sure they talk." She frowned. "This might mess up their friendship."

Dilly came over with a book and climbed onto Mercy's lap. "Read stories."

Ethel turned three circles and collapsed on the floor at Mercy's feet.

Elle laughed as Mercy did her best to shift her belly to accommodate Dilly. "It won't be long before your lap disappears and she won't fit."

"We'll snuggle on the sofa then, won't we, Dilly?"

"Ya-huh." She stuck the book up in the air by Mercy's face. "Stories."

"I'll leave you to it," Elle said. "I have some shopping to do. Oh, and I'm going to dinner and a movie tonight with Shandy Camden and Brianna Bowler. Do you know them?"

Mercy rolled her eyes. "Shandy wanted Clay for a while there. Brianna was in some of my classes at Welcome High."

"Shandy had a bit of thing for Clay before your sister snatched him up," Elle said. "But you're saying she tried again recently? What happened?"

"I won." The gleam in Mercy's eye screamed devilment and made Elle grin.

"I see," she said with a nod. "We had lunch the other day after bumping into each other in the women's clinic. She was great to talk with. Shandy, Brianna, and you are the only people from school who're friendly. Anyone else who remembers me is hostile. I hoped you might want to join us for the movie, but I guess not."

"I'd feel weird hanging with Shandy," Mercy said. She scrunched up her nose.

"I get it," Elle agreed with a nod. "Clearly you believe my brother's a prize, but as his sister, I say not so much." She let the teasing comment hang in the air as she stepped outside to the back deck. She heard a muffled objection from Mercy, but laughed and waved bye-bye to her niece.

The twins had been happy last night when they'd had their video chat. Liam had been his usual bubbly self and Jorja had been enthusiastic about their baby sister. She'd held nothing back and Elle couldn't remember how long it had been since Jorja had been unreservedly joyful. Jorja had been allowed to hold Angelica for as long as she wanted and had helped with her bath. Jodie had promised lots of activities through the coming weeks.

Elle, naturally, had her doubts, but if Jodie hanged herself with all the rope she'd been given, too bad. And Ben would be there every night after work. If the kids weren't getting along with Jodie he'd step in. He loved the twins as much as Elle did.

This change could be good for everyone. *Suck it up. Ben might be right.*

At loose ends, she wandered across the backfield toward the Bowler place. It seemed strange to have nowhere she had to be, or no one waiting for her or needing her.

No wonder she wanted an affair. She had to have something to, occupy her mind and hands. Whew! The memories of touching Logan freely, of holding him with her arms and wrapping him tightly between her thighs brought a heat to her face she hadn't felt in years.

Tuesday glowed like a beacon. As she climbed over the fence to the Bowler property, she heard distant barking from the rescue dogs. Maybe she should take one home. Mercy had taken Ethel home and look how that had turned out. Dilly had a pet to play chase with and Ethel had a good home.

She remembered the brown orphaned pups found at the roadside. If she let one of them pick her, she'd have a steady, loving companion. The twins would love having a dog and with all the space around the house, they'd have lots of places to walk it.

Elle'd have a pet that needed her. And no one could take a dog away; not its mother, not its father, and not its grandparents. The petulant thought gave her no comfort at all.

LOGAN STARED INTO THE mirror while he shaved on Saturday morning. The conversation with Elle yesterday afternoon rolled through his head like a ball in a pinball game: bouncing, shooting, rolling, pinging, and lighting up his brain.

Dinner the night before with his parents had been a distracted meal and conversation. By the time he'd left, Logan's mother had looked curiously at him. Several times his dad seemed about to ask him something then clamped his mouth shut. At least they hadn't needed him to chase after Jamie or do anything that required clear thinking.

Logan had been in a fog; the long evening filled with thoughts of Elle's proposition. An old-fashioned term, *proposition* was the only word that fit her suggestion.

He stared at his reflection. Could he be pulled into an affair with Elle Foster that would go nowhere? His feelings for Elle were different from anything he'd had. Could he walk away free and clear after weeks with a woman he *liked*? Because he did like Elle. She was tart and hard-shelled with a sweet center. She came with more baggage than most men could handle and still, she pulled at him.

Give your head a shake. He was overthinking it. They were good together, had fun, supported each other and understood each other. At least he hoped Elle got him. She understood his need to help his brother. She gave great advice and no matter what happened Elle handled her setbacks like an adult.

Never mind that he was her boss. Never mind that they were in completely different places about having children. He had to face it; ultimately they were wrong for each other.

Elle must be suffering a strange reaction to all the changes with her children. She was likely worried about being lonely. Maybe she felt a summer fling would fill the gaps.

None of that mattered.

Elle had asked for an affair and she wanted an answer. Tuesday loomed and in spite of all the reasons he should say no, Logan knew he'd take her to dinner. They'd share a nice bottle of wine, some good food, and easy conversation. He nodded, happy with the decision. She'd probably enjoy an evening out.

Then back to his place.

His place. The guy in the mirror needed new sheets and stuff. When he'd moved home to Welcome he'd bought the bare necessities because he'd left the household goods with Trish. He had one set of sheets and a blanket; an ugly one he'd picked up off a clearance table. When he got it home he realized he'd bought a twin size instead of the queen size he needed. He hadn't bothered to exchange it. His mother had chuckled and asked if he needed help.

He'd said no, naturally. What grown man wanted his mom involved in his linen purchases?

His semi-adequate decorating was not the impression he wanted to give Elle of the way he lived. If he hurried, he'd have time to make his home look like he actually lived there and liked it.

He taught clients the importance of staging a house for sale. But staging one to make it looked lived in was another matter.

Armed with his phone, he walked the main areas of his house, taking photos.

Then he sent them all to Mercy with a text message that read:

Logan: "Help me make this place into a home."

After a few minutes he got a text back:

Mercy: "I'll help. Hang tight. Be right over."

Chapter Nineteen

DILLY RAN THROUGH THE rooms in Logan's house exclaiming about every piece of furniture she found. Fortunately, Logan didn't have a lot. One room was totally empty. It was the smallest bedroom and perfectly sized for a nursery. It had been painted a cheery light green with yellow ducklings on an infinite march behind their mother. Someone had had an eye for the natural world. He'd had the pretty scene covered with a neutral, but warm, gray.

Now he regretted the loss of the plump little birds. Dilly would have loved them and they'd have occupied her while Logan and her mother walked the rest of his ranch bungalow.

"Find a cheerfully colored carpet and aim to match two of the colors in throw cushions for the sofa. Same with drapes. They don't need to be custom." Mercy indicated the fireplace mantle. "Something for there. Not too big. Again, keep the color in mind. You want to warm the place up."

He scrolled through the home décor page on a website. He passed her his phone. "Like this?"

"Yes. Perfect." She scrolled a bit. When she gave him back his phone, he saw she'd gone to the linen page. "And this is a nice comforter set. Mind you get at least one throw cushion and make sure you buy two extra pillows to use with the shams that come with the set."

He had a vague notion she was teasing him, but he was too tense to be sure. "And this color's okay? Not too dark?"

The image was of steel-gray linen with a couple of red lines that dramatically sliced through the color. He liked it, but he was a guy and Trish had kept their bedroom light and flowery.

"You said you wanted this place to look like you enjoy living here. Like it's your home."

"Got it. The bedroom should look like mine, not as if a woman lives here."

"You keep your kitchen tidy and any woman would appreciate that," she said with an approving smile. "Make sure you buy some nice, thick towels for the bathroom. Toss a matching mat on the floor in front of the shower and we're done." Dilly zoomed into the living room and bounced on the leather sofa.

"Mitser Logan, where's your toys?" The mash of words from Dilly took a moment to come clear to him.

"Where *are* your toys," her mother corrected. "Mister Hughes doesn't have toys, Dilly."

Dilly's pretty face scrunched into a picture of disbelief.

Logan laughed and then crouched to her level. "I have no toys because I have no children, Dilly. No one lives here who would play with toys."

Her happy eyes dimmed with concern. "Oh. You should get some toys then maybe someone would come to play."

"D'you think so?"

"Ya-huh." She threw her arms around his neck and blessed his cheek with a kiss.

And this, *this* was what he wanted: little arms around his neck, sweet breath washing his face, warm, happy eyes next to his. It might not be every man's dream to have children, but being adopted already made him different from all his buddies. He picked Dilly up and swung her around as she giggled.

"I'll see what I can do about getting some toys and maybe my own children to play with them. Would you play with my children, Dilly?"

"Yesss!!" The squeal came loud, high, and right against his ear.

"We'd better go, my mom's expecting us to go shopping with her," Mercy said.

He set Dilly onto the floor and she reached for her mother's hand. "Logan, don't expect to get what you *really* want from Elle." Mercy squinted in concern. "It won't happen."

He nodded. "Elle told you about our plans for the summer?"

"Yes, just as you texted me about this decorating tear you're on." Dilly tugged at her hand. "Don't be disappointed if things don't last any longer than she said."

"It's fine," he muttered. After a breath, he continued. "We'll have a fun summer and when Jorja and Liam come home, I'll step away. No harm, no foul."

Mercy looked relieved. "And your house will look much nicer for your efforts here today." With that said, she took Dilly out the door, leaving him in his empty, empty house once more.

LATER THAT EVENING, Elle met with Shandy and Brianna at the Welcome Bar and Grill. The entrance was typical. Two benches on either side in dark wood with a stand for a host. Music from the bar side thumped a country beat, while the grill side of the restaurant was quiet and softly lit. Most of the restaurant tables were empty. "Brianna Bowler, meet Shandy Camden."

"You look familiar," Brianna said and offered her hand. Shandy took it and gave Brianna a warm smile.

"I haven't been in this place in years," Elle commented as she surveyed what had once been the grubbiest beer hall for miles. "It's changed."

Shandy gave her a sly glance. "Bar or grill? What's your pleasure?" She waved to the divided sections.

Elle grimaced. "I don't want to see that bar ever again," she joked. The décor was barnyard chic with barn board wainscoting and checkered tablecloths. She could smell the comfort food and her mouth watered.

"Old memories die hard. Grill it is," Shandy said and led the way to a table by the window.

Brianna suddenly brightened. "Oh! Now I get it. This is where...?"

Elle flushed and pulled out her chair. "Not one of my finer moments."

Both of the other women laughed like old bawds and took their seats. Elle looked from one woman to the other and joined them with a self-deprecating chuckle. Soon, Shandy and Brianna were laughing and comparing notes on men and dating, an area of life that Elle had little experience with.

They ordered drinks and when they arrived, Elle offered a toast to new friends. After they sipped and nodded, Elle admitted her lack of dating experience. "I got together with Tad so young and then Ben came along. I was too busy with my children to date, let alone have any relationships. I was easy pickings for Ben."

Shandy leaned in. "You haven't missed out on a thing. It's hard being a single mom."

Brianna nodded. "It's hard being single, period, but better than being with the wrong guy. I've fallen into that trap more than once. Now I'm more wary." Her lips turned down at the corners.

"I've avoided men for some time, ever since the last guy I thought might turn into something good turned to someone else," Shandy commented breezily. She waved to their server to request menus.

Elle sucked in a silent breath. *Clay, Shandy was talking about Clay and Mercy.* All she could do was nod. "Have either of you started something that you knew would go nowhere?"

"From the get-go?" Brianna asked. "No. I tend toward being hopeful and optimistic and then a few months later, see the light. I've had my share of losers."

"Oh," Elle said with a nod. "Shandy?"

"You mean like a short-term thing? I've had a resort romance or two. Nothing but fun. But like sugary treats, after a while, they lose their allure." She rested her chin in her hand and swirled her straw through her drink. "Why?"

"Nothing. I just wondered about affairs in general."

"I avoid married men," Shandy offered.

"Me, too," Brianna said and opened her menu. "Not that they haven't tried, but, I figure if they cheat once they'll do it to me."

"Ben cheated," Elle confessed, but since both of her friends assumed that an affair meant with a married man, she decided not to mention Logan and her plan.

After the murmurs of sympathy about Ben, Elle shook herself. "Enough of this maudlin talk. Let's decide what movie to see."

Chapter Twenty

TUESDAY WAS THE LONGEST day Elle ever lived. That included delivering a single baby and a set of twins. By the time her workday ended she was on edge and a smidgen insecure. Logan had spent the day out at the Springhill Meadows site and his absence had made her jittery and nervous. *That's right, blame Logan for your self-doubt.*

She'd earned her insecurities; by being thirty-three, a single mother, a woman with two exes who'd left her with their children to raise without a backward glance. There had been no attempts to reconcile with either Tad or Ben. No on again, off again times.

Tad had run home to the parents who'd never supported him rather than stay with her and Daniel. Ben had abandoned her, Jorja, and Liam for a gullible young woman who now seemed nice and sweet and kind. *Ugh.*

Oh, yes, and her body definitely showed the effects of two pregnancies. Her face had lines bracketing her lips and crow's feet had crept in where they didn't belong. The vertical line that bisected her forehead when she frowned seemed to take longer to clear every day.

She was a wreck and Logan had best see the truth soon or she might develop feelings for him.

Logan must be having second thoughts about the summer. He'd avoided her all day to let her down gently.

All she had to do was act as if nothing was wrong; that she wasn't disappointed. She decided a text would be the easiest way to move through this awkwardness.

Elle: "Closing up in a few minutes. Do you need anything before I go home?"

Logan: "Just your preference. Steak or seafood?"

She couldn't help herself and texted back her surprise.

Elle: "We're still on?"

Logan: "Pick you up at 7."

Elle: "OK."

All her angst had been for nothing. Oddly deflated and feeling the fool, she shut down the office computer and closed for the day.

When she got to her car, she texted Daniel.

Elle: "Are you staying with them for dinner?"

Daniel: "Pork chops."

Elle: "That's a yes, then. See you later."

The Murdochs would have Daniel until ten when they'd agreed to always have him home unless there were special circumstances. She'd have three whole hours with Logan.

On a date.

With her boss.

Two of her rules blasted to smithereens, and she didn't care. She might be all the things she'd focused on while she was fretting, but she was still, above all, a woman, and the prospect of dinner with an attractive man who wanted her thrilled her to her toes. But there was one more text to send before she drove home.

Elle: "Steak."

LOGAN MADE A RESERVATION at the steakhouse, although midweek, it was likely they wouldn't need one. He wanted to be certain this evening went off without a hitch. He wasn't sure if they'd end up back at his place after dinner or if she'd shy away.

Get a grip. Elle will tell you straight out what she wants. He'd be at dinner with Elle Foster, not some coy first date. If she wanted to hit the sack with him she'd say so.

God, he hoped she said so.

His phone buzzed with a text. Elle. He dragged in a breath and hoped she wasn't canceling.

Elle: "Need to be home by 10. Take two cars?"

Logan: "See you there."

He parked in the steakhouse parking lot several minutes before seven, like an anxious, horny kid with too much riding on one evening.

Apparently, Elle felt the same way because she parked in a corner of the lot less than a minute after he did. Cheered, he walked over to her car and watched her climb out.

"You look fantastic," he said as he neared. She wore a figure-hugging top with a loopy, saggy neckline that flashed cleavage as she strolled toward him. Her tight black skirt skimmed over her curvy thighs and down to her knees. He wanted to run his hands around to her butt and hold her while he kissed her stupid.

Logan stepped up and did exactly what he wanted to. Her mouth opened under his and when he slid his hand to her butt, she leaned into him. She welcomed his kiss, sighed into his mouth, and sucked his tongue. And then, then, Elle Foster slid her hands to the back of his slacks and dragged his hips to hers.

"To hell with the steak," she said next to his ear. "Let's go to your place." Her eyes shone brightly into his. "We have three hours and I don't want to waste a minute in a restaurant."

He trailed his knuckles across her cheek and she tilted toward his hand. A mini-van pulled into a nearby spot, its lights highlighting them.

"Follow me, it's not far," he said. They separated and he noticed as she walked back to her car that she turned her face away from the couple who climbed out of the mini-van. Elle didn't want to be seen with him. A burr of disappointment rode with him all the way home.

Again, he watched Elle climb out of her car and saunter up to him. This time, she smiled and linked her fingers to his. The kiss she gave him was light, with no hint of what she'd shown him in the parking lot.

"Nice place," she said, with an admiring glance across the front of the rancher. Then she swiveled her head to take in the street. "Very suburban for a man who lives alone. I expected a sexy condo or upscale townhouse."

"I've had both in Tacoma," he said as he unlocked his front door. He ushered her inside. "Now, I'm looking to the future." The house screamed "family home" and it was exactly what he wanted. "Three bed, two bath, with a bright basement." He pulled out his phone. "Make yourself comfortable, I'll be a moment."

He called the restaurant, canceled their dinner reservation, and convinced the maître-d to have their meals delivered. He ordered for Elle and grinned with each thumbs-up she gave him as he placed their orders for steak, baked potatoes, and a side of vegetables. Simple, but he knew the food would be perfect. Elle flashed him jazz hands when he asked for delivery in an hour and a half. When he finished the call and slid his phone to the kitchen counter, she walked into his arms. "Thanks for thinking of that," she said. "I expect to be very hungry ninety minutes from now."

"Hungry but satisfied," he promised. He cupped her head in his hands and smoothed his thumbs over her cheeks. "I've thought of this all day." He was already hard and wanting her and it showed in his kiss.

She opened her mouth for his tongue and he lost himself for long moments. The feel of her, warm and curvy and soft— so soft— went to his head. She'd used a scent he didn't recognize but he'd never forget; flowery and subtle and inviting. It was on her neck where he nuzzled the delicate skin below her ear, between her breasts when he lifted them to lick at their softness. Her nipples beaded to hard points and he suckled one, then the other.

"Too rough?" he asked.

"Never," she murmured against his mouth.

By the time they got to his bedroom, they were half-undressed and ready. "I'd like to go slowly," she said. "But I'm not sure I can."

He chuckled at the anxious tone in her voice. "Next time," he promised and lifted her in his arms. He set her on the bed and followed her down into the softness of the new duvet. He stripped off the rest of her clothes reverently as if he were undraping a work of art.

They'd been rushed in the office and he hadn't taken the time to appreciate her curves and valleys. Elle was lush and lovely and for now, here, she was all his.

FOR TONIGHT AND THE coming weeks, Logan was hers. She watched as he carefully removed her skirt, tugging it down her hips, to her thighs and then off. When he pulled the material away from her feet, he lifted one and kissed her instep, sending a shock wave of sensation to her core.

"My God, that's sexy," she said as he blessed her other instep with another kiss. He grinned the same pirate grin he'd used on her in his office and she melted like butter in a hot pan. She shifted in restless need and raised her hips to get her panties off. He helped and scented the bit of material before dropping them with the rest of her clothes.

"Your scent." He shook his head. "I can't get enough of it." The look he gave her burned with sensuous need and earthy desire.

She reached to undo the tab of his slacks. "Off," she muttered. "Now." While he obliged, she pulled the downy covers back and revealed clean, crisp sheets. "It's a shame to dirty these," she said with a sigh. The luxurious feel of the silk made her head spin. She'd never felt anything like it.

"All for a good cause," he said as he climbed up her body and settled heavy and hard against her. "And when I sleep here tonight, they'll smell of you. Beautiful, sexy, mysterious."

"Oh, Logan. Lo—do me like you mean it."

"I do mean it. I want this summer with you more than anything I've ever wanted before."

There was danger here, but she was too aroused, too involved to hold the thought. And then he carried her down into a vortex of loving that took her to depths she'd never explored.

Logan Hughes was more pirate than anyone knew. He took and took, draining her essence, stealing her mind, and then, just when she thought there was nothing left, he replenished her fully.

By the time Elle walked out the door to go home, Logan had taken her apart and put her together again in a whole new way. She was too sated to worry about it now. She would dissect her new self tomorrow when she could think again.

DANIEL SLOUCHED INTO the kitchen later than usual. Without the twins and their early morning energy, neither Elle nor Daniel had to be up and at it by six. She'd managed a sleep-in until seven, something that hadn't happened for her in years. Every muscle still felt like liquid, her lips kept tilting up at the corners and she hummed as she padded around the kitchen getting out the makings for breakfast.

"Why're you so happy?" Daniel asked with a yawn.

"Nothing special. I just got to sleep in a bit and it feels great." She let her hair fall over her face to hide the flush his question brought on. She'd flashed on how satisfied she'd been in Logan's arms the previous night. She'd hated to leave him, but she wasn't up for Daniel learning about them. Not yet. If ever.

"How's it going with your grandparents?"

"Okay. She's pretty cool. But he's a real pain. So tough. Especially on her. He gets onto a topic and can't get off."

"For instance?" She wanted to know the inner workings of the Murdoch family so she'd know if they were affecting Daniel in a bad way. She broke a couple of eggs into the frying pan and held up two more to see if her son wanted any. When he nodded, she broke them, too.

Daniel slid two pieces of bread into the toaster. "It was weird yesterday. I finished mucking out the stalls and was washing up in the sink in the barn. He came in and glared at me like I'd just stolen a horse or something. I said hi and even called him Grampa and he started spewing stuff."

"Like?"

"He yelled at me about my grades, said how disappointed he was, and that I couldn't have the car all summer. That's when I realized he thought he was talking to my father."

"Oh. I guess he can't keep some things straight. It's a symptom."

"He was so mean. Vicious."

A spike of sympathy for Tad rose. He'd been subjected to his father's degrading comments his whole life. And yet, he'd still run home rather than face the responsibility of caring for Daniel.

"How does he talk to you when he's aware of who you are?"

"He doesn't say much of anything. Mostly, he watches me like he expects to catch me doing something wrong or bad. I don't know if he trusts me being in the house."

"But Susan's okay?"

He nodded. "She keeps him focused on what's really happening. When his mind wanders off, she brings him back gently." Daniel's face flushed. "He's still a pretty strong guy, though and I'm a little worried he could hurt her. Did he ever hit Dad?"

"I don't think the abuse got physical. Tad never mentioned that. But with Graham's mind going, anything could happen. Does Susan have help with him?"

"She's talking about having a nurse move in. I think she should. I don't like leaving her alone with him."

Elle's heart contracted with love. Daniel cared for his grandmother, in spite of all the lost time. "Would you like me to talk to her?"

"Maybe. I don't know." He sighed and reached for a mug. Sloshed coffee into it. "I can't be there all the time."

Elle cocked an eyebrow at her coffee-swilling eldest but he ignored it. The eggs drew her attention and she slipped them onto plates. Daniel buttered toast.

"If a time comes when your grandfather is agitated and you want to spend the night, let me know. I'd be okay with that." If Daniel had to stay over, maybe Susan would accept she needed twenty-four-hour support.

"I've got to see Clay," he said. "He's helping me get my bike into shape." He ate his eggs and toast, left his dishes where they sat and headed for the door.

"Hey, you forgot to put your dishes in the dishwasher."

He smirked at her over his shoulder as he opened the door to leave. "Nah, I didn't forget. I figure you miss the twins so much you need something to do."

"Hah hah."

But Daniel was already out the door. Pride in her son swelled in her chest. At fourteen, he was more adult than a lot of forty year olds. He'd taken a lot of knocks in his life and had his share of shocks, but he was rock-steady and dependable. Having the Murdochs take an interest in him could take his life along different paths from anything she'd imagined for him.

Checking the time, Elle decided it was not too early to call Susan. But it wasn't Susan who answered the phone. It was the man himself, Graham Murdoch III.

Chapter Twenty-one

"MISTER MURDOCH THIS is Elle Foster calling. Is your wife at home?" Elle hadn't expected the man himself to answer the phone. Maybe she should have waited until later in the day to call.

"Why are you calling?" His tone sounded brusque as usual and part of her wanted to shrink from the sheer power in his voice. But Graham Murdoch had always had people cower before him, probably expected it. This man had bullied Tad and now Daniel had concerns about his behavior. Elle refused to turn meek in the face of his demand.

"I want to talk to Susan. Right now," she blustered back.

"Who do you think you are talking to me that way? You're nothing but trailer trash and you leave Tad alone. He doesn't want the likes of you." Time had slipped away from Graham Murdoch and a stab of sympathy filtered through her shock.

A soft, feminine voice came from the background and then Elle heard a muffled sound as the phone must have been passed from one person to another. The next voice she heard on the phone was Susan's. "Good morning, you have Susan Murdoch here."

"It's Elle, Susan. Sorry to call so early." She hesitated. "I told Graham it's me, but—"

"I heard," Susan interrupted. "And I apologize."

They fell to silence because, really, what could be said?

After a moment, Susan spoke. "Is Daniel not coming today?" Concern threaded her words. "Did we keep him too late last night?"

"Yes, he's coming. He enjoys his time with you," Elle assured her. "He's worried about your situation with Graham and now, I am, too." Graham had sounded deeply disturbed at hearing from

Elle. "Given what you told me about Mr. Murdoch's father, we're concerned that Graham could become agitated and physical."

"I see." Susan drew in a long breath. "You think he'll hurt Daniel, the way Graham's father hurt Graham. Do you want to stop Daniel's visits?"

"No, that's not why I'm calling. Daniel is concerned for your safety."

"Mine?"

"Daniel says you've talked about having a live-in nurse. He'd like to see that happen sooner rather than later."

"My grandson is worried for *me*?" Breathy surprise came through the phone. "I don't know what to say."

"Tell Daniel you'll find someone as soon as you can. Also, if you feel you need him there overnight—" she sighed because she was handing off *another* child—"then it's all right if he stays until you find a live-in nurse."

Another silence and then Susan sobbed. "I'm overcome by your kindness after all the years we denied you. We were cruel and thoughtless. I blame myself for allowing. . ." She trailed off with another sniff and a wobbly breath. "Well, I can see where Daniel gets his maturity and compassion."

Elle appreciated the compliment but couldn't address it; not now, with Susan trying to collect her composure. "I'll pack Daniel's toothbrush and cologne," Elle said. "Let him stink up your bathroom for a while," she quipped in an attempt to lighten the tone for Susan's sake.

Susan chuckled weakly and when she spoke, it was with warm humor. "Yes, I know the scent. He must bathe in it." Gratitude shone through her words.

"That's his body wash," Elle said with a smile in her voice. But she grew serious again. "This is only until you find live-in help and I expect you to hire someone as soon as you can."

"I will. I've put it off for too long. Lately Graham denies he needs medication. He's forgotten he has high blood pressure and he's tried to flush his pills. It was lucky I caught him beforehand."

The situation was worse than Daniel thought. Susan must be overwhelmed. "You *all* need help," Elle said in a comforting tone.

"I'll get it, rest assured."

"I want my son back soon," Elle said and hung up. She looked around the spacious living area and shuddered. A few weeks ago she had four children living with her and now she was staring at empty space. Life was strange.

HALF AN HOUR AFTER opening the office, Logan finished his call and glanced at the clock. Maybe Elle was late because she felt awkward about last night. The time with her had been more than he'd hoped for but less than he wanted. He wanted Elle to spend the whole night with him, not just a couple of hours.

Logan wanted her to sleep with him, wake up with him. He wanted to make her breakfast and watch as she picked up a piece of crisp bacon and snapped it in two with her perfect white teeth. Then he wanted to kiss her and taste bacon on her tongue. His fantasy popped as the door opened.

"Daniel will be staying with his grandparents for a few days," Elle said in a brisk, efficient tone as she walked in. "Maybe a week—" she paused for a breath "—or two."

"What?"

She hung a sweater on the coat rack in the corner. "Susan's hiring a live-in nurse and until then Daniel's staying over there. Graham needs more supervision and Daniel wants to pitch in."

Logan settled back in his chair. He raised his eyebrows. "Oh," he said vaguely. Daniel would be gone, too. And Elle would be alone. She'd hate it. "You're okay with this?"

"I have to be." She dropped her purse to the floor and settled into a chair across the desk. "But yes, I'm okay with it. Daniel's grown attached to Susan and he's worried Graham may become agitated and physical with her and he wants to be there in case she needs help."

"That's a lot for a kid to take on." Especially for people he'd only met recently. But then, he had Elle for an example. Hadn't she done the same for Clarissa?

Elle's shoulders sagged. "I agree it's a lot to take on, but Daniel brought it up himself. He's a responsible kid, even when something is *not* his responsibility." She blinked and smiled. "I couldn't be more proud of him."

"You'll be available to spend the night with me." Daniel's temporary exodus brought Logan's fantasy to the forefront.

"Do you want that?" Her cheeks grew pink as he watched.

He controlled his excitement; kept it out of his voice. "Our time's short. We should make the most of it."

The sexy way she canted up one corner of her mouth made him hard. "Good idea," she said mildly. "Last night was perfect but too short." Her eyes flashed with warmth. Elle felt the same way he did about the start of this summer fling.

His phone rang and he took the call. "I'm needed out at Springhill Meadows," he said after he hung up. "Call me later to tell me what you'd like to eat tonight."

"I'll make homemade pizza," she offered. "The twins' favorite."

He bent to kiss her forehead on the way past. "You miss them."

"So much," she agreed with a sigh. "But we'll have a video chat later today. By the time I get to your place, I'll be full of news from them." She raised her face to his and he couldn't resist another kiss. She firmed her lips and kissed him back with deadly appeal.

"Later," he said, too eagerly. He didn't want to spook her, but damn, she'd made him happy.

"MOM!" JORJA ACTUALLY pushed Liam off-screen with an excited screech. "Angelica wanted me to pick her up today and Jodie let me!"

"So what?" her brother said. "Dad let me help him fix his truck today." Liam shoved his way back onscreen while Elle chuckled at their antics.

"I'm happy for both of you," she responded. "What else did you do today?"

"Went swimming at her parents' house," Jorja said. "We had fun." She squinted at the screen and Elle watched a frown form. "They want us to call them something."

"Who?"

Liam leaned in and lowered his voice. "Jodie's mom and dad want us to call them grandparents."

"I see." From the looks on their faces, her children wanted her opinion or permission. "Do you like them?"

"Yeah, I guess," Liam said.

"They're nice," Jorja said cautiously. Elle hated that Jorja felt wary of the changes that had happened for all of them. The family relationships that were forming all around her children were out of Elle's control. Whatever friendships developed for her kids with this other family were not her responsibility. She couldn't interfere.

"You call them whatever you feel comfortable with. Something will come to you and it will feel natural. What does Jodie think?"

"She'd like it, but she said the same thing as you." Surprised, Elle decided to move the conversation into more fun territory. "Did you dunk each other's heads in the pool?"

"Yes!" They said in tandem. "And Billy and Lori showed us how to jump in the deep end," Liam yelled.

"Is that so? Did you hold your breath?"

They nodded. "Billy and Lori are real nice," Jorja said with a wide smile.

"I'm glad."

"Bye, Mom!" Liam stepped away while Jorja looked around the screen at someone off to the side.

"Jodie wants to talk to you, okay?" her daughter asked. "Love you, bye." And she blew Elle a kiss before skipping off.

Jodie wanted to speak with her.

And Elle wanted to talk to Jodie.

LATER THAT NIGHT AS Elle draped her leg over Logan's hairy one, she sighed into his neck. He tucked her head under his chin and held her close and warm. Heaven. It had been a long time since she'd slept with a man. She'd forgotten how warm another body could be, how the scent of lovemaking could settle her, make her feel cozy and cared for.

"Jodie's handling the twins well," she said. "Ben's spending more time with Liam than I'd hoped and her parents are interested in forging a bond."

"How do you feel about that?" Logan craned his neck to look at her. The steady rise and fall of his chest made her safe and lethargic after making love.

"There's a toddler inside me who wants to throw a tantrum," she admitted. "But that'll pass. I accept that they have an extended family now. This summer will be good for all of them." For once, Ben had had a good idea that panned out. After talking with Jodie she realized the young woman seemed genuinely interested in the twins and their welfare. "I miss Jorja and Liam, but this time is important for them and their dad. And Jodie," she added as an afterthought.

Maybe Jodie should be more than an afterthought. She would play a big role in Liam's and Jorja's lives. Whatever resentment Elle still felt had to be buried deep to make this work. For the twins' sakes, she'd dig down as far as she needed to make sure her leftover anger never surfaced again.

Logan's scent under her nose and the silky feel of his chest hair calmed her. Her mind drifted as sleep came.

LOGAN LISTENED TO ELLE'S breathing even out as her head relaxed onto his chest. She constantly amazed him with her outlook. She took everything in stride and never let her emotions dictate her reactions. He wasn't sure if he could handle having his children living part-time with someone else.

His belly clenched at the idea of his children. When he thought of them now, he saw them with Elle's inky black hair and brilliant-blue eyes. He tried to overlay the image with his own hair color but his limited ability to imagine the color change failed.

All his life he'd wanted what he felt he'd missed; a link, a physical connection to someone. He wanted to share DNA with a person he loved and who loved him. It was probably childish, but he'd felt this way for so long he couldn't see anything else. He'd accepted his feelings long ago.

When he'd been ten, a buddy down the block had a baby sister. Her eyes matched her brother's exactly. Logan had been shocked because no one in his family shared any features.

Not that he and Jamie weren't loved. His parents loved them both fiercely. Logan had never lacked support or encouragement. Even Jamie would admit they'd been blessed with love growing up.

This estrangement with Jamie hurt their parents. But the depth of their love had pushed them into their most difficult decision. Underneath, Jamie had the same bedrock of love that Logan had and they all prayed that he'd miss his family enough to get clean. They prayed that love would win.

While Elle slipped deeper into slumber, Logan felt restless and oddly alone even though he held her close. He considered how his parents would cope if Jamie was lost to them for good. He thought about how a child could bring them back to laughter and joy. His child.

And if he didn't have a child? What then? The woman in his arms had as many valid reasons for not having more children as Logan had for wanting them.

Family meant everything. He'd spent his life appreciating that simple truth. With Jamie teetering on the edge of disaster, Logan wanted a family of his own more than ever.

Chapter Twenty-two

TWO WEEKS AFTER DANIEL left home, he returned without fanfare. Elle bit her lip to stop from crying when she saw him climb out of Susan's car with his backpack. Susan followed him into the house.

"He's yours again," his grandmother said with a soft smile. "Our newest nurse, Harrison Good, is working out well. Graham wouldn't listen to any of the female nurses we tried. But Harrison has a way about him that works."

"The guy's voice sounds like a foghorn, even when he laughs." Daniel contributed from the hallway. He'd taken his gear back to his room.

"I'm glad," Elle said to Susan, and she meant it. From Daniel's reports life had been difficult while the family had attempted to integrate different nurses into Graham's routine. While he'd slept at the Murdochs, she'd seen more of Daniel than she'd expected. He'd stopped by the office at lunchtime occasionally and joined her for dinner when she'd eaten with Clay and Mercy.

Daniel had escaped the tension and pressure of the Murdoch home by visiting Elle, whereas Susan had to stay in the house. The more she'd heard about the various nursing staff coming and going, the more Elle had come to admire the older woman's inner strength.

Not that she'd forgotten how little support Susan had given Tad as a boy. But at that time a bully had controlled everything in their lives. Now that the bully had become dependent on Susan, she showed more compassion than Elle would. Plus, she was giving Daniel a life he might never have had.

"Do you have time for coffee?" Elle asked Susan.

A wide smile broke across the older woman's face. "For the first time in too long, I have. Harrison is swimming with Graham and then they'll go for a walk. I have at least two hours to myself." She sounded surprised at the gift of time.

"What will you do with two whole hours?" Elle asked.

"Get a manicure," Susan said dreamily and with all the anticipation of a kid at Christmas. She took the mug of coffee that Elle offered. "I have my appointment and a few errands to run. Thank you for allowing us to have Daniel for this long. I'm grateful. He's a pillar of patience. Without a word of complaint, he followed Graham as he walked the house in the middle of the night. I'm afraid I'd become too exhausted for his midnight wanders."

Daniel returned to hear the compliment and reddened. "Walking with him was easy enough. He talked to me like I was my father in a way that I doubt my dad ever heard. He was kinda nice."

Susan looked startled. "Really?"

"Wow," Elle said.

"He told me his hopes and dreams for Tad, but maybe he forgot my name and used that name instead."

Susan's eyes sparkled with unshed tears and she focused on drinking her coffee for a moment. "That's lovely, dear."

Daniel gave Elle a significant look. He had more to tell her later.

A car pulled up outside, a car door closed and a moment later a hand pulled open the screen door. Logan stepped inside, held up a grocery bag, while his face held a cocky smile. "Steaks, wine, and me for dinner," he said and then froze as he took in the scene. "Oh, hell."

Susan stood immediately and slung her purse strap over her shoulder. "I'll see myself out," she said with a smirk she tried to hide by ducking her head.

Elle groaned and Daniel stepped up to Logan, shoved his face close to Logan's and then tilted it to the side. "Got a steak for me?"

"Actually, I do. They came in a three pack." Logan sidled past her son and gently set the bag on the counter. He opened it and pulled out a bottle of good, red wine. "None of this for you, though."

Daniel snorted. "Fine." He settled on a stool and leveled a look at Elle. "So how long has this been going on?"

"Nothing's going on," Elle blurted.

Logan glanced at Daniel and gave him a look. "Tell her."

"Logan called me a few days ago and filled me in."

"What?" She glared at Logan. "Why?" He broke their agreement. Worse, he didn't tell her.

"Because your son deserves to know."

"Right," Daniel interjected. "I do."

Had Logan told him that it would end when the twins came home? But she couldn't ask, not with Daniel giving her an assessing look. She had to be careful not to set a bad example for Daniel. It was one thing to date a few times and decide the relationship wouldn't go forward, but quite another to set an end date on a sexual affair.

"Okay," she said to Logan. She flicked a glance to Daniel. "We're seeing each other. Satisfied?"

"I told you this would happen," Daniel said, with smug conviction. "He got to you. But he's smarter than he looks and called me to clear it first."

His patronizing tone made her eyebrows climb as high as they could. "Clear it first?" She pivoted toward Logan. "Really," she drawled. Not a question, more like a stab.

Logan had the grace to flush, but Daniel looked confused.

"Daniel, I don't—" Logan began.

Elle cut him off with a raised palm. "Zip it."

Logan shut his mouth.

"Daniel," she said in a soft, but warning tone that brought him up short. "You don't have a say in my personal life. You made your doubts clear to me before. I put due consideration into my decision to see Logan and you have no right to clear it or deny me my choice. This will come as a shock, but just because you have a penis doesn't give you more rights than a woman, or the right to patronize me."

Her son blanched.

Satisfied that she'd made him think twice about his attitude, Elle dismissed the conversation by opening the fridge and rooting out the makings for a salad.

LOGAN AND CLAY HAD only managed to run together sporadically, so when Clay called Logan late on Monday afternoon, he jumped on the invitation. They started as usual but midway through the run, it turned into a footrace, with Clay beating him by a nose. They both walked in circles to cool off and Clay cleared his throat in a way that signaled he wanted to talk. "What?" Logan asked. "Something on your mind?"

"You're seeing my sister."

Logan squared his shoulders. "I see her every day at work."

"Not what I mean." Clay's response to Logan's square off was to get in his face. "Your car goes past my house at all hours. Until Daniel came home you wouldn't leave until dawn. Spill it."

"Ask Mercy. Or your sister."

"What would Mercy know about it?" But the light of understanding dawned. "Elle told her?"

Logan nodded. "When it started weeks ago."

"My wife kept a secret? For weeks?"

Logan gave him a *duh* look. But at least Clay had moved off the affair question and focused on his wife's ability to keep secrets.

"But why keep it quiet? There's no reason you and Elle need to sneak around. You're both free. You're a good guy and you've even won Daniel over."

"You'd best ask Elle." He would not tell Elle's brother that this affair would be over at summer's end and that she, not Logan, put an end date on it. "The twins aren't aware because they're away." It was the best he could come up with. "She doesn't want them to know."

"Okay." Clay narrowed his eyes. "I get that. I had my concerns about Dilly getting attached to Mercy at first. Come for dinner tonight."

Logan swallowed hard. "I'll check with Elle."

Clay slapped him on the back. "Of course you will," he said with a pleased chuckle. "Any smart man who wants to keep his woman checks first."

"Can't argue with that," Logan said.

"CLAY KNOWS NOW," LOGAN said to Elle on his phone as he walked back to work, sweaty from the run. Elle was still in the office, but she'd be closing up shortly. He planned to head home for a shower but figured he'd best tell her about this new development immediately. "He came to the conclusion on his own."

"I made a mistake letting you stay over."

"I don't sleep well without you." *Crap.* He'd said that out loud.

She sucked in a breath. "Me, neither, but we should have been smarter."

"We slipped up. We're not made for secret affairs."

"You'd be a lousy cheater." She laughed into his ear.

"That's right," he said. "Someday, I'll make a faithful husband and doting father."

"Yes, you will," she said faintly. "You'll make some woman very happy."

He let the comment hang between them.

"I've got to go. The twins expect a video chat." She ended the call before he could mention having dinner with Clay and Mercy. He considered heading upstairs to the office, but he decided to let Elle stew about the doting father comment.

He sent her a text about Clay's invitation and got a response immediately.

Elle: "Not tonight. Dinner with Shandy and Brianna."

The three women had formed a posse of sorts. They enjoyed the same movies and spicy Indian food. Elle considered it a treat to go out with them. Mercy had declined invitations because she claimed her advancing condition made theater seats uncomfortable. But Elle said Mercy felt weird about Shandy because Shandy had once wanted Clay. He had vague memories of Clay and Shandy sharing coffee at the bakery and taking their children to play at the park together.

BEFORE SHE HEADED OFF to dinner with Shandy and Brianna, Elle traipsed across the backyard to Clay's house. She saw him lighting the grill on the deck and hailed him. "I'm going out with friends for dinner," she said as she approached. "But thanks for the invitation." She stepped up beside him.

"Why couldn't you tell me about Logan? I approve, by the way, not that you need my approval."

She snorted. "Thanks, please explain how that works to my son." She forged into her reason for this private conversation. "I understand why you think it would work out for me and Logan. He's a great guy and I like him a lot."

His head reared back and his face darkened. "But?"

"Logan wants children. His own children. I'm not giving anyone any more children."

"I see." He ran his hand across his jaw. "You both accept all this and still see each other?"

She flushed. Stupid to flush like a girl. She had nothing to be ashamed of. "Yes, until the twins come home. Things could get messy and I don't want them disappointed."

A light shone in Clay's eyes. "You don't want them hurt if Logan disappears from their lives."

Clay had had the same doubts about Dilly being hurt if Mercy returned to her career in Hollywood. They'd sorted out that whole thing admirably.

"Having a baby is not the same as compromising on where you live the way Mercy did. You either have a baby together or you don't. I choose not to have more children."

"Why not?"

The question came out of left field and hit her broadside. "The answer's obvious. I already have three by two different fathers."

He cocked an eyebrow.

"Don't look at me like that. Tell me with a straight face that when I showed up with Clarissa that you assumed she was mine and that I'm a baby factory. If I have a child with Logan, that's exactly what I'll be."

"Logan's a better man than the ones who came before."

"What's that got to do with anything? He's the best man I've ever known," she said, hurt leaking into her voice. "But children, *my children*, deserve better than what I can give them." She turned abruptly and stalked off, back to her car so she wouldn't be late for dinner.

Irate, she continued to berate herself as she drove. She wasn't a good enough mother to handle more children. Look what her return to Welcome had done already. Her children were scattered. They'd taken on new families and left her as if she were nothing.

What kind of mother was she that her own children chose to leave her? Heartsick, she sobbed into her hands and then climbed into her car. She needed to gather her composure before she drove. No one should see her like this, least of all her friends.

She swiped at her eyes and then repaired her makeup in the rearview mirror. By the time she reached the restaurant that served the best East Indian food for miles, she felt composed again. Well enough, actually, to pull off a whole evening without Brianna and Shandy guessing anything was wrong.

They waved to her from the far end of the busy eatery. As she pulled out her chair to sit, they spoke in tandem. "What's happened?"

So much for makeup repair.

She sagged into her seat. "My brother knows more about my private life than I want him to and he's got opinions about it."

"Oh," Shandy said while Brianna nodded beside her. "Brothers can be a pain."

"Especially happily married ones with a baby on the way. He seems to think I should—" She cut herself short. She hadn't shared much about Logan. The only thing she'd told them was that she wanted to keep her new relationship quiet.

"What?" Brianna asked. "Bring this thing you're in to light? We're dying to know who he is."

"I'm not," Shandy reassured her. "You've got more to consider when there are children and going public can be the wrong thing for everyone until you're sure where it's going."

"Oh, I know where it's going and it's going to end," Elle said in a spiteful tone.

"I'm sorry," Shandy murmured sympathetically. Again, Brianna nodded and patted Elle's hand.

After a quick glance at each other, her friends spoke at once.

"Is he being a jerk?"

"Or has a wife suddenly come out of nowhere?"

Elle propped her chin in her hand. "There's no wife, but he wants children and I can't see myself doing it all again."

Shandy nodded sagely. "I would. I'd love another baby or two. But that's me. And, to be honest, I haven't had the financial struggle you've had. I'm far from wealthy, but I never need to worry, either."

Brianna watched Elle closely. "I'm not sure what I'd do in your circumstances, but you know what's best for your family."

"This will all be over soon and things will go back to the way they were. The twins will come home, school will start, and I'll be fine."

"Hey, being alone isn't the worst thing in the world," Shandy said in an atta-girl tone.

"That's right," Brianna agreed.

"I'm not in the mood for a rom-com. Finding true love isn't what it's cracked up to be." After they ate, she left the others to go to the movie without her.

When she got home, Daniel had the television on and gave her nothing more than a brief wave as she wandered into her room and threw herself on the bed.

Adulting felt way too hard.

The earlier conversation with Clay burned her soul. His idea that she could give Logan a family showed how little he remembered about their lives growing up. Clay needed to see what a lousy mother she was. He, of all people, should understand her fear that she'd turn into their mother.

Besides, what did Clay know about being a single parent? She rolled over and blindly faced the ceiling. *Oh, wait.* Her brother knew exactly what it was like. He'd been raising Dilly alone when Mercy had wandered into their lives.

She pulled out her phone and texted him.

Elle: "Do you remember what they were like?"

Clay: "Of course."

Elle: "Did they hate us?"

Clay: "You want to do this now?"

God, no, she never wanted to think about her parents and how she and Clay were raised. Digby and Belinda Foster had shown Clay and Elle almost no love. Who would want to go back there even in their mind?

Elle: "I think I need to."

Clay: "On my way."

She scooched to the far side of the bed next to the wall to give her brother room, because she was damn sure not airing this shit where Daniel could hear it.

Chapter Twenty-three

NOT TEN MINUTES AFTER texting Elle that he was coming over, Clay crawled onto the bed with her. She lifted her head so he could slide his arm beneath her neck. They linked hands in a comforting hold that had saved them many times when they were children. Tears leaked down from the corners of her eyes as Elle drew in a sobbing breath at the feel of Clay's old, familiar support.

"They didn't hate us," he said into the quiet that wreathed them. "They hated themselves."

"You think?"

She listened to the steady thud of his heartbeat and let the heat of his body and his dear scent drift over her. Her brother had grown into a father who'd learned to be a man by default because he loved his baby girl, his new wife, and the new life they'd made. It was hard to credit that such a man could grow and blossom from the childhood they'd shared. "You're a good man," she whispered. "I'm not sure how you did it, but you've overcome everything they ever did to hurt us."

"So have you," he said, which made her snort in derision.

"I've made a mess of my life and the lives of my children. Sure, I don't hit or belittle them or expect them to take care of me, but I didn't give them what they need. I can't keep their lives stable and I never will."

He tilted his head to look at her face. She looked back, not sure what he looked for. "You don't remember much, do you?"

"Of course I do. I remember all of it."

"You remember Mom leaning on you, making you do all the chores, the cooking, the laundry, and stuff."

"Yes." She couldn't see where he led, but his face was earnest so she followed. "I also remember Dad being hard on you. And us running to Karen to spend the night."

He nodded. "I remember that, too. But you're forgetting that on top of all the other things you had to handle, you took care of me. You protected me, covered for me, got me out of the house when the shit hit the fan. You had a sixth sense about how things would go."

"It wasn't hard to read the signs of a blow-up. Mom getting snarky about where he'd been. Dad barking at her."

"Yeah, the barking. He barked like a dog and said that was what she wanted; a dog on a chain in the yard." His tone turned amused as if laughing about those brutal arguments could somehow lighten their effects.

"When the barking started, I'd grab your hand and hit the door running."

"You saved us." He tucked her head into his shoulder. "You did that, Elle. And that's what you've always done. You've turned Daniel into a great kid who shows compassion and concern for people who never bothered with him before. Jorja and Liam are wonderful kids who are never stifled, will never lack confidence, and are always ready to laugh."

"Jorja's too serious. She takes on too much worry."

"That's her personality, not the effects of your mothering," he said in a soft rumble meant to soothe her. "Besides, having Liam for a twin means that one of them has to be the cautious one. Liam's a pistol."

That made her smile and warmed her heart. "He is, isn't he?" Liam was her rambunctious, happy, little daredevil.

"When I was on my own with Dilly, I was convinced I didn't have a clue about fathering a girl. She was willful and difficult and flew into tantrums. Then Mercy came along, a woman with no experience with children. But she saw something the rest of us missed. She came at Dilly with a different perspective. Using her memories of what it was like for her to be in the pageants, she finally convinced her mother and me that Dilly needed a break. Dilly needed to be herself, not another Mercy."

"Did the tantrums stop?" She felt the bob of his head when he nodded.

"She turned into a sweet thing once we let her be Dilly."

"And all this is to say what? I need to let my children go? Because I've done that. Daniel spends more time with his previously disinterested grandparents, and Jorja and Liam were too busy having fun today to take my video call." That had bummed her out, made her feel deserted.

"And Logan. What are you doing with him? He's a good man and I'm surprised you're leading him on."

A stab of something ugly went through her. "I'm not leading him on. He knows damn well I'm a lousy choice for a mother."

He tensed. His whole body went rigid. "I thought we covered that. Weren't you listening?"

"Doesn't mean I believe it," she admitted. "My being with Logan is nice. Neither of us expects this to go on for long. We want different things. I'm not prepared to give him what he wants. When this ends, we'll move on with no hard feelings." She was glad that Clay knew about her relationship with Logan. She could breathe easier around her brother. Having secrets never felt good. Or right.

Clay cleared his throat. She braced because her brother was gearing up for something. "We all know what Logan wants. What do you want?"

Oh, crap. "Do I have to answer now?" She didn't have a clue what she wanted. Not from Logan, not from her brother, and not from life. She'd spent the last years too busy with her family to consider her needs.

"Think about it and get back to me. Or, better yet, tell Logan." With that, he climbed out of the bed, kissed her forehead and turned to leave.

"Thanks, Clay. I needed this."

"Maybe I did, too."

The old comfort they took from each other by talking out their fears had helped. Their positions had been reversed this time, though. When they'd been kids, she used to climb into Clay's bed, rest his head on her shoulder and talk him through their fears. It was good that he remembered how deeply comforting those times were and had offered the same comfort back.

LOGAN'S DOORBELL RANG as he shoved the last bite of a bagel into his mouth. He had his other hand on his front doorknob. He opened the door to find Jamie on the other side.

"You're on your way to work," Jamie said. "This is a bad time."

His brother had shaved, wore clean clothes Logan didn't recognize, and looked clear-eyed. "What happened to you?" he asked as he pulled the bagel out from between his lips.

Logan's worries about Elle, his schedule for the day, his hopes for a couple of house sales, all disappeared in the face of Jamie's return. "Never a bad time when you show up looking like this." He stepped back to invite his brother inside.

A ghost of a smile rimmed Jamie's lips. "Thanks." He raised his hands in surrender. "But I won't come in."

"Okay." Whatever he wanted, Logan thought, afraid of spooking him. Jamie looked nervous and scared. "Have you seen Mom and Dad?" Logan asked.

Jamie shook his head no. "I'm not ready to see Mom."

"Okay."

"I want you to know I'm trying. It's hard but I'm living with a couple of other people who are further down this road. They're strong and keep me stronger than I've been before."

"Is living with former addicts wise?"

"They've been clean for over ten years each and they've done this before, had people come and stay, I mean." He blew out a long breath and ran his fingers through his freshly cut hair. "They're good people. But they don't let me lie to them, or to myself. This is what I need." His chin firmed and his eyes stared back into Logan's with determination.

Logan nodded because there was nothing else to do.

"Mom and Dad let me get away with a lot," Jamie said. "Too much. I need to learn to be strong from people who've learned the hard way. Please let Mom and Dad know I'm not on the streets. Not using. And I'm working hard. Not for them, for myself." He lifted a corner of his mouth in a shaky grin. "I'm working the way I should have all the other times, but didn't."

Logan nodded. "I'm glad. Really glad. I want my brother back."

"Me, too. I'll get there. You can believe it this time." Jamie's eyes welled up, but it was hard to see because Logan's were damp, too.

"Can I give you a lift downtown? I'm going to the office anyway."

"No thanks. I've got to find my own way."

Logan drew his brother into his arms and gave him a long, hard hug, a couple of slaps on his shoulder and let him go. Then he shut his front door, set his back to the wall and dropped his head into his hands.

He was afraid to hope, but this time, *this time*, looked different from all the other times. He pressed his thumbs into his eyes. They came away wet. Then Logan drew in a ragged breath and called his parents. His dad answered. "I'm coming over," he said. "Jamie was here."

When he arrived at his parents' house, he explained immediately about the visit at his front door. "Jamie could be okay this time?" his mother asked.

"He's got a long way to go, but he looked good. He's had a haircut, a shave, his eyes are clear. He looked me right in the eye. He seemed steady."

"Is he eating all right?"

Logan smiled. "Yes, Mom, Jamie's eating." He explained about the people Jamie was staying with. "They've got years of sobriety behind them and understand what he needs."

"He's not in the shelter, then."

"Apparently the shelter recommended these people. They've helped others by taking them in. Jamie says they can't be fooled, that they're strong, and won't put up with lies."

His father nodded. "Good. He needs to stand on his own two feet when he's able. We're not what he needs right now." He shifted his gaze to Logan's mom.

She nodded. "Right. Sometimes loving him isn't enough."

Logan drew her into his arms and gave her the same hug he'd given his brother.

On the way back to his car, Logan's father joined him in the driveway. They stood together, each one scanning the neighborhood. Logan wondered which houses would be sprouting signs on their lawns in the coming year. He hoped more than a few of those signs were his.

"How're things with you?" his dad asked. "Business good?"

"It's great, Dad."

"I don't remember if I thanked you for moving home when you did. We needed you here and you stepped up. I appreciate it. We both do."

"I'm glad I came home. Welcome's a good place to live and I see potential for me here."

"Not a lot of nightlife for a young man on his own." His father looked in the opposite direction as if butting his nose into Logan's life was tough.

It must be hard because his father rarely asked about personal stuff.

"I'm not lonely, Dad. I am seeing a woman." But for how long? Hanging on until the end of the summer seemed too hard. He wasn't sure he could make it that long and come out intact. "I'd like a family," he said. "Welcome is where I want to raise children. Finding the right woman who wants the same thing is the issue. The woman I'm seeing now doesn't want children."

That brought his father's gaze back to him. "No?"

"She has three and doesn't want more. She's three years older than I am and started her family early."

Dad nodded and looked at his shoes. "Who's to say the next woman will be able to have any? Children don't always come along just because you want them. Sometimes you need to find another way."

"You and mom did a great job with Jamie and me. But I can't help wanting to see a resemblance to me in my children. My eyes, or my chin or my hair."

"I understand." His father's voice went low and gruff. "At first, when your mother wanted to adopt I said no. I wanted what you want. It's natural." He cleared his throat. "I was stubborn for too long, pining for people who would never exist." He gave Logan a put-upon expression. "You have no idea how stubborn your mother can be. Look how long it took for her to push Jamie to work on recovery without us gilding his path."

"She did the right thing."

"Anyway," his father said with a fond smile, "once I saw you and Jamie, none of the physical traits I wanted to share mattered. Your trusting eyes were all I needed." He cleared his throat and his voice went rough with emotion. "When you adopt, you open yourself up to whatever your children will be. You set aside the stuff about where they got their musical talent, or interest in sports, or math or what-have-you. As a father you allow your children to develop as they will, without pre-conceived expectations."

Logan tried to see his point. His parents had spent years trying to conceive. Science had failed them, so his father had had no choice. It was adopt or not be a father at all.

"If this woman already has children, then you'd still be parenting," his father pointed out. "You'd still see them grow into adults you helped shape in some way. Even if they don't look a bit like you."

But Jorja and Liam already had a father determined to stay in their lives. And Daniel was mostly grown. Logan doubted there was anything he could teach him.

Except how to drive. Logan shuddered. But Daniel's life had taken a new direction with the Murdochs involved now. They could afford to buy him a new car, give him a living allowance or a trust fund.

"Life should be simpler than this," Logan said around a sigh.

"It rarely is, son. It rarely is."

Chapter Twenty-four

LOGAN TEXTED ELLE WHEN he climbed into his car.

Logan: "We need to talk."

Elle: "Yes."

Logan: "See you at work in ten."

Elle: "I'm already here."

He checked the time and saw the office had opened an hour ago. Jamie's visit had thrown off his timing, but he was happy he'd been able to deliver some good news to their parents. He had a feeling Jamie would be in touch more regularly now and when he felt strong enough he'd visit Mom and Dad, too.

One problem of the day handled. The next would likely kill him.

ELLE WAITED IN THE office with nerves stretched to the breaking point. There were only three weeks left of the summer break and she had to end things with Logan. She couldn't see him, sleep with him, eat with him, or *laugh* with him any longer. Best to cut ties while they still could.

But she couldn't quit working with him. Turned out, she enjoyed her job. She liked the variety and the contact with people. She liked seeing Logan build his business and got caught up in his enthusiasm.

Ten minutes after Logan's text Elle broke into a sweat. Right on time, he stepped through the office door. He couldn't meet her eyes and her belly dropped with dread. It was over.

"So," she said quietly, "I think we both know what we need to say." He was dressed in his usual dressy-casual style with a lightly checked shirt and beige slacks. His sleeves were rolled to his elbow and his forearms drew her eye.

He nodded and a muscle jumped in his jaw. "I want what I want." He looked as if someone had just killed his cat. "I can't stop myself from wanting the whole thing: a wife and kids, a dog, and coaching whatever sports my kids want to play."

"It all sounds beautiful. Perfect for you." Her brother's question rolled through Elle's mind, rumbling and heavy and hard. Clay had asked what she wanted and she still couldn't say. But, she was damn certain of what she didn't want. She did not want Logan's dream family. "Should I look for another job?" Her belly clenched as the words popped out.

His eyebrows bounced up. "Of course not. This was never about convenience, or us working together or me expecting sex from an employee. I want you to stay." He sighed. "In fact, I've ordered you a desk. You'll need to go to the store and pick out a chair that suits you." He looked toward the window vaguely. "A comfortable chair is important," he muttered.

"Okay." Why were they talking about office furniture when her heart was breaking? "Should I go now?"

"If you want. I'll be out at Springhill for the next few days."

"Good. That's for the best."

"What'll you tell Daniel?" He assessed her.

She wasn't sure what she'd say to her son. "Daniel will figure it out when you stop coming around. I'll tell him then. He'll be relieved."

His face fell. She'd hurt him. "Not because he doesn't like you," she explained. "He warned me early on not to have more children. Not for you or anyone. He's far more grown up than I realize sometimes."

Logan nodded. "Okay. So you handle the furniture delivery and I'll be at the other end of the phone if you need me. Keep in touch," he said and walked out.

That was when she collapsed into a pool of misery. Half an hour later, her face wet, her throat feeling like barnacles had taken up residence, she sent out three texts, all with the same message.

Elle: "It's over."

An hour after that, Mercy, Shandy, and Brianna blew into the office like three warrior queens. Elle had washed her face, fixed her makeup and combed her hair but they still tutted and took stock. "I'm fine," she blustered, wondering if she should have waited and told them one at a time. But repeating the same sorry tale three times held no appeal.

Mercy took a seat first, easing her body into the chair gingerly. "I'm never sure if I'll fit into an armchair like this one," she said with a groan. She'd plumped a lot over the last weeks. Her face was rounder, her neck looked heavier, but her chest had blossomed. Her sister-in-law looked happy and pregnant and sad for Elle. All at the same time.

Shandy was the first to respond to Mercy. "Don't worry about it," she said. "You can lose weight after the baby. As long as your doctor's okay with your weight gain, it's all good." Mercy gave her a glance but then smiled shyly.

"Thanks. The doctor's happy enough. I was underweight before."

Brianna spoke next and reassured Mercy how flush and pretty she looked.

It came to Elle then that no one had mentioned her loss. Good. She didn't need to hear platitudes or lies. She needed to know that she could feel normal again soon. "I have an errand to run. Care to come with?" she asked the trio.

"Of course."

"Sure."

"I'll drive," Shandy said. "Where to?"

"I'm to go try on office chairs. Logan bought me a desk." She waved toward an empty space along the wall, where she assumed her desk would reside. She stood and her friends stood with her.

"Thanks for being here," she said, looking into their faces in turn. "Last time I got dumped I was alone." She'd had to keep things together for Jorja and Liam's sake. Daniel had been angry at Ben and she hadn't been able to talk to him without causing an explosion. Eventually, she'd given up.

"Logan *dumped* you?" Mercy blurted. The other two women looked equally appalled.

"No, not exactly," she admitted. "It was mutual, but it sure feels like a dump." It felt permanent like there was no going back, no way around the roadblock to the future. No way to start again. *Oh, Logan, we never should have started.* "I wish we hadn't ever begun. It hurts to know I've hurt him, too."

Shandy stepped close, put her arm around her and smiled shakily. "I suspected it might be Logan. You never actually told me." She slanted a glance at Brianna.

"I guessed he was interested in you when we first met at my mom's place. He couldn't keep his eyes off you."

Logan had liked her from the first time they'd met and she'd been snarky. "I was rude to him when we met. I wanted him to back off, but he wouldn't." Now, look at them.

"Two people in pain is the worst," Shandy said. "But you didn't want the twins to know and now they never will. They'll never get attached to Logan or lose him. This is for the best."

Elle agreed. "By the time they come home in three weeks, I'll feel like my old self." Losing Logan *was* for the best. In the long run, she'd accept that they'd done the right thing. It was getting to that point that might kill her.

By noon, they were in the store and Elle was spinning in a chair, her feet off the floor and her hands clutching the arms. "This is the one," she said, pressing against the lumbar support. "This is the support I need." She looked at the faces of her watchful posse. "And I'm not just talking about the chair."

Shandy flushed prettily, Mercy bent and pressed her lips to Elle's forehead and Brianna sighed heavily. "Good," her younger and oldest friend said with a smile. "Logan and you deserve every happiness. And if that means separate lives, then that's what's best." A sadness lurked under her words, but Elle didn't have the emotional strength to ponder what it meant for Brianna.

"I forgot you and Logan are friends," Elle said, wondering if Brianna would be the one to give Logan the life he wanted. If that was how things panned out, Elle would handle it.

"Buddies since high school," Brianna admitted.

Mercy frowned. "Didn't you have a thing for someone who wasn't Logan?"

Elle perked up. "That's right, Brianna, you did. Wasn't it Jake Morrow?" She recalled Brianna asking Elle for advice at the time, but nothing came of it. Brianna had left Welcome after high school and Jake? She didn't know what happened to him because she'd also abandoned Welcome.

"Jake's a friend of my ex-husband." Shandy piped up. "They keep in touch." A curious light glowed in her eyes. "Jake still lives here."

"Oh?" Brianna said airily. "That's right, Logan told me that. I forgot." But the flush in her cheeks called her a liar.

Mercy shook her head. "Elle, if you've decided on this chair," she said, bringing everyone back to the matter at hand. "Then I need a ladies' room and some lunch. In that order."

"And then you'll need the ladies' room again," Shandy said with a warm chuckle.

Mercy laughed. "You're right." The smile in her eyes was infectious as she looked at Shandy.

It seemed the leftover pique between Mercy and Shandy over Clay had dissipated. Elle was glad. She liked and enjoyed the company of both women and would hate to see any friction between them over her brother, of all people.

THREE WEEKS LATER ON Friday morning before the Labor Day weekend, Elle waited by the door watching for Ben's vehicle. The twins were due home any minute and her heart thumped hard with anticipation.

The weeks after her breakup with Logan had dragged until yesterday, when, for the first time, she'd slept a full night. Her subconscious must have decided it was time to think clearly. She needed to carry on normally with Jorja and Liam.

Daniel waited with her, antsy and excited, although he'd never admit it. To keep her mind occupied she'd been grilling him about the Murdochs, but there was no real need. Susan and she talked fairly regularly now and they'd developed a rapport Tad would never have believed possible.

"I want to focus on science," Daniel told her. "I think."

"Oh?" This was the first she'd heard of Daniel focusing on anything. He was a good student, but not an overachiever. She'd never noticed that he'd had an affinity for one subject over another. Some would call him well-rounded, she supposed.

"Clay has offered me a job next summer in his clinic. We talked about what sciences I'd need for vet school."

"Really?" Surprised and pleased, she grinned and ruffled his hair. "Imagine that."

"I like working with the horses. They're pretty cool."

"I bet."

He nodded and went back to playing a game on the laptop while she sat in disbelief. Daniel had grown by leaps and bounds, physically and emotionally, over the summer. He towered over her now and would soon catch up to Clay in height. His shoulders were less bony and his legs and arms had filled out. She blinked and had an image of him as a man.

She wanted to cry because Tad would never see it. But Tad's mother would, and she drew comfort from that.

By mid-morning, she'd about given up that Ben would ever arrive when she saw a car approach up the driveway. She stepped outside and joy nearly broke her in two. Her babies were home, back where they belonged.

Safe and sound and hers again. All hers. That wasn't right, but she'd been parted from them for weeks and she needed to clutch them to her chest and never let go.

That was what she did, as soon as her babies climbed out of their father's pickup. Ben jogged to the back of the truck to unload their bags while Elle enfolded them in her arms.

"Mom!"

"Mommy, we missed you." Jorja's breath, moist and warm, blew across her neck. Elle wanted to drink it in and hold her little girl forever.

"I missed you both so much." She kissed them again and again until even for Jorja, it was too much. They both giggled and moved back.

"Jodie wants us to come back for Thanksgiving!" Liam looked expectantly at her, looking for a yes, but Elle was too surprised to do more than stare at her ex.

Ben set their backpacks on the front step. "About that, we hoped we could set up a new visitation schedule."

Everything in her stilled in rigid denial. "They've been gone all summer—"

But Ben wouldn't let her deny him and interrupted her. "True, but we're hoping we could have them Thanksgiving and Easter and for summer breaks."

She did a quick mental tally. "Leaving me with all of the Christmas break and spring break?"

"I get that it's more than we discussed when we agreed on visitation but it seems fair. And they should see Jodie and Angelica regularly, don't you think?"

"While you may think this is fair, I want some summertime, too. You can have them for a month."

"Six weeks."

"Five." She felt cornered with the twins watching them avidly. Jorja looked pained by the negotiation and Liam looked sorry for speaking up. She crossed her arms. "You've never been this thoughtful before; more of a seat-of-your-pants guy," she observed. "This must be Jodie's idea."

Ben had the grace to flush. "She loves them and they like her a lot."

"I'll talk to Jodie and sort out dates." Then she faced the twins. "Take your backpacks inside, please. Daniel's waiting to see you." They scampered into the house and she heard squeals and laughter as they greeted their older brother.

Ben shuffled his feet. "Daniel's still pissed at me," he muttered, referring to Daniel's continued refusal to set eyes on his stepfather.

"He is." She couldn't soften Daniel's reaction to Ben. Her ex understood how badly he'd hurt Daniel when he left.

"I'm sorry about that. About all of it. I should never have let things happen with Jodie. But when they did and she became pregnant, I couldn't mess up another life."

Elle could point out that *things* hadn't happened with Jodie—Ben had arranged his affair—but why belabor the semantics. Ben believed he'd had no choice and that his feelings for Jodie had overcome him. Angelica was the result. "You couldn't mess up her life, so you messed up ours," she said softly. "I've wondered what I did to make you look her way in the first place." Had Elle ignored Ben? Taken him for granted? Demanded too much or not enough?

Odd, but for the first time in a long while, getting answers to those questions didn't matter. Because she no longer cared. She'd moved on, moved past her grief and anger and disappointment.

"Yeah, I messed everything up. And I'm sorry, but you didn't do anything wrong. It was all me. I'm the one who pursued Jodie for no good reason." Ben sighed and looked off into the middle distance as he gathered his thoughts. "But you've handled everything like a trouper. You're a class act, Elle. The twins are happy and well-adjusted. Anyone can see that."

Heat rose in her cheeks at the compliment. But Ben wasn't finished.

"I'm starting a new job as site manager. There'll be more money for support. If you need anything over and above, ask me. We'll work something out." His lips thinned. "I know you've had it rough."

She must be dreaming. All these confessions exploded in her head. She couldn't take everything in. Ben had taken full responsibility for their breakup and promised more support and wanted to see more of the twins. She should pinch herself awake. But the dream was way too good to miss. "Okaaay," she drawled. "Thanks for the offer. I'm doing better now that I'm working." Still, she'd remember Ben's offer if an emergency cropped up.

"Jorja told me you've got an office job. Never thought I'd see that."

"I have a good boss." Logan was the best. He hadn't blinked when she'd told him she needed the morning off to see the twins and get them settled. In fact, he'd told her to take the whole day. The thought of him still hurt, but now that the twins were home, she'd feel more complete.

Because she hadn't felt complete since Logan and she had made their decision. She shook her head to clear the unwelcome thought away.

"How's the baby?" she asked to lighten the mood.

"Beautiful. I see some of Jorja in her."

"You always said Jorja looked like you." In spite of her hair and eye color being Elle's, Ben had claimed their daughter as all his. She smiled at the memory. "Remember when she was born? How you crowed like a rooster?"

"That's how I felt. I've never been happier," he confessed. "Angelica came at a dark time and I wasn't sure how things would work with you and my children." His eyes dampened. "Elle, thanks for sharing them, in spite of how I treated you and what an ass I was."

"Stop. It's done." She couldn't take any more. How could things sort out this well for Ben while she ached for Logan? Life had blessed Ben and she'd been kicked in the teeth. Again.

Chapter Twenty-five

BY THE END OF THE BUSINESS day, Logan was antsy to learn how the twins' return had gone. But it wasn't his place to ask and Elle wouldn't appreciate hearing from him on the subject. They'd managed to avoid any personal conversation for the past three weeks, but it killed him more each day.

Last night, he'd swiped right on a dating app and met a woman at a café. She'd looked nicer in her photo than she was. She'd picked apart every other woman in the place. They'd shared a table and had a coffee at the same time, but other than that, they left the same way they'd arrived. Alone.

He stood looking out his living room window, with a beer in his hand, when he saw a familiar junker pull up on the street to park in front of his house. Elle.

He tore open the front door and hurried down the walkway to the sidewalk. As she climbed out of the car, he asked, "What's wrong? Is it the twins? Did he return them as promised?" His heart clattered like a window shutter in a hurricane. And then it tore away when he saw her face.

Elle looked stricken.

He'd kill Ben. Find him and tear his guts out.

Logan ran to her and took her hands. "What'd he do? I've been worried all day that he'd decide to keep them." People did terrible things when they wanted to punish the other parent.

"No, no. Logan," she said with a shaky smile. "Jorja and Liam came home. They're in bed fast asleep. Daniel's with them."

"Then why are you here?"

"Because I want to be," she said simply. "Let's go inside."

He let her lead him back up the walkway, confounded by her arrival and the spark in her gaze. He wasn't sure if it was humor or fear or something else entirely.

But Elle wanted to be here, so he followed her into his house and shut the door. "Now what—"

She cut him off by kissing him square on the mouth. It was awkward and her teeth smashed against his lower lip, but it was a kiss. From Elle.

He set her away from him. "What are you doing here?"

"If you can't tell I'm seducing you, I must be doing it wrong."

"No." He stepped away and walked into the living room. Running his hand through his hair in frustration, Logan spun to face her. She looked shaky and alone, but determined. "Again, what are you doing here? We had an agreement not to do this, to move on."

"I can't and I don't want to." She sidled closer, but he refused to fall into whatever trap this was.

"I'm not looking for an affair," he said. "I won't sneak around with you. Unless something's changed, I need to find a woman who wants what I want." He couldn't be clearer, but Elle's lips canted up in a secretive smile.

"Something has changed," she murmured and kept moving slowly toward him. He stepped back again. She stalked him across the room.

"What? You still have three children, you still work for me. You still don't want—wait—what? You've changed your mind? About kids?"

She nodded easily and the simple gesture broke him. While he stood stunned she planted another kiss on his lips. This one was gentle, coaxing, and he groaned against her mouth. Her breath caught as he deepened the kiss, still unable to process what she'd said.

Children. Elle Foster wanted his children. He tore his mouth from hers. "Are you sure?"

"I'm sure."

"What happened?"

"I'll tell you after we get started on this baby thing. I'm not getting any younger. I turned thirty-four last week."

"Tell me all about it later," he mumbled against her lips.

LOGAN MUST HAVE FIGURED things out by the time she mentioned her age because he took complete charge. One second they were kissing sweetly, deeply, and the next she'd been swung up into his arms. He jogged with her against his chest through the living area, down the hall, and into his bedroom. Once there, he dropped her unceremoniously onto the unmade bed.

She took a quick assessment of the room. Clothes had been tossed onto his dresser and a chair in the corner. She laughed as he climbed on top of her. This was the pirate she remembered from before. Rough, ready and demanding, Logan stripped off only the essential items of clothing: her shorts and panties and his slacks and jockeys. Her T-shirt was shoved up and he undid the front catch of her bra.

Then he fell on her while she laughed and kissed everywhere she could reach. "Logan," she breathed.

"Elle. My Elle." He suckled her breasts, drawing her womb up tight. She widened the opening between her thighs so he could settle there. She'd missed the weight of him, the scent of him. She missed him, Logan.

Missed loving Logan.

"I want this," she said on a husky note. "I want you. Always. Love me, Logan. Just love me."

He froze over her. "I do love you, Elle. More than anything. More than potential children. If you don't want any more babies, I'm okay with that. I get it."

Making promises in this moment had been too easy for her. She'd made lots of mistakes, most of them, in fact, while she was aroused and ready. "Stop," she said clearly.

He'd been nudging at her entrance, but he pulled back and rolled off her. He threw his arm across his eyes and blew out a huge breath. "Don't change your life for this, Logan. Not because sex is clouding your judgment. Decisions made in the heat of the moment usually turn out bad."

She rose on her elbow and lifted his arm away to look into his handsome, confused face. "You still don't get it. I. Want. Your. Children."

He stared up at her. "You're sure?"

"If you still want me and all my baggage." Maybe he'd already been dating. He was determined to have his suburban wife and kids. Maybe he'd set things in motion elsewhere.

"What changed?" He shifted away and his eyes went cool.

She hadn't expected the question. "I have. I've had the worst year. Because of Ben's departure, my decision to take Clarissa and then hand her back as agreed, and seeing how much more the Murdochs can do for Daniel, I lost my confidence. Lost everything I believed about myself. Before this year, I was brave and forged ahead no matter what happened to me.

"I lost *myself*, Logan. I began to believe what my parents told me when I was a kid. I would be a lousy adult, a bad mother and would never be important to anyone."

"Oh my God," he tenderly cupped the side of her face. She tilted into his hand.

"Let me finish."

He nodded, but his eyes were bright with compassion. Not pity.

"When the twins came home, I realized how happy they are. And then I looked at Daniel and saw him as the man he's going to be."

"You did that, Elle. You're a wonderful mother. Can you blame me for wanting you to mother my children? You're gentle and kind and smart with them. You're loving and firm and guide them."

"It seems odd that I'd forget all that, but I did. I lost my way."

"And now, with me?"

"I want to do it again. I'm only thirty-four. Lots of women wait until this age to start their families. Imagine how easy it will be with two of us and all my years of experience."

He chuckled then and pulled her atop him. She straddled his hips and watched his eyes glaze with desire. "Elle. My Elle."

"My Logan," she whispered as he entered her. "My loving, generous, Logan. Love me with all my doubts, all my fear."

"You're the bravest woman I know. I'll love you forever."

ONE YEAR LATER

"One more push, Elle and all this will be over," Logan urged. He glanced over his shoulder to where the nurse held baby number one. "Everything okay there?"

"Absolutely, Mr. Hughes." Relief and fear warred inside him. "Elle, are you okay?"

But Elle focused on the last push and with a mighty grunt that came from deep inside, she brought baby number two into the world. A squall that sounded like the one they'd heard only moments ago rose up and then she looked at him with tears in her eyes.

"You're crying," she said. And he was. Fat tears filled his eyes so it was hard to see her beautiful, shining face. "I love you."

"I love you. Now, can find out their gender?"

"Yes, I wanted to wait until they were both here. I still say I won our bet."

The nurse who stood behind him passed the swathed baby to him and handed over a blue cotton blanket she'd been hiding. "Welcome your son to the world, Mr. and Mrs. Hughes."

The doctor slid the second baby up to Elle's chest for a cuddle. "A girl," she breathed. "Another beautiful girl." She chuckled and looked up at him again. "I won! Jorja and Liam will go crazy when they find out we've had another pair like them."

Logan bent and kissed her, his heart so full he was sure it would burst. Life had just become a whole lot of everything he ever wanted.

"It's a good thing you married me, Mr. Hughes," Elle quipped. "Because there's no way I want to be a single mother with five children." She held his wet cheek in the palm of her hand, the same way he held her heart.

"You'll never be a single mother again. I'll always be there for you and for all our children. Yours are mine and these are ours. Forever," he vowed.

An hour later the room had filled with friends and family. Clay and Mercy held his son so that Dilly and her baby sister could peer at his sweet, scrunched-up face. Daniel, Jorja, and Liam leaned over the bed to see his daughter in their mother's arms.

His parents had held both babies right away and cried tears of absolute joy. His brother, Jamie, stood in awe next to them.

Susan Murdoch stood in a corner, quietly enjoying the moment beside Shandy and Brianna.

Logan looked at his wife across the bed, caught her eye, and said. "My Elle is tired and needs her rest. And I need to catch my breath."

After much kissing and hugging as they all said their goodbyes, he was suddenly alone with his wife and babies. "Will you tell me their names now?"

"First names to be decided, but I'd like to use your parents' names for the middle." She held both babies, her eyes soft with love. The one in the blue blanket began to wail which triggered his sister. "And so it begins," his wife said with a chuckle as she kissed their soft heads.

Life, his life, couldn't be better than this.

The End

PLEASE ENJOY THIS SMALL sample from

Craving Jake Return to Welcome Book 3 by Bonnie Edwards

Stalking wasn't always a bad thing, Brianna Bowler told herself. Not when it happened by accident. Seeing Jake Morrow from afar three times in one month could be called a coincidence, couldn't it?

But this was the first time she'd seen Jake with his girlfriend. From across the street, Brianna froze in shock as they stood in front of the fire station together.

Jake had always been easy on the eyes and fifteen years hadn't changed that. Jake had black, untamed curls and deep blue eyes, and if she were close enough she'd see his spiky black eyelashes that looked like inky starbursts. Women would kill for those eyelashes. In fact, they paid swank prices for extensions that looked just like the ones Jake grew on his own. It wasn't fair.

But she was distracted from the real reason she stood numb and still at the open trunk of her mom's car.

Jake's girlfriend was petite and slim and looked like a chirpy little sprite in her skin-tight activewear cropped pants and her kicky cross-trainers. And her dark curling hair made her look like a little sister or cousin. She'd just bet the gorgeous specimen of femininity also had blue eyes.

Not to mention she looked much, much too young for him. Even from across the street and up the block Brianna could see she was a very young twenty-something. Young and fresh and pretty and perfect.

Brianna had already heard they lived together. She tried not to scowl, but Jake should be ashamed of himself. He was over thirty and this girl-child was an entire generation behind.

She shook off her dark emotions and bent to her task. And yes, her chest always clenched when she hefted bags of dog food and dumped them into a car trunk. Her eyes always smarted and her breath always caught.

Four bags later, she dusted the kibble dust off her hands and closed the trunk lid. She studiously kept her eyes away from the fire station's open front doors, where Jake and his perfect girlfriend stood, probably talking about what to have for dinner together or what shows they'd be binge-watching tonight. The ordinary stuff of lives lived together.

She didn't miss that part of a relationship, not at all. She'd left Anthony behind in Seattle and he'd been content enough to be left. Whatever they'd shared had run its course and she was free now. Single again, and not looking at Jake Morrow and his cheerful, chirpy child-sized girlfriend.

On stiff legs, she marched to the driver's side door and climbed inside the car. Slipping on her sunglasses, she sniffed as her side vision caught a quick kiss on Jake's cheek from the sprite. The woman had to go on tiptoe to do it. Fine. He liked them young and tiny. Everything Brianna wasn't. As her mom said, Brianna was statuesque, an old-fashioned word for tall and square-shouldered.

Not that it mattered. Not anymore. She was *so* over her high school crush. Had been for years.

Actually, she was glad Jake had found someone. After what happened all those years ago, it was a wonder he could find any happiness at all. She revved the motor a titch too hard in agitation.

Bowler's Dog Rescue needed a new truck, but she and her mom hadn't had time to even look at them. Until they bought a newer pickup, the rescue had to rely on her mom's ancient econobox that Brianna had learned to drive in high school.

She added the truck shopping chore to her mental list and squealed the tires as she took off. At the squeal, she winced and felt as if she'd whipped the poor old car like an old horse, poor thing.

She settled her shoulders. The squeal wasn't that bad, she thought, a mere chirp, hardly noticeable, she decided.

Brianna hated drawing attention and she feared her childish response to Little Miss Perfect had done just that. She drew a deep, calming breath and forced her hands to relax on the steering wheel. Gossip ran rampant in Welcome and her attempt at ripping up the road could be commented on.

She liked her hometown, she did. But returning to Welcome hadn't been as easy as she'd hoped. People seemed disappointed in her as if they'd expected her to set the world ablaze when she'd left. Nothing could be further from the truth.

Brianna had snagged a decent job in a field that was quickly disintegrating in a world that valued rumor and gossip over the truth. A fact-checker for a news team on a radio station, Brianna had developed mad skills and contacts, but little respect and no job security. When her mother needed help for a few weeks to recover from knee surgery, her boss had refused to give her the time off.

With her relationship stalled on neutral, she'd looked forward to coming home. Now, she wasn't so sure she was in the right place to be happy.

"I'm glad to be home in Welcome," she said to Beau, the rescue's mascot, who sat shotgun, tongue lolling out of his wide, grinning mouth. The pit bull's eyebrows shot up at the sound of her voice.

She wasn't sure who needed convincing, herself or the dog. "My mom needs my help and no one will chase me away again."

Beau groaned in agreement like he always did.

"No one," she emphasized with a glance at her rearview mirror, "including Jake Morrow and his sprite," she said with determination.

Beau farted and stuck his nose to the cracked-open window.

"I'm glad you agree," she said as she opened her window, too.

WAS BRIANNA BACK IN Welcome for good? She'd been here for at least a month. Jake Morrow watched her out of the corner of his eye as she picked up the last bag of dog food and stowed it in the back of an old car. Her mother's car if he wasn't mistaken. She must be visiting because she sure as hell wouldn't have moved back permanently.

"Thanks, Jake. I'll see you later," Theda raised her lips and caught him on the cheek before he could swing his head out of the way. He used his palm to swipe off the orange lipstick she had on this morning. Theda was messy in more ways than one.

"Sure. Let me know how the apartment hunt goes today."

Theda's wide, blue eyes moistened. "I'm baking your favorite pie today. Stop by the bakery when my shift's done and we'll bring one home."

"Sure," he replied. It was useless to point out that the pie baker was the owner, Alyce Markham. Theda's use of the truth was fluid and it came and went like the tide.

Besides, his mind was on Brianna and his gaze followed her mom's old car as it belched fumes down Main Street. Theda used his distraction to grab his jaw and raise her lips to his. Surprised, he allowed the kiss for a fraction of a second.

She took his hesitation as an invitation and wrapped her arms around his neck, pressing her body to his. He set his hands to her forearms to disengage.

She clung.

He tugged free.

And then he turned and walked into the station.

Doug Marton, his partner, waited with a sly expression on his face. "Theda still living at your place?"

"Not for long. She'll find something." Doug must have witnessed Theda's clinging kiss. "Don't bust my balls. She's a sweet girl, just slow to get the message." He never should have opened the door to her when she appeared, wet and bedraggled, six months ago, claiming she had nowhere else to go.

But Jake had always had a thing about damsels in distress and Theda had had that whole lost little girl thing down pat. It hadn't taken long for them to move beyond roommates to something more. That *something* wasn't working for Jake anymore.

IF YOU ENJOYED *Loving Logan* and have ever found a wonderful romance by reading reviews, please pay that joy forward by sharing a few words about how *Loving Logan* made you feel when you closed it. A review doesn't have to be long, or a retelling of the plot, just a few words on how you felt when you finished. Did you sigh at the end? Feel happy?

The next book in my Return to Welcome series is *Craving Jake* and tells the exciting, suspenseful story of Jake and Brianna.

If you want to hear about exciting new releases and deals you can subscribe to Bonnie's Newsy Bits on my website. Readers can download a free e-book when they subscribe.

Over 40 romance titles are listed on my website at https://www.bonnieedwards.com/.

Don't miss out!

Visit the website below and you can sign up to receive emails whenever Bonnie Edwards publishes a new book. There's no charge and no obligation.

https://books2read.com/r/B-A-JXD-BFET

BOOKS 2 READ

Connecting independent readers to independent writers.

Did you love *Loving Logan*? Then you should read *Craving Jake Return to Welcome Book 3* by Bonnie Edwards!

Returning to Welcome was easy...staying will be a challenge. Especially when someone is determined to drive her out.

Brianna Bowler has returned to Welcome to help run Bowler's Dog Rescue. She's also doing everything she can to set aside thoughts of her high school crush who appears to be with a perfectly perfect sprite of a woman. (Not that she minds how opposite she and the sprite are. Really, she doesn't.)

Paramedic Jake Morrow has a woman in his house, cooking, cleaning, clinging—and irritating the hell out of him. He'd felt sorry for her, injured, alone and broke, and offered to help. Big mistake

Jake set himself apart from everyone who used to know him. He can't take their pitying looks, their sympathy, or their avid interest in his tragic past.

What would really make his day? His ex-girlfriend finally moving out. But Theda won't take his word for it that things are over.

What's worse is Brianna Bowler's return. Their shared secret and attraction burns between them as Jake accepts that things aren't quite right with his ex. A break-in at the dog rescue, smashed windows, and a stolen laptop all add up to serious trouble for Jake and Brianna.

All Jake's protective instincts rise as the strange events take a deadly turn and Jake knows his loner life will never be good enough again.

Some women can't be set aside, not even for their own good...but others want revenge.

About the Author

Bonnie Edwards has been published by Kensington Books, Harlequin Books, Carina Press, and more.

With over 40 titles to her credit, her romances have been translated into several languages. Her books are sold worldwide.

Learn about more exciting releases and get a **free** romance by subscribing to her newsletter, **Bonnie's Newsy Bits** through her website.

https://www.bonnieedwards.com/

Cheers and happy reading!

Bonnie Edwards